Fantasy Books by Vaughn Heppner:

Cain

(Lost Civilizations: 8)

by
Vaughn Heppner

ISBN: 9781080969265

-PROLOGUE-

The patriarch of two peoples stood on a hill looking down into a valley of tall waving grass. A large herd of horses grazed there, some of the finest chariot horses in existence.

The patriarch was Lord Uriah from the ancient line of Seth. Uriah was over five hundred years old, as his blood ran true. He was considered a big man, with a close-cropped white beard and a red-tinted nose. He had been drinking hard the previous night, and it showed in his bleary eyes.

He was the patriarch of Elon, the country said to produce better charioteers than the nomadic Jogli, those sons of Cain. He was also the patriarch of hilly Shur, but only in the sense that he had sired Shur, a son who hated his father. For countless years, the clans of Shur had proven a thorn in the side of Elon.

A bigger man than Uriah finally reached the patriarch. The man who had trudged up the hill was huge, with twisted oak-like muscles and crooked talon-like fingers. He, too, had white hair and strange blue eyes that smoldered like a volcano ready to spew its rage. He was Lod, a tiger of a warrior who believed himself to be the blade of Elohim. Once, he had slaved in the galleys of Poseidonis for twenty long years, pulling the weighted oar through pestilence, famine and fevers as the other wretches around him perished within a year or two. At the slave oar, he had received haunted visions from Elohim concerning breaking teeth and the shattering of Nephilim bones. These days, Lod dreamed of marching through Shamgar, burning it to the ground as he hunted to slay the First Born, Gog the Oracle.

Lod could not claim a special bloodline. He did not know who his mother and father had been. He had grown up as rat bait in the canals of Shamgar. Though that had been long ago, the lessons he had learned in the garbage-strewn canals had been burned into his brain.

"Look," Uriah said, indicating the horses.

Lod squinted. The horses that had been grazing all looked up. They all looked in one direction. Lod craned his head. The horses had spied Joash.

A slender man in a blue tunic strolled through the tall grasses in the valley. He heaved a stick at times. A huge hound would run, pick up the stick and race back to Joash, handing it back. If Joash took too long to throw the stick again, the hound barked at him.

Transfixed, the horses watched the interplay.

A stallion soon neighed, a magnificent Appaloosa.

As if that was a signal—and perhaps it had been—the horses in Joash's path began to trot out of the way. The young man did not seem to notice. Neither did the dog. The horses did not trot in a frightened manner, but almost reverently, as if they held Joash in high esteem.

Finally, Joash noticed the horses. He halted and waved to the herd.

Several stallions reared, pawing the air as they neighed shrilly. The rest of the herd neighed as well, as if in greeting rather than anxiety. Then, the horses returned to their grazing, as if they had been waiting for the young man's acknowledgement.

"I wanted you to see that," Uriah said quietly.

"The presence of Eden yet remains on him," Lod said in a rough voice.

"Maybe. But that isn't why the horses reacted like that."

Lod pulled at his beard, finally glancing questioningly at Uriah.

Like the two of them, Joash was a seraph, called by Elohim to resist the Nephilim. Years ago, Nephilim giants had captured young Joash, using the lad to find a fiery stone once stolen from the Mount of Heaven and taken to Earth. Joash had found the stone in the Valley of Dry Bones, and he had held it afterward so the giants could gaze at it. They had attempted to accustom themselves to heavenly glory so that they could successfully slay the Cherub guarding the

2

Tree of Life in Eden. The giants had yearned to eat the fruit from the tree and become immortals.

Joash had held the fiery stone long enough that its shine began to radiate from *his* features. Because of that, he had reclaimed an ancient ability lost by Adam when Elohim had driven him from Eden; communicating directly with animals. It had proven instrumental in Joash's thwarting of the Nephilim plan back then.

"Sometimes," Uriah said, "a shine, a glow, is still evident on Joash."

"I have seen it," Lod said.

Uriah nodded. "We are going to war, my friend. At last, we shall attempt to destroy Gog's armies and pull down Shamgar the Wicked, salting the ground so it never grows again."

A terrible glint appeared in Lod's eyes like that of a holy prophet about to pronounce doom. The fire in his heart leapt at the news.

"We three are the only seraphs," Uriah said. "I will lead the first host while the two of you remain behind gathering the second."

"What of Shur?" asked Lod. "Won't the hill clans attack Elon once they know that you and the host are gone?"

"The hill clans have agreed to send warriors with me. Joash spoke to their elders. He convinced them."

"This is wonderful news."

Uriah put a hand on one of Lod's forearms. "We are the three seraphs, but Joash is worth more than the two of us—and I do not say this lightly."

"What you say is hard to fathom."

"You are the blade of Elohim. You have slain more than your share of Nephilim. Your adventures are legendary and often strange indeed. I highly esteem you, my friend. Never doubt it."

"I am Elohim's to command. If I have become so proud that you must mollify me first, by saying such things—"

"No," Uriah said, interrupting. "It isn't that. I'm clarifying the situation for both of us. Gog is wounded and less powerful than before, but he is still incredibly dangerous. He will call upon grim powers. We can be sure of that. Yet, in the end, this will be a contest of sword and spear, of excellent generalship and new stratagems. Gog will throw necromantic-fueled sorcery at us. That is why we as seraphs must be in many places at once."

Lod nodded.

3

"Here is my point," Uriah said. "Joash is the key to victory. We must use his special abilities to give us an edge against Gog's soldiers."

"Use how?"

"Before I tell you, I want to hammer home your part in this. You are a champion, and you have the best chance of slaying any one Nephilim. But producing champions of war and rapine is not mankind's strength. That belongs to the Nephilim. Thus, we cannot rely on having better champions than they do on the battlefield. We must use our strengths against their weaknesses. That means Joash."

"So…?"

"Your task in the coming war is keeping Joash alive."

"And?"

Lord Uriah put his right hand on Lod's shoulder. "Keep him alive, as I'm certain Gog will send assassins ordered to slay Joash. You must remain at his side and slay anyone who would destroy our chances for victory."

Lod heard the words, and part of him rejected the idea. He wanted to lead the host that defeated Gog's minions. He wanted to lead the warriors that bearded Gog in his den deep under the Temple of the Oracle in Shamgar. He wanted to be the one that stabbed the First Born to death.

Thus, in his heart, Lod fought Uriah's idea…until he looked down in the valley. Joash and his dog had passed the horses. The equines all watched him, and then, as one, the horses began to nod their heads.

An unsettling feeling coursed through Lod. Was that a sign from Elohim? The idea choked him, and he found it impossible to speak.

War, war against Gog and the forces of Shamgar—abruptly, Lod went to a knee and bowed his shaggy head.

He found his voice then: "As the blade of Elohim, I swear to defend Joash to the best of my ability. If it is possible, I will protect him until Gog's blood drains from his body."

"Amen," Uriah said. "Let it be so."

PART ONE
THE GATHERING

-1-

NINE MONTHS LATER

Giant mocair trees swayed in the nighttime darkness, monsters of the jungle with creaking branches and millions of rustling leaves. They surrounded a solitary man sitting in a small clearing before a crackling fire, roasting a monkey on a spit.

The aroma of the meat would surely attract jungle predators, but the man seemed unconcerned.

He was massive, like an overdeveloped wrestler of Nod, with an incredible breadth of shoulders and thickly muscled arms. He wore a leather vest and pants, with boots on his feet and a sword belted around his waist. He had thick yellow hair, a lion-like beard and brooding black eyes like drops of scorched oil, staring moodily at the mocking dancing flames.

Cain had come this way for a reason. He was weary of life, of the long march of years where everything changed but him. He had begun existence near the beginning of days, when a petulant entity had demanded sacrifices done in an unreasonably particular way. It was the entity's boast to have formed the first man and woman from clay and breathed life into them. Worse, this god of Eden had honored Cain's brother because his brother had truckled to the vain being's whims.

Cain stared at the dancing flames, remembering the distant past. He had slain his brother, and the angry god had cursed him, putting upon him the mark of Cain.

That mark blazed in his black eyes, the gaze of a maddened killer; the first killer of Earth. Never again had Cain tilled the soil, as the ground had become like flint to him. He became a wanderer, stopping long enough at times to build a city or found a clan such as the Jogli nomads. Then, he would depart, often with enemies trailing him, eager to spill his blood. Many times, he had turned at bay, slaughtering his foes. He was forged through violence and destined, some said, to die by the sword when the day of vengeance finally arrived. Until then, he remained as he had been on the day of Abel's murder.

The flames danced and mocked him, seeming to hiss, *"You are alone, Cain. Houses, monuments and nations grow and then decay, yet you remain the same. All around you things perish, yet you vainly struggle to find meaning."*

As he sat upon a rock, Cain moaned low in his throat. The weight of centuries pressed against him as the futility of life had finally become overwhelming. Vain, vain, everything was vain. Nothing that his hand found to do satisfied him for long.

Cain closed his eyes as the weariness suffocated his soul. He had come to this desolate jungle because he could no longer stand to be around people. The uselessness of it all—

Thick droplets of monkey grease sizzled as they fell into the fire.

Cain's eyes flew open. He had preternatural senses, and his muscles and other bodily functions were knit together better than anyone alive. Not only did he have the accumulated knowledge and skills of centuries, but he had also been born from two perfect humans.

There was something in the jungle...

Cain bent his head. The sizzling had abruptly torn him from his brooding. He had come this way to be alone, to let the futility of existence fill him with the resolve to finally put an end to meaninglessness.

He had thwarted the garden god once before—he would do it again by breaking the curse one way or another.

From out in the darkness, Cain sensed...hostility. Hostility directed at him.

6

He looked up, straining to see past the firelight. He could see farther and better in the dark than an ordinary mortal. He concentrated on the middle areas of the giant mocair trees surrounding him. The branches seemed to sag as if something heavy stepped or shifted upon them.

That wasn't just the wind, which had died down.

Cain pulled a bear cloak from his belongings behind the rock. He settled the cloak upon his shoulders, half wrapping it around him. Something had disturbed his brooding, and he would make that something pay for its affront. Hidden by the bear cloak, the fingers of his left hand curled around the hilt of the sword belted at his waist.

The sword, of Caphtorite steel, had been taken from the corpse of the then-First Sword of Caphtor. People had acclaimed that one as the finest swordsman on Earth. Cain had proven him second best, although the man had certainly owned the best sword Cain had ever carried.

The emanations of hate redoubled—Cain could feel staring eyes and the hot desire for teeth to sink into his flesh.

Despite the darkness, he peered more closely up at the trees, but couldn't penetrate the dense foliage to see his oppressor. The emanations...Cain shook his leonine head. The emanations did not come from a leopard or python. A thinking creature yearned to devour him.

That was strange and ominous.

Again, droplets of monkey grease sizzled into the fire. The terrible futility that had engulfed Cain moments ago retreated into his tormented soul. In its place, the killer instincts resurfaced. If the secret watcher wanted to eat him, that one would pay for the attempt with his *life*.

Despite Cain's former wishes, an ancient tension coiled in his gut as he readied himself for mayhem. As often happened with him, it was a quick transference from one state to the next. Berserker-like bloodlust seethed just under the surface. When others thought to use or hurt him—

A coconut thudded upon the soil several feet from the fire.

Cain didn't jerk or shout in surprise. Clearly, his enemy wanted him to panic. That wasn't going to happen.

A second coconut thudded near the first.

Cain waited. He had time. A half-insane smile twisted his lips, and his eyes shined madly. Time—he had time, more than any creature on Earth. That included the First Born and their Nephilim children. He—

A third coconut and then a fourth thudded onto the soil.

"Are these gifts?" Cain roared up at the trees.

There was no answer, but several midlevel branches swayed up and down as if heavy creatures moved upon them.

Cain scowled. Would men climb so high in the dark? He did not believe so. What would—?

An eruption of wild hooting gave him the answer. He listened with a discerning ear. That sounded like… great apes, creatures on par with gorillas but more intelligent. Great apes were big but leaner than gorillas and ate meat at times. Had he stumbled onto their favorite territory, or did they believe him harmless because he was alone?

At that point, a huge hairy beast jumped out of a mocair tree. Cain saw it in the darkness, the body hurtling down more than forty feet. The great ape landed on the soil farther back than the coconuts. It grunted, using all four limbs to absorb the shock of landing.

Cain exploded into action, letting the bear cloak fall from him. He grabbed a fiery brand from the blaze, hurling it at the great ape.

The beast stood nearly as tall as he did, although it was stooped and hairy, and sported incredibly long, gnarly arms. The knuckles pressed against the soil as the beast opened its jaws and screamed at him, displaying baboon-like fangs. The great ape seriously outweighed him and despite Cain's legendary strength, if the beast grabbed him, he would be like a child in its arms.

The spinning brand struck the great ape's face. It screamed anew in panic and pain, stumbling backward as it clutched at the burning brand.

Before the ape could recover, Cain crossed the distance between them, thrusting with unerring accuracy and viciousness. The razor-sharp point sliced through fur and flesh, sliding past protective rib-bones to pierce the ape's heart.

The creature thrashed in agony, swinging its long arms, trying to grapple with Cain.

Cain ducked as he jerked back, yanking the sword from the doomed beast. The great ape crumpled to the bloody grass, a twitching dying mass of flesh and fur.

Ape screams erupted from the trees, screams that promised searing vengeance against the killer on the ground.

Cain understood, backpedaling into the firelight, snatching another brand from the flames, setting himself for a fight to the death.

Three apes leaped from the trees, rocketing to the ground where their fallen brother lay dead. Each beast thudded hard, swiftly gaining its bearings. More jumped. More landed, until a band of them hooted and screamed in rage at him as they surged up and down. It was a terrifyingly barbaric sight.

Cain gripped his sword in one hand and the brand in the other. He laughed insanely. It galled him that simian monsters should put him to death after all these centuries.

The great apes danced around their fallen brother, as they worked themselves into a killing fury, screaming ape epithets at him.

Cain snarled, willing himself to charge anew. He doubted that he could frighten them, but better to die attacking than waiting. Better to laugh at death than whimper as he huddled in fear by the fire.

A new monster landed on the ground, one that upset Cain's calculations. This one was bigger than the great apes and stood straighter, like a man. A long red cape billowed at his back, and a thick belt girded his hairy waist. A short heavy scabbard held a sword with a black, leather-wrapped hilt protruding. The creature wore sandals, with leather bindings wrapped around his hairy calves.

The shock of the sight stilled Cain's charge and stirred an old memory. The thing before him was clearly a blasphemous comingling of man and beast. That meant supernatural power of some kind, whether sorcery or *bene elohim* magic. He had heard of Tarag of the Sabertooths, a so-called First Born conceived from the seed of a *bene elohim* and a sabertooth. There was another like Tarag, although of lesser stature. That one was called…Sagoth. Sagoth led great apes as Tarag had led sabertooths. Cain couldn't remember if Sagoth was Nephilim or half-Nephilim.

Normal berserkers were like prey in a spider's web when the battle madness overtook them, unable to think until the fight was over and they collapsed exhausted. Cain could move in and out of

9

his rages, and in a display of mental prowess, he forced his tongue to form coherent words.

"Sagoth," he called.

The hooting, screaming and dancing had grown louder and wilder. Fifteen or more great apes surrounded the corpse and their leader with his billowing cape.

A new thought flashed in Cain's mind. Maybe he could charge again and scatter the apes through surprise. Then, he would kill Sagoth—

"Cain," the half-human, half-ape creature said in a tortured manner. "You *are* Cain, aren't you?"

Cain nodded sharply, surprised at the recognition. Few men knew him these days.

"I have come to speak to you," Sagoth said.

Cain had to concentrate to understand the creature's words. Once he did, he wondered how Sagoth could possibly know he would trek through *this* jungle at *this* time. Since the possibility of that struck Cain as absurd, he did not ask the obvious question. Instead, he waited for more information. He willfully lessened the intensity of his grips around the fiery brand and sword.

"Put down your weapons," Sagoth ordered.

Cain did nothing of the kind.

"I can order my apes to disarm you."

The threat stirred Cain's already stoked rage. "More will die if you do," he said thickly.

"Kill another of my tribe, Cain, and..." Sagoth's threat drifted into silence. For the first time, the Nephilim seemed frightened.

The great apes must have sensed his unease, and what happened next showed his mastery over them. The dancing, screaming apes slowed their weird performance as they grew quieter. Finally, they stopped altogether, panting as they stared at Cain.

"You must join me," Sagoth said. "I am allowed to force you if you don't agree."

Allowed? The unreality of the situation, perhaps the uniqueness of it, stirred Cain's curiosity.

"Who sent you?"

Sagoth cocked his simian head. "Gog did. I thought you realized. All surely know that I belong to the Order of Gog."

Cain's gut tightened. He had heard of the evil order and its chief. According to what he knew, Gog the First Born was the son of Magog the Accursed. Magog had come down from the Celestial Realm, a so-called fallen angel that had mated with a mortal woman of Earth to sire Gog, among others. Cain seldom ventured among those with the blood of the high, as they conceived of such things. They were too conceited and arrogant, and they were always stronger than men and usually more cunning.

The fallen ones like Magog were the *bene elohim*—the sons of God. They no longer lived upon the Earth, as there had been a war ages ago when the Shining Ones had descended to the mortal vale to drag the rebels to Tartarus, one of the regions of Hell. The First Born of the unnatural unions between the *bene elohim* and women still remained on Earth to torment humanity. But there were no new ones anymore, just the old ones like Gog and his brothers scattered throughout the world.

Cain had no desire to speak with Gog, which presumably would entail going to Shamgar the Wicked. This part of the jungle was near the pirate city, but Cain had taken pains to avoid its immediate environs.

"Will you come with me?" Sagoth asked.

Cain shook his head.

"You—" Sagoth stopped talking as he looked away. After a moment, he turned to the great apes.

Cain set himself for battle.

Sagoth hooted and chattered. The beasts cocked their heads as if they understood him. To Cain's surprise, the apes turned away from the fire by ones and twos and melted into the forest. Branches dipped and leaves shook as the apes climbed into the mocair trees. At last, Sagoth stood alone with Cain.

With the immediate threat gone, Cain lowered the point of his sword.

The hybrid creature drew the red cloak around himself as he marched into the firelight, the heavy scabbard slapping at his side.

"I will join you," Sagoth said.

For an instant, Cain debated plunging his sword into Sagoth's breast. The instant passed as the Nephilim settled onto a different rock.

11

"The meat is ready," Sagoth said as he eyed the dead monkey on the spit. "Let us eat."

Wasn't eating monkey-meat a cannibal act for Sagoth? Cain didn't plan on asking, nor did he plan on sharing his hard-won meal with the intruder.

"Hurry, Cain. I dislike charred meat. Raw is always better."

"What about the ape I slew?"

Sagoth turned swiftly. "You will not eat him."

"That wasn't the question. I slew him. Must you now try to slay me in revenge?"

Sagoth appeared to struggle with the question, opening his ape-like lips several times. Finally, he said, "I have a message from Gog. He instructed me to tell you that you would want to hear the message."

"How would Gog know that?"

Sagoth had turned away, no doubt to stare at the corpse in the darkness. He turned back, closed his eyes and moved his lips silently. Was he praying for the great ape or telling himself something?

After Sagoth was done with the silent litany, he opened his eyes. "You'll have to hear the message to understand how Gog would know."

Cain's nostrils flared. He had come this way to think deeply. That would have to wait a little longer, it seemed.

The man tossed the brand back into the fire as he stood. He lifted the spitted monkey and measured the portion he would give Sagoth. He would listen to the message, and if he didn't like it, he'd kill Sagoth and take his chances with the great apes.

-2-

Cain watched sidelong as Sagoth cracked the monkey bones and sucked out the marrow. Afterward, the hybrid creature tossed the bones into the fire and wiped greasy fingers on his fur.

"Is there a problem?" Sagoth asked, noticing Cain's scrutiny.

"Do great apes often eat monkeys?"

"When they can catch them."

Before he'd eaten, Cain had stuck his sword point-first in the dirt. He now withdrew the sword from the soil and brushed the dirt from it with his fingers. Then he set the blade on his knees.

"Do I frighten you?" asked Sagoth.

Cain simply looked at him.

"You're unusual for a man. Usually, men quake in terror upon seeing me. Often, I am the last thing they see in this life."

Cain waited, unimpressed with the boast.

"You must weigh almost as much as I do," Sagoth said. "I'm taller. You're thicker, built like an arena wrestler of Nod. I would think you could snap a man's back if you wanted. And your hands— those are a strangler's hands, they say, big and powerful."

A transformation began in Cain's black eyes—once more becoming the eyes of a maddened killer. Few could match his gaze for long when he unhooded what truly lay in his soul.

Sagoth tried, but the Nephilim son of Gog grew visibly uneasy as he looked into Cain's eyes. Perhaps he felt a need to speak, to threaten.

"One word," the Nephilim said, "and my brethren will descend from the trees in a rage. If I will it, they will tear you limb from limb. You will be powerless to stop it."

A sinister smile twisted Cain's lips. By choice, he seldom mingled with Nephilim or their children. The few times he had been in their presence—Cain shook his head. He wasn't going to think about that lest he give himself away.

The fire in his eyes lessened as he hooded their intensity. It was time to hear Gog's message. "We have eaten together," Cain said. "Thus, we are under truce."

The hybrid creature sat straighter and expanded his chest, slapping it. "I am Sagoth of the Great Apes. This is my domain. My brothers await my command, and more are coming. I am also Gog's chief beastmaster, the greatest of my kind in Shamgar. Thus, I will say if we have a truce or not, as I am in command here and you have slain one of mine."

"Do you have a message or not?"

The Nephilim bristled. "You keep a sword on your knees because you fear me. I understand, and I will permit it…for now."

"The message," Cain said, as if bored. "Give it to me."

Sagoth swept the last of the cracked monkey bones from his lap and jumped to his feet.

Several unseen great apes in the trees hooted loudly from above.

Sagoth turned toward the darkness and hooted, speaking in what might have been a great-ape language. He seemed to derive comfort from the display, turning back to the fire more relaxed than before.

"I have come from Gog, the First Born of Magog. Are you familiar with Gog's gift?"

Furrow lines appeared on Cain's forehead. He nodded shortly, remembering.

A First Born, his Nephilim offspring, and the half-Nephilim offspring after that possessed a gift of the blood of the high, yea, unto the third generation. The gift of the blood—the blood of the *bene elohim*—was chaotic in application. One of the blood could run without becoming weary. One could heal in a supernatural manner. One could summon hawks. Gog could see into the future, sometimes, in a spotty fashion. It was a laborious process and took sacrifices to grease the way. He was called Gog the Oracle because of this, and many journeyed to Shamgar in order to beg of Gog a glimpse of their future. For a price—often a grave price—Gog did so, binding yet another person to his shadowy kingdom.

"Gog is the mightiest First Born on Earth," Sagoth said. "Any who wish him harm fail in the end because Gog sees their hidden plans. Gog is supreme, and men tremble at his displeasure."

"During my trek, I've heard rumors, ill tidings that concern Gog. Men say he is blind."

"Lies!"

"Men say he lost a son on the Isle of the Behemoth."

Sagoth's simian lips pushed outward in annoyance.

"Men say Gog lost many beastmasters that time," Cain added. "Is that why you are now the greatest in Shamgar?"

"Have a care, Cain. If you anger me beyond enduring—"

"By your own admission, you will do nothing. Gog sent you to find me. He needs something from me. If you harm me, at the least, Gog will strip the fur from your hide in a beating you will never forget."

The Nephilim recoiled in fear, although he recovered fast enough, giving Cain a haughty glance.

Cain did not nod to himself, but he knew he'd guessed right. After endless centuries of life, he could read people—and hybrid beasts like Sagoth—with pitiful ease.

"Gog told me to tell you the truth," Sagoth said slowly, almost as if speaking to himself. "He said you can sniff out the truth and uncover lies. Is that true?"

"Yes."

Sagoth nodded, and he seemed to regain his poise. "There is one who is like a gnat to Gog. That one is called Lod the Seraph."

Despite himself, Cain inhaled sharply. A seraph was supposedly called by Elohim to fight the evil ones, usually Nephilim and their children. Some believed that a seraph's "inner flame" acted as a shield against Nephilim magic and more common sorcery. Cain did not like anyone summoned by Elohim. He wanted nothing to do with…with the godling of Eden or his servants.

Cain thus spoke harshly, "Is this Lod from the line of Seth?"

"I do not understand the question."

"It doesn't matter. What's Gog's message?"

"You have heard of Lod?"

"No. Now, what is the message?"

15

Sagoth cocked his head. "You became distressed after I spoke about Lod. You must have heard of him."

"I said I have not. Now, get on with it, beastmaster."

Sagoth's simian brows furrowed. In the end, he shrugged his powerful shoulders. "It is said that Lod has an uncanny knack or is unusually lucky. Perhaps the One…" Sagoth shook his head as his words trailed away. "Lod has an uncanny knack. Men speak truly when they say Gog was blinded. Lod did that, underneath the Temple of the Oracle."

"If Gog is blind, how can he see into the future?"

"Lod blinded Gog's physical eye. The seraph did not steal Gog's mystical art."

The way Sagoth spoke… Did that mean Gog had been one-eyed? Whatever the case, "The First Born must hate Lod," Cain said.

Sagoth laughed mirthlessly.

"Ah," Cain said, beginning to understand. "This blinding is why you've come, isn't it?"

"I can tell you this. Gog has a plan to trap the seraph. Gog yearns for Lod's return to the Catacombs below the Temple."

"You still haven't told me what any of this has to do with me. If Gog can still use his supraocular sight, let him use it to capture Lod."

At that, Sagoth started breathing deeply.

It took Cain a moment to realize the Nephilim had become frightened by his suggestion.

"Gog instructed me to tell you the truth," Sagoth said slowly. "I obey my master, nothing more or less."

"You're not talking to me," Cain said, looking around. "Who else is out there?"

"No one but my brothers," Sagoth said. "They would warn me if anyone else approached."

Cain's eyes narrowed. He sensed truth from Sagoth, but he also knew that the Nephilim had just spoken for another's ears. Sagoth feared Gog. Gog could read the future…sometimes, anyway. The First Born might see a future where Sagoth displeased him by what the hybrid said. If that future displeased Gog deeply enough, Sagoth would die, maybe in a hideous way. Thus, Sagoth had just spoken for Gog's ears because what the hybrid was going to say might anger the First Born.

16

That was strange, and thus it intrigued Cain anew. He had lived so many centuries, so many endless years that he seldom saw something new under the sun. Mostly, life bored him. This situation...

"Go on," Cain said. "Finish your message."

"Lod is slippery like an eel. His seraph power protects him from Gog's future sight. There are hidden paths that Gog cannot pierce. Still, common spies have learned that Lod is gathering an army in Elon. Therefore, Gog cannot send his Nephilim champions to drag Lod to Shamgar for punishment. And he does not desire to use assassins to kill Lod too soon."

"An Elonite army, you say? Is that army headed for Shamgar?"

"War has already begun. Settlements in the southern coastal hinterlands have fallen to Lord Uriah's host. The rulers of Dishon and Pildash have become fearful. Perhaps as bad, too many Nephilim champions have perished in fruitless enterprises these past few years. Chieftains and warlords have forgotten their secret pledges to Gog."

"You're saying that Gog's shadowy kingdom isn't as powerful as many once believed. Lord Uriah's host must have wounded Gog's prestige, made him seem less powerful than men thought."

"The latest setbacks are minor things."

"No," Cain said. "I don't think so. You wouldn't be here otherwise. What else happened to encourage men against Gog?"

Sagoth hesitated before saying, "Dagon failed to tame the Behemoth."

"Dagon is a son of Gog?"

"He was...until Lod slew him. Gog tasked Dagon with the quest of taming and bringing the Behemoth to Shamgar. With it, Gog's soldiers would have swept the land of his enemies. Now, Gog is resorting to other means."

"You still haven't said what any of this has to do with me."

"You are Cain, the greatest human warlord in existence."

"I've led victorious armies in the past. But those soldiers are all dead. I have turned my back on imperial conquests. These days, I am no more than Cain the Wanderer."

"You are much more," Sagoth said earnestly. "What man could have charged my brother as you did? I should have foreseen that, but I did not believe—no matter," the hybrid said abruptly. "Gog

17

requires your presence in Shamgar. He has plans for you, plans for his good and your good."

Cain studied the Nephilim, and he considered the situation. Finally, he said, "I have grown weary of battle. Even less do I wish to lead Nephilim 'champions' in war."

"You do not understand. Gog has mighty captains of war. He has tough soldiers. What Gog requires from you is tricking and capturing Lod."

Cain stared at Sagoth, finally nodding in understanding. "I'm not a Nephilim. I'm a man. Thus, I can freely walk into Elon if I so choose."

"You and a band of hardy warriors under your command."

"You spoke about this being for my good. I realize how such a thing would help Gog, but how does any of this help me?"

"Gog can pay richly for your services."

Cain laughed sharply. "What do I care about silver, gold or gems? They are colorful pieces of dirt to me, nothing more. What do I care about ruling a captured city? Administration is one of the most thankless chores in existence."

"Gog would pay with an oracle."

Cain shook his head. "I have no need of oracles."

Sagoth's manner became sly as he leaned forward. "What if the oracle of Gog could see the manner of your death? What if you could know the limit to your endless existence?"

Cain's mouth dropped open. Could he gain sure knowledge about the cessation of his endless wanderings through life? The idea took him by storm. He had always known that he could kill himself. Yet, he could never bring himself to do that, as it wasn't in his nature. Neither had anyone proven strong, cunning or swift enough to slay the first killer on Earth, the man with the curse of Elohim upon him.

"You intrigue me, Sagoth."

"You will come with me to Shamgar?"

Cain wondered about the wisdom of entering a city belonging to a First Born. Men said Gog was bigger and more powerful than an elephant.

"I could head straight to Elon instead," he countered.

"Gog told me you would say that. He bade me say, 'You must come to Shamgar to learn why Lod is so important to you.'"

18

"Important to me how?" asked Cain.

"I do not know, but Gog does."

"Did Gog foresee my coming to this spot in the jungle?"

"Of course."

"Did he foresee me going with you?"

"Gog would not tell me."

"Why?"

"I do not know."

With his left hand, Cain grasped the hilt of the sword in his lap. He raised the sharp blade.

Sagoth's eyes grew wide and wary.

For a moment—for pure spite and the chaotic restlessness that lay within him—Cain debated plunging the sword into the apeman's chest. Instead, he turned it and slid the blade into his belted scabbard. He would take a risk, a bold risk that he would never have dared even a hundred years ago. He would enter the city of Gog and speak to a First Born in his lair of power, there to collect something very precious indeed. And if Gog should attempt to play him false—

For the barest fraction of time, a feral light shined in Cain's eyes. "Gather your beasts," he said. "We'll start tonight. I'm eager to speak to your master."

His ancient enemy—boredom—was shoved away once more. Cain would plunge back into life and see what Gog and Lod could give the oldest man in existence.

-3-

Cain, Sagoth and his great apes threaded through the hinterland jungles said to lie behind Shamgar and before the Hanun Mountains that fed the countless streams that trickled their way to the Suttung Sea. The mountain streams joined in the lower regions, turning into sluggish waterways. Crocodiles, sliths and other predatory beasts inhabited this region. Mosquitoes and flies hovered in clouds, descending to torment the apes in particular.

In an area where the soggy ground finally became impassable, Cain parted company with Sagoth and his apes. Several Nebo tribesmen waited in flat-bottomed reed punts.

The Nebo were stone-age primitives who worshiped Magog the Accursed as a god. In the Accursed War against the Shining Ones, the Nebo had fought for the *bene elohim*. Perhaps as divine punishment, they continued to live in squalor in the wettest parts of the jungle, doing the bidding of Magog's most notorious son.

Cain gingerly climbed aboard the largest punt. The Nebo wore loincloths and were hairy, although not as hairy as the great apes had been. The Nebo universally had forward sloping foreheads and beetling brows. They would not look at nor speak to Cain, but they clearly did everything they could to make the journey as easy for him as possible.

The Nebo poled the punts beneath a maze of towering branches and across the sluggish rivers, avoiding crocodiles, hippos and large saurian monsters with elongated necks and needle-sharp teeth. On the third day, the tribesmen reached a waiting flat-bottomed swamp barge. There, a priest from the Order of Gog greeted Cain.

20

The priest had a shaven pate with a trident symbol tattooed on his forehead. He was Flay Rank, torturing captives with a flaying knife, perhaps to ready them for skull magic, a horrific form of necromancy.

Cain disliked the priest from the start. The man was too servile with him and tyrannical with everyone else. At his orders, whip-masters lashed the poor souls manning the barge's oars, forcing the chained slaves to propel the craft as fast as possible.

The barge soon surged into a wider but still sluggish river. Two days later, the priest shook Cain awake as he slept on a hammock in back.

The barge had reached the swamp-side of Shamgar. The city of pirates was situated in a swamp many miles from the great Suttung Sea. The swamp was the first layer of protection for those living in the city.

Shamgar was one of the most disunited cities of Earth. Individual pirate lords controlled most of the strongholds, keeping their ships and stolen wealth behind high stone walls and iron-barred gates, using the canals that crisscrossed the city to reach the river that would take them to the sea.

The barge used the city canals and moved past the strongholds, heading toward the center of Shamgar and its famous acropolis. The center held the main marketplace, which was controlled and patrolled by Gog's minions. The canals widened near the acropolis, a towering rock that held the terrifying Temple of the Oracle. In the rock's depths lived blind Gog.

"I bid you eat now, sir," the priest told Cain. "Gog will desire your presence as soon as we land."

Cain did not reply, but he ate roasted lamb, sugared peaches and carrots. He drank several flagons of beer and belched afterward. By that time, the barge docked, and the priest led Cain across the gangplank to a waiting delegation of three, black-robed acolytes of Gog.

These three were different from the barge priest. They were taller, leaner with longer heads and an obvious stain upon their souls.

Cain recognized it instantly. These three were skull practitioners, necromancers. They also had the taint of the blood of the high in their veins. They must have been of the fourth or fifth generation. None had a supernatural gift, but had to practice magic the hard way,

21

through spells, incantations and skull weaving. Each of the three wore black eye shadow and a cowl thrown up to protect them from the sun and perhaps from sight of the Overlord. That would be their name for Elohim.

Cain noticed something else. Each of the three was drugged—perhaps by ingesting purple lotus—the glaze showing in their hooded eyes.

"You are Cain," the leader said slowly. "I am to take you at once to the Temple."

Instead of acknowledging the words, Cain looked around. The plaza and steps were devoid of people. Several bronze braziers sitting on tall tripods glowed with heat. High overhead in the sky seagulls drifted lazily.

"Are you ready, lord?" asked the priest.

Cain inhaled deeply through his nostrils. This might have been a mistake. Gog ruled here, a First Born. Still, there was no turning back at this point.

Cain snapped his fingers and motioned for the priest to start walking.

The three, lotus-drugged acolytes of Gog did not appear to take offense at the command. The priests raised their arms and tucked their hands into the opposing voluminous sleeves. They turned slowly and just as serenely headed for the stairs. They did not see if Cain followed but walked as men going to their certain doom.

Cain continued to look around. Once he reached the stairs, however, his concentration changed. Now, he sensed something powerful and malignant, something brooding with an intensity greater than his own. That was Gog, no doubt. The First Born must know he was here.

The three priests led Cain up broad steps to gigantic wooden doors that led into the Temple of the Oracle. The doors were barely ajar. The three picked up torches, lofting them high to fight the immediate gloom as they slipped within.

Despite himself, Cain swallowed audibly. A sense of evil struck him, and a greater sense of power. Yes. He was the first killer, perhaps the greatest swordsman humanity had ever cast up. His will had started the art of murder. He was cursed by Elohim and had wandered the planet for endless centuries. But the being radiating this was—stronger by far.

22

I should not have come.

The feeling increased as the priests led him through a vast chamber of gigantic idols towering as tall as mocair trees. The idols—Cain recognized several; Moloch the Hammer, Magog the Accursed and Abaddon the Destroyer.

Cain shivered. He knew how all this had started, which meant he had a part in it through his distant great-great-great granddaughter Naamah. The fallen ones from the Celestial Realm had lusted after women, beautiful Naamah and her long dark hair in particular. The *bene elohim* and later the children of their seed had haunted humanity from the start of their original descent onto the mortal plane.

"I am Cain," he whispered to himself, as if that was answer enough.

The priests left the vast cavern of idols and turned onto a downward slanting ramp. They marched into the mountain, into the depths of the Temple of the Oracle. At the bottom lay the Catacombs where Gog entombed those he most hated. Once, Lod had lain down there. Somehow, the seraph had escaped, blinding Gog in the process.

How that must gall the First Born.

The air grew cool and moist, and doomed souls screamed from a torture chamber. Later, demented animals roared. Rumor told of necromantic experiments upon poor beasts, turning them into fearsome monsters that could terrorize a battlefield.

Perhaps Gog searched for a replacement for the Behemoth.

Perhaps the most ominous thing was how the very darkness surged inward against the flickering torchlight, pressing closer and closer until Cain had to close the distance to the three in order to see where he was walking. The acolytes moved in a leaden manner. One of them moaned, although he ceased instantly as something vast moved through the inky darkness ahead of them.

"Gog," the chief priest intoned. "Gog is coming."

The three halted. Cain stopped behind them. They had let him keep his sword, which he had judged a mistake. Now, Cain realized, the sword didn't matter. Gog was coming. He could hear a heavy sliding tread. The sense of raw power billowing over Cain…

The killer struggled to lock his knees. Cain knelt to no one. He did no one's bidding but his own. If he were going to die, he would die free and unbowed.

Grunting, realizing he could hardly move, Cain strove to reach his sword. Gog was mighty. Gog was supreme in this place. A snarl of desperation twisted Cain's lips. He clutched the hilt of his sword, and he prepared to draw it.

"DO SO, GNAT, AND I WILL DESTROY YOU." Gog's words boomed through Cain's body, making his bones shiver.

The three acolytes fainted, dropping to the tiles as if dead. Their torches clattered, one of them guttering out. The other two still flickered, casting but a semblance of their former light.

Cain's hand dropped away from the hilt. He did not draw his sword. Neither did he drop to his knees. He waited, knowing that Gog stood just outside the torchlight.

Coming here had been a dreadful mistake.

-4-

"You are wise, gnat," Gog said, his voice pitched low so it no longer shook the man. Yet, the bass was so low and ominous that it had a new terrifying quality. The voice indicated that Gog was as big as an elephant. It came from higher up in the darkness, which had to mean something.

Why did Gog hide in darkness? Why didn't he want anyone to see him?

Like an automaton, Cain forced himself to move. He stooped low and scooped up a torch, waving it from side to side as he stood. The flame increased, but the amount of illumination remained the same.

Cain sensed the play of magic around him. Gog was keeping the light low.

"I have come," Cain said, forcing himself to keep from wincing. To his own ears, he sounded bombastic, and he did not like that.

"I sense unwarranted arrogance in you, Cain."

The man waved the torch back and forth again. As he did, he thought furiously, finally settling upon his plan for dealing with the First Born.

"Why shouldn't I be arrogant?" asked Cain. "Who else has Gog summoned? Who else has Gog given such a promise because he has a foe no one can kill?"

"Do not *presume* upon that."

Cain could feel the conceit radiating from the First Born. Gog was a creature unlike any on Earth. He had size and power. He wielded powerful magic. Yet, one of the seraphs had blinded him, had thwarted his will. Did that cause Gog to fear?

25

Cain did not like the question because it came too close to home. The god of Eden had power. There was no sense in denying that. Did that mean the god of Eden was the Creator of All? Did that mean all life should worship Elohim? Would that one truly judge everything at the end of time? Did that mean power, riches, women and wine were only transient pleasures of this life? Was Lod a servant of such a god, and did that bode ill for Gog, for Cain?

"You are quiet," Gog rumbled. "You fear something. I have indeed summoned you, as you can provide me a service. I know men, and I know they love to bargain for what they want. You want knowledge, Cain, knowledge that will never do you any good until the moment it happens."

Cain opened his mouth, his breathing quickening.

"I speak of your death, Killer."

Cain nodded.

"Do you desire death?" Gog rumbled.

Cain closed his mouth and strove with all his might to pierce the inky darkness. For just a moment, he spied a rubbery tentacle—a huge thing as thick as a man's body—waving through the darkness.

"NO!" Gog said, in the booming voice that vibrated in Cain's bones.

Once more, the darkness billowed toward the torchlights and almost consumed their illumination.

Gog grunted as if the exhibition cost him strength. "Do not seek to see that which I do not grant you."

Cain noted the threat and what lay behind it and waited.

"You would do better to grovel before me," Gog finally said. "I tire of your spurious display of vainglory."

"I will not grovel, but I think you could slay me if you desired."

"*Bold* Cain, *proud* Cain, *arrogant* Cain the Killer. You defied...the Overlord. That pleases me. You have gained much through that defiance. For instance, you are as you were long ago. You have healed from countless scars. I wonder...if someone blinded you, would your eyes grow back?"

Cain said nothing.

"You are unique among men," Gog said at last. "You can stand in my presence without wilting. Few of my children are capable of that. I wonder if you are still human in the accepted sense of the

26

word. I suspect you are the oldest being in existence. That is strange, very strange."

Cain lowered the torch, growing weary of holding it so high.

Gog sighed. "It has been a long, long time since I have spoken to another First Born. It has been many years since I walked upon the surface. You have strength of character greater than any I have spoken to, greater than my lost son, Dagon."

Cain dipped his head.

"I...find it strange speaking to one of power," Gog said. "I could crush you easily enough, but then I would waste a great opportunity."

On the floor, one of the priests stirred.

"No," Gog said. "None shall remember this."

Cain staggered back as a black tentacle slid into view. It curled around the priest that had stirred, raising him high.

The priest must have come out of his drugged stupor, for he looked around wild-eyed. "Please," the priest whimpered.

Once more, Gog grunted, drawing the tentacle and priest into the darkness. The priest shrieked once, awfully. Seconds later, Cain heard the chomping of teeth, the grinding of bones and terrible sucking and slurping noises. A jet of blood flew into the light, splattering onto the tiles.

Finally, Gog belched, and said, "Ah... That's better, much better."

By an act of will, Cain kept himself from shivering or blanching.

"I am Gog," the great one said. "My will is supreme in this place."

Cain waited even as he yearned to depart the inner mountain and flee from Shamgar.

"You and I shall speak plainly with each other," Gog said. "We hate the Overlord. Is that not so?"

Cain nodded.

"He has taken too much on himself. He does not let a being stretch and do what he desires. He hems in because he thinks to make us truckle to his will. I have refused. You have refused. Each of us in his own way has made the refusal stand. Thus, I admire you, Cain. Oh, surely not to the degree that you think I should, but I have respect for your actions."

"I—"

27

"A moment," Gog said, "a warning. Speak only the truth to me, for I am uninterested in lies from you."

"What do you want from me?"

Gog sighed deeply. "I want vengeance," he said quietly. "I wish to torment the one who…who…stabbed out my eye, my only eye."

Cain could hear the anguish but did everything in his power to hide that knowledge from his features. Gog wanted to remain in darkness for a reason. Look how he'd slain and eaten the priest because the man might have heard something.

"Lod did this to me," Gog said in his quiet voice. "Oh, how I hate the gnat. How I yearn to hold him close and whisper all the horrors I am about to commit upon his person and soul. But Lod eludes me. He is clever, using others to do his dirty work. He hides in Elon even as he urges Lord Uriah to storm the hinterlands. I have grown weary of their attacks and wish to turn the tables on them."

"Your beasts—"

"Do not interrupt me. My hatred for Lod courses through my veins like hot lava. I would gladly sacrifice Shamgar if I could hold Lod again. I would go down to Sheol if I could torment Lod until he croaked his last."

"Your hate is strong."

Gog had begun to breathe heavily like a great bull about to charge.

"I understand your hate," Cain said.

"It is strange. At first, I was going to squash you like a bug for speaking just now. But I hear the truth in your words. Yes. I imagine Cain knows how to hate. We two are good haters."

The cold fires in Cain's eyes awoke.

"You have changed," Gog said. "I feel it. Yes… I feel the hatred radiating from you. You are not like other men. You are different, elemental and driven. I have done well in summoning you. Know this, Cain, that Lod holds a special purpose for you."

Cain was skeptical.

"I stumbled upon a truth regarding you in one of my oracles," Gog said. "I began to study you, seeking your futures. Many of those were hidden from me, although I uncovered a time that you would travel near Shamgar. Thus, I sent Sagoth to fetch you. I believe that you can bring Lod to me. In fact, I have seen Lod and you in

28

Shamgar together. Thus, you will succeed if you choose to go to Elon."

"Interesting," Cain said. "But how does that help me?"

"You do not seek silver, gold or gems. You desire to break the curse set upon you by...*him.*"

Cain nodded as elation and fear beat through him.

"Your futures are shrouded in mystery," Gog said. "To break the barrier, I need a powerful soul—a seraph, preferably."

"Lod?"

"Yes. If I sacrifice Lod on the altar and use his soul to power my gift, I believe that I can break through the barrier and see what you desire to know."

"When and how I die?"

"If that is your wish, I can tell you. But I will need Lod to do it."

Cain averted his gaze as the possibility enticed him. Would Gog keep his word? He sensed that the First Born would do so. Hadn't Gog foreseen his victory? Indeed. To know when and how he would die...for many centuries, he had longed to know that.

"Yes," Cain said. "I will do it."

"Ah... Then attend me, Cain. First, though, throw down your torch and stamp out the other."

Cain threw his torch onto the tiles and stamped it out. Without hesitation, he stamped out the last torch, throwing himself into darkness. He sensed Gog sliding next to him, and he felt a heavy tentacle resting on his left shoulder. At that point, Gog leaned low and began to whisper into his ear.

-5-

On the other side of the Suttung Sea from Shamgar were the rolling plains of Elon, prime chariot territory. There, between the Huri Forests and the Hills of Paran—where the clans of Shur held sway—Lord Uriah ruled. Many of the charioteers of Elon, archers of Huri Land and stern hill-warriors of Shur had joined Uriah in a crusade against Shamgar and its allies. Those Gog-allies included the coastal cities of Pildash and Dishon, thousands of Nebo tribesmen from the swamps and many mountain mercenaries from Arkite Land.

Upon Uriah's arrival in the region, a third of the troops levied from the coastal cities of Carthalo and Bomlicar joined his host. The best soldiers from those cities remained with the galleys that guarded the sea-lanes against Shamgar pirates and privateers.

The urban levies proved to be indifferent fighters, but the importance of the coastal cities lay in their ability to supply Uriah's host with food, drink and credit. Because of that, the original host remained in one body instead of scattering to search for needed supplies.

Thus, the first battle against the men of Dishon proved deceiving. The warlord of Dishon waited what he considered an appropriate period, letting time whittle down the barbarian host. Finding enough food to feed thousands of hardy warriors usually proved too much for fur-clad savages—that was how the warlord envisioned Uriah's host. Hunger often drove savages to despair, and then many barbarians deserted.

Finally, the warlord marched the city army into the Dishon hinterland, having boasted how he would roast his prisoners over fire-pits until their corpses shriveled and charred. Unfortunately for the warlord and his army, he missed a message from Gog by a mere three days. The message said on no account were they to go inland or to give battle to Uriah.

At the Battle of Three Creeks several days later, a tall warrior with a princely face, green eyes and long red hair led four squadrons of chariots. He was Herrek of Teman Clan, a great-great-grandson of Lord Uriah. He wore chainmail and had thick wrists wrapped with leather. Herrek led the charge, but the shield wall of Dishon held, and from the flanks, hired Arkite archers peppered the swirling chariots stymied before the shield wall. From his battle-platform, Herrek gave the signal, and trumpets pealed. The charioteers turned their carts and fled, whipping their horses in seeming panic. A few of the chariots broke as wheels shattered against rocky creek shores. The charioteers flung to the ground by the crashes scrambled upright and sprinted after their fleeing fellows.

The watching Arkite mercenaries threw down their bows, yanked out their stone-tipped clubs and yipped their battle cry, giving chase. Likely, none thought he could outrace a horse, but the idea of looting the nearby Elonite camp fired the notorious Arkite greed.

The warlord of Dishon shouted at his tribunes to hold back the men. The spearmen of Dishon did not obey but dropped their heavy shields and also gave chase. They didn't want the mountain mercenaries getting all the camp loot.

The streaming mass of Arkites and Dishon city levies raced past a great knot of trees in the center between the three creeks, and scrambled up a steep bank. There, at the top of the bank, the front-rank men halted in confusion.

Huri archers in a waiting row let their flint-tipped shafts fly, striking many.

The Arkites were fierce warriors, however. Their champions bellowed, waved their newly won iron weapons and charged the damned archers. Scrambling city men of Dishon panted as they raced after the faster fur-clad barbarians.

Then, hill men of Shur rose up from hiding before the Huri archers. They drew short swords and steel-headed tomahawks—gifts from Lord Uriah at the start of the campaign. The clansman of Shur crashed against the disjointed Arkites. Both sides fought fiercely, but the men of Shur had the numerical advantage. What was more, the weight of their numbers slowly pushed the mixed Arkite and Dishon soldiers back toward the steep bank.

The Huri archers had reformed, running close to the edge of the fighting. They shot skyward, raining arrows down upon the enemy's heads.

The Arkite mercenaries and Dishon spearmen broke, jumped down to the creek and raced for safety.

At that point, the last part of the trap swung shut. The princely Herrek had led the charioteers. They had re-formed earlier and driven around the area, parking near the knot of trees, jumped down and waited. As the fleeing enemy raced toward them, Herrek drew his famed short sword and shouted the war cry. The Elonites boiled out of the wild grove behind him. That proved too much, as Shurites and Huri men had jumped down the bank to surround the milling enemy forces.

The butchery began, ending when the last Arkites threw down their weapons and begged for mercy.

Since Lord Uriah led the host, a small party remained to guard the loot and prisoners. The rest set out that night to surprise the soldiers garrisoning the coastal city. Uriah pushed his tired warriors, with equally weary Shurites and Huri men piling onto the chariots. Uriah used the speed of his advance and the captured golden shields of Dishon's city guard to trick the unsuspecting defenders.

Two days after the battle, Herrek led Elonites in stolen golden armor and shields, forcing a Dishon survivor among them to shout up the password. The great land gate of Dishon creaked open, and Herrek led his disguised warriors through it.

The champion of Teman Clan lost half his men in the struggle to keep the gate open. It took that long for charging Shurites to reach the gate and boil inside, pushing back the city defenders.

Then, the rest of the host marched through to sack the city, as the hill warriors of Shur and the Huri men went wild, looting, raping and pillaging for three drunken days. It was a terrible spectacle, one Uriah proved incapable of stopping.

Herrek and his men saved half the populace, and it almost cost a rupture of the host. Herrek slew two Shurite champions, who thought to brush past him and rape the women he was protecting in the main city temple. That led to hot words and vile oaths. But in the end,

Uriah raged at the Shurite chieftains the next morning, demanding to know if this was how Elohim wished them to wage war.

The chieftains knew shame, although Uriah wisely let them keep their stolen treasures and newly captured slave girls.

Afterward, Uriah installed the city levies of Bomlicar and Carthalo in Dishon. They would hold the captured city and defend it against any relieving force sent by Gog to reclaim it.

Now, however, many Shurites wished to go home. "Look how we have slain Elohim's enemies. We have done our part." They were gorged with slaves and loot and sated with killing. Now, they thought about returning home with glory. Uriah persuaded them to stay, and he took the main host from Dishon back into the hinterland.

A new enemy general led a new enemy force, as the former Dishon warlord had died from his battle wounds. The host of Uriah soon marched through burned land, finding poisoned wells and smoky, ashy fields. There were no more slaves to catch either, as the people had fled at word of their coming.

Despite the complaining, the host crossed boundary stones that marked the hinterland of Dishon from Pildash. If anything, the desolation and destruction here proved worse instead of better. Now, too, sliths flew high overhead. Men muttered that those were gifts from Yorgash of Poseidonis. The trained pterodactyls surely spoke to the Gibborim handlers, telling the Nephilim children of Yorgash where and how the host of Uriah moved upon the ground.

As if to confirm the rumor, three nights later, crazed dire wolves—two to three times the size of normal wolves—raided a nighttime encampment. Soldiers of Gog struck next, hacking and slashing, murdering stumbling warriors rising from the ground where they slept.

Herrek was on guard to the west of camp. He blew the trumpet and led his men in disciplined attack, marching in a shield wall through camp. They slew seven dire wolves before an eerie cry caused the rest to race away into the night. With the wolves went the Nephilim attackers.

Herrek's guard had slain one of them—the reason they knew the identity of their foes.

The next morning, Shurite chieftains bitterly accused Herrek of deliberately marching slowly so the Nephilim and dire wolves could slay more of their people. Herrek hotly denied he would be so base, but wondered if maybe that was how Shurites thought.

It might have come to a duel, but Uriah halted the proceeding.

The next day, several clan chieftains of Shur gathered their warriors and marched from the main host. When Uriah arrived in a chariot, demanding to know the meaning of this, they told him they were going home. They had done their part. They did not plan to die in this foreign land.

After a few moments of silent thought, Uriah let them go with a warning. "We face Nephilim now. United we win. Divided we fall. We must keep our resolve. Because I only want willing warriors, I bid you well, men of Shur. You fought hard for a time, and for this, I thank you. Go in peace."

Half of the men of Shur who had originally marched with him now departed, mumbling in their beards, trying to decide if Uriah had insulted them. In the end, they were glad to leave.

Wisely, the enemy Nephilim leader did nothing to the deserters. No doubt, he hoped more of Uriah's host would follow them.

"What now?" Herrek asked Uriah in the command tent that evening. "Soon, we won't have anyone left."

Uriah sat back on his stool, dipping his drinking horn into a barrel of beer. He had wrapped himself in a white cloak. He quaffed the beer and dipped the horn again.

"We captured Dishon," the patriarch said at last. "We marched into Pildash territory, hoping to strike while the iron was hot. But Gog had someone else ready to face us. I don't think we can catch the rest of his forces by surprise. Thus, we should prepare for a grind."

"I don't understand," Herrek said.

"I would be surprised if you did. We've been moving fast like a chariot host should. We beat Gog to the punch and captured one of his key allied cities. That was a great coup. We're not going to do the same to Pildash, and we need to capture that city before we attempt our approach on Shamgar. In the old days, we could stop here and call it a victory, a grand victory. But Gog's prestige is lower than it has ever been. This is the moment. We must rally the countryside to us and show all men that we can defeat and destroy the Nephilim."

"Yes, but how?" asked Herrek.

Uriah lofted his horn and drained it. "By winning. We've won, and then we took a hit. That frightened too many of the hill men. We must make sure we don't take another dire-wolf-Nephilim hit like that again. That means we switch to a deliberate advance."

"Giving Gog time to gather reinforcements," Herrek complained.

"Yes. That means we also need reinforcements, and we need an element of surprise to help us regain the initiative."

"Do you have an idea?"

Uriah grinned at his grandson. "Indeed, I do."

"Will you tell me?"

"Not yet," Uriah said. But in his heart, he was counting on Joash acting faster than planned. That was another reason he had told Lod to stay with Joash. Two seraphs should be able to block Gog's supraocular visions. He wanted Joash's part to remain hidden as long as possible, because he wanted that which Joash could bring them to remain a surprise against Gog for as long as possible.

Uriah set aside his horn. It was time to pen a missive and send it by courier back to Elon. They needed to speed the process and get the special weapon onto the battlefield. Herrek had a point. How long could he keep these various tribes and clansman together as a coherent host, and large enough in number to capture Shamgar? He had to win before he ran out of time.

-6-

Cain slipped away from the pirate city on a bireme at night. Hardy rowers propelled the galley through the dark swamp as pirates held huge lanterns aloft at the prow. They reached the Suttung Sea before dawn and continued west. When the sun rose, nothing but green water surrounded the bireme in all directions.

Without a word to captain or crew, Cain climbed down a net thrown over the side of the galley. He descended into a launch the bireme had towed from Shamgar.

The launch was a sturdy boat with the forward part enclosed, holding their supplies for the next part of the journey. The launch had several rowing ports and a small mast and sail, although no oars were set in the pins and the mast was stowed along the outer left side of the boat.

The launch's crew consisted of two abnormal people. The first was a small woman named Ceto. She wore a cowl over her head, showing an albino face with eerie red eyes that looked up once before she stared at the launch's inner ribbing. She wore a brown robe, hiding her form, but the few times she moved, Cain gained the impression that she had misshapen shoulders and a crooked back. He could sense something else, too. She carried the blood of the high, making her half or a quarter-Nephilim. If half, she would have a supernatural gift unique to her.

Gog had sworn she would be instrumental in Cain gaining Elon sooner rather than later. The massive swordsman was dubious, but he knew how much the First Born desired Lod. Thus, he would believe for now.

The second person was lean like a vulture and wore a black robe like a priest of Gog. Neret had a hood, but it was thrown back to reveal his features. He had a narrow head with sunken cheeks and sinister black eyes that swirled with evil knowledge. Like the woman, Neret belonged to the Order of Gog.

Cain did not know the rank of either in the Order. He didn't particularly care to know, either.

Neret also had a Nephilim heritage, but more diluted than the woman possessed. He must be of the fifth or sixth generation. He would not have an inner gift, yet he exuded the stench of necromancy.

Cain nodded to himself. Neret must have stowed specially prepared skulls aboard the vessel. Had the man stuffed the skulls himself or purchased them from a stronger necromancer?

According to Gog, Neret was a spymaster, one of his best. The man would know those who had come to the Oracle and bargained for a vision. Such people came from everywhere, even from Elon, Huri Land and the Hills of Paran.

"I have secret allies everywhere on Earth," Gog had boasted.

"I believe you," Cain had said. "But will they help us while we're so far from Shamgar?"

"That is why I'm loaning you Neret. None who has made the secret oath will refuse. They paid too dear a price for the oracle. If they think to recant, Neret will help them remember the penalty for failure to fulfill their pledge."

Soon, the pirates untied the ropes holding the launch, climbed aboard the bireme and used long poles to shove the smaller craft away. Afterward, galley oars reappeared and stroked the green waters as though to a drum beat. The bireme turned, heading back in the direction of Shamgar.

"Well?" asked Cain.

Ceto looked up but wouldn't meet Cain's gaze. Finally, she shook her head before cowering once more.

"Neret?" asked Cain.

"Tell me what to do, Lord," the spymaster said in an oily voice. "I have seldom been abroad and never in so small a boat."

Cain was standing near the mast slot in the middle. He licked an index finger and held it high. There was hardly a stir of wind. The placid sea had said as much. The sail would prove useless until they had a breeze in the right direction. Staying here wasn't going to help either.

Cain moved with easy grace, having sailed many times. He picked up an oar and slotted it into its spot on the gunwale. He did the same on the other side.

"Take an oar," he said.

"Lord?" asked Neret.

Cain turned, peering into Neret's eyes. It was as if he looked into Neret's soul. Cain saw the evil, the delight in torturing helplessly bound victims, the silent chuckle Neret made when twisting a caught victim in a net of lies. Cain also saw the skill Neret used when casting a necromantic spell and the secret fear the spymaster had if he should stumble when applying heartless skull magic.

Neret bowed his head as he shivered, perhaps in real terror. Without another word, the robed spymaster scrambled to his place, sitting beside Cain on a thwart.

"Stay in time with me," Cain rumbled.

Neret nodded hastily.

The two began to row, and immediately Neret had trouble keeping up with Cain's powerful stroke.

"L-Lord," the necromancer panted later. "I'm exhausted."

"Row, damn you," Cain said in a low voice.

Neret continued, and the launch moved sluggishly through the sea. After half an hour, Neret cried out as the oar slipped from his blistered palms. He moaned as he stared at his bloody hands.

Cain stopped rowing and glanced at the trembling necromancer. As he did, he noted that Ceto secretly watched from her place near the tiller, although she remained in a huddled mass. He wondered if he should beat the necromancer for his weakness. The man feared him. Did he also want Neret to hate him?

"Wash your hands in the sea," Cain said. "The salt will help heal them. Then—"

"Lord," Neret said, "this is a disaster. I cannot cast a spell with bloody hands. Until they heal—"

"Put them in the water," Cain ordered, interrupting. "Use ointment afterward and then wrap them. Do it now!"

Neret scrambled to obey, using bloody hands to pull his sleeves back, revealing skinny, tattooed arms. He plunged his hands into the sea. It must have stung, but he didn't utter a word. After washing them and applying ointment, the necromancer wrapped them in mummy cloth.

The swordsman watched Neret. Finally, Cain grunted, reached over and grabbed the fallen oar-handle. Sliding into the middle position, he righted the two oars and began to row with both of them as if this were a mere rowboat. The launch began to move, going much faster than before. Cain leaned forward, set the oars into the sea and pulled back in an expert fashion. Clearly, he knew what he was doing. He began breathing harder, but he did not sweat. For over an hour Cain rowed. It seemed as if he could row forever, as if he possessed an inexhaustible fount of strength.

At last, Ceto straightened enough to watch. "You mustn't tire yourself, Lord," she said.

Cain did not acknowledge her words.

Ceto licked her pale lips before pressing them together. She closed her red eyes and concentrated. Suddenly, her head snapped up. She opened her eyes and crawled across the inner ribbing until she was near Cain's booted feet.

"Lord, if you would row north, that would be better."

"Better how?"

"We would skirt near the edge of Vergelmir Deep then."

"The hunting grounds of Nidhogg?"

"Nidhogg is dead."

Cain raised his eyebrows.

"Several years ago, our enemies slew him, calling a leviathan to do their bidding."

An odd feeling stirred in Cain. At first, he did not recognize it. Then, he understood that a pang of fear stabbed him. Who were these people to have done such a deed? The servants of Eden's god had been busy it would seem.

"Please, Lord," Ceto said. "It will be for the best."

Cain turned the launch until it headed north toward the legendarily haunted waters of Vergelmir Deep. He continued for some time, tirelessly pulling the oars.

"Lord," Ceto said.

There was something new in her voice, something strong and certain.

Cain pushed the oar handles down, lifting the oar blades from the sea. He set the handles in loops, and then worked one oar into the launch and then the other.

Ceto shed her robe, letting it fall to her feet. She was misshapen, as he'd suspected, with twisted shoulders and a hunched back. Worse, she had glittering marks here and there on her naked body.

With horror, Cain realized those were scales like on a fish. Her hair was like seaweed. When she leaped overboard, he saw webbing between her toes.

Ceto pierced the water's surface with a splash, disappearing from sight.

"Look," Neret whispered half a minute later. He pointed with a wrapped hand.

In the distance, Ceto surfaced. In the time that had taken her—Cain knew he could not have swum nearly so far.

Once more, the woman dove out of sight.

Time passed, and Cain debated drawing his sword, slaying Neret and rowing to the northern shore of the sea, which would place him on the southern edge of Giant Land. He would escape this mad land of Gog. He would—

"I see her," Neret said.

Cain looked up, and he blanched. Four, no five, long-necked sea-saurians headed for the launch. They had dark, rubbery skin and flashing needle-like teeth. Ceto clung to one of their necks, and she appeared to be laughing. The creatures were bigger than the river saurians he'd seen while with the Nebo on their punts. The creatures were each almost as long as the launch. That meant each of the sea-beasts was many times smaller than Nidhogg—

Abruptly, Cain understood. These must be Nidhogg's spawn. That's why Ceto had wanted him to head toward Vergelmir Deep. Had that been the spawning grounds—waters?

Soon enough, the five sea-saurians swam around the boat. They glided effortlessly with fins in places where legs should be. Ceto laughed and waved to Cain and Neret.

Neret glanced in horror at Cain. Cain smiled at Ceto and waved back at her.

Soon, the bizarre woman coaxed the monsters near the launch. If any of them decided to crash against the boat, it would stove in the sides.

Ceto petted the creature carrying her before she slipped off and swam back to the launch. She cast webbed hands onto the sides.

Cain hauled her naked body into the boat. He was very aware of each of the sea-saurians eyeing him. Ceto might have sensed their unease because she scrambled up and waved to them, crying out in clicks and whistles.

Then, she seemed to understand that she was naked. She went to her robe, slipping it on. Wearing it, she climbed onto the sealed area and opened a hatch. She drew three long heavy ropes, casting each into the sea.

"Do you need help?" asked Cain.

Ceto did not answer. Instead, she slipped off the robe and dove back into the sea. The beasts crowded around her.

At her bidding, three of the sea-saurians each slipped its head and long neck through a loop. The other two watched.

"Are you ready?" she called back.

Cain cupped his hands around his mouth. "Ready," he shouted. "Are you staying out there?"

"For now," Ceto shouted.

Cain turned to Neret. "Sit down. I have a feeling we're going to go fast."

Neret obeyed.

A few moments later, the three sea-saurians began to pull, towing the launch faster and faster until it fairly skipped over the waters.

Cain crawled out to the front of the boat and shut the hatch. He took Ceto's robe with him. The woman was strange beyond anything else he'd seen that resembled a human. She was much stranger than Sagoth.

This—Cain sat back near the tiller. He thrilled at the speed of the craft. And he realized why she had brought five monsters with her. They would switch out with each other, thus ensuring the fastest voyage possible across the length of the Suttung Sea.

Gog was running short of time, and this voyage might help thwart Uriah and his barbarian host of charioteers and hill men. Lod was busy doing something important back in Elon. Gog not only wanted Lod as a captive, but the First Born wanted to know what his spy service was warning him about as a possible blow to Shamgar's hold of the eastern shores of the Suttung Sea.

-7-

Almost two years ago, Lod had freed Joash from Nephilim captivity, removing the bronze mask his captors had locked in place. Joash had returned with Lod to Elon, there to heal from the wounds received at the hands of his captors. Joash had recovered rapidly, in large part because of the care of his wife, Adah of Poseidonis. That was fitting, perhaps, as Lod had rescued Adah many years before from the island kingdom of the First Born Yorgash and his hideous Gibborim children.

Lord Uriah and the crusading host had left Elon quite some time ago. Since then, Lod and Joash had been busy with the secret project. It had been going well, and now, possibly, would go even better according to the news from the Huri tracker they'd just invited into their lodge.

"My news is ten days old," the Huri said, a lean warrior with gray-streaked hair. He wore a thrice-curled boar tusk on each arm, proving him a mighty hunter indeed, as he would not have worn the adornment unless he'd slain the animal himself.

As a gift for his troubles, Joash gave the Huri an iron-tipped spear and a sharp iron knife.

"You are generous," the old hunter said.

"I appreciate good news," the young man said as they ushered him into the lodge.

"It could be a trap," Lod said after the Huri departed. "This would be just the thing one of Gog's minions would devise to draw you away."

Joash shook his head. "It isn't a trap."

42

"How do you know that?"

Joash seemed confused. "It's no trap," he repeated. "I just know."

Lod had already learned how hard it was to argue with the slender young man once Joash made up his mind. Joash didn't get a mulish look and never raised his voice, but once he decided a thing, there was no turning him.

Lod admired that in the man, and like everyone else in Havilah Holding, he liked Joash. He was also one of the few people who spoke freely to the shiny-faced seraph without stammering or becoming nervous. The mark of Elohim clearly rested on Joash, and everything about his character proved he was good. Maybe Lod spoke so easily because he was the blade of Elohim. He'd led a darker path through life than Joash, repeatedly staining his hands with the spilled blood of his Elohim-hating foes. Lod was certain Joash communed directly with the Lord Above. There was so much wholeness about the young man, even though he had been through Hell as a Nephilim captive on more than one occasion.

Lod had also been through hell as rat bait and later a galley slave of Poseidonis. The experiences had stamped him with harshness and bitterness at times. It had also turned him into a fierce warrior, eager to attack and smash the enemy.

Joash had learned other lessons, learning to feel sorrow for those held captive and wanting to help the downtrodden. He fought when he had to, but he didn't relish battle and bloodshed as Lod obviously did. Maybe that was why animals loved him so much. Maybe Joash had found more of Adam's original innocence from before the Fall of Man. Maybe he had gone deeper into the hard places with Elohim beside him, instead of latching onto Elohim as the last hope to drag him from utter despair, as Lod had done when he'd descended into madness.

In this instance, concerning the news from the Huri tracker, Lod listened to Joash, before hurrying from the lodge and making arrangements. Two hours later, five chariots careened from Havilah Holding. They used the road to Nearer Tarsh on the Tarshish Sea.

Joash drove his own chariot with Adah laughing beside him. Behind the chariot raced a pack of hunting dogs. They bayed with delight, often looking to Joash as he flicked the reins. The horses pulling Joash's chariot glanced back at him almost as often as the hounds did. The horses did not hold back but raced freely because Joash asked it of them.

The journey only took three days because at each holding, Joash switched horses. The hounds had trouble keeping up the fast pace. Thus, Joash asked each of the charioteers if some of the hounds could ride along with them.

Every one of them agreed, even Lod.

On the third day of the trek, the small company of chariots raced past towering trees, the border between Elon and the southern Huri Forest.

Lod warily eyed the gloomy woods. He still suspected the Huri tracker who had given them the news. Any moment, he expected archers to race out and launch arrows at them. He expected Huri hounds to race for the horses. It was the chief reason why he'd agreed to let several of Joash's dogs rest in his chariot. He wanted the hunting dogs ready to fight to the death for their master.

None of that happened, however.

Toward the end of the third day, a driver shouted, pointing at the wine-dark Tarshish Sea at the distant horizon. The land of Elon separated this body of water from the inland Suttung Sea. An hour later, the same driver pointed out the spires of Nearer Tarsh, one of the greatest trading cities in this part of the world.

They passed through the main city gate by nightfall and lodged in a grand house. It belonged to a chief merchant of Nearer Tarsh, one beholden to Lord Uriah and also a friend to the present ruler of Caphtor. Over two hundred years ago, Uriah and his followers had emigrated from tall-walled Caphtor, a city, men said, had been founded by Seth, the third son of Adam and Eve. The ancient city of Caphtor was hundreds of leagues south, across the Tarshish and then the Great Sea.

The Elonites, including Lod, slept deeply that night. He trusted the hunting dogs to give the alarm, if needed.

In the morning, Lod and Joash, with the charioteers in tow as bodyguards, left the merchant palace and went down to the main slave mart by the waterfront. They were looking for a particular group of slaves, ones that had threaded past the southern forests of Huri Land. That was where the Huri tracker had seen them, talking to the slavers. After a three-hour search, the company found the slaves in the stockyard of a silver-mining magnate who had

44

purchased cheap bodies to dig for silver in subterranean pits to the north.

"This is terrible," Joash told Lod. "Someone already bought them."

"Hang on, lad," Lod said. "I see the magnate with his slavers. Leave this to me."

Joash eyed the over-muscled warrior and looked again at the magnate. He was a rich man in an ermine fur coat that reached the ground. The magnate had a heavy gold necklace and many expensive rings on his fat fingers. The slavers around the magnate were beefy men with hook-knives and coiled whips hung on their belts. Lod would not like such men or the lord who employed them.

"Let me join you," Joash said in a reasonable tone. "I could…learn a few things by watching you."

Lod grunted and almost said no, but finally shrugged, muttering, "If you wish. But make sure the rest of the men tag along. I don't trust slavers."

"Of course," Joash said.

Lod thus led the group of Elonites to the magnate and his men. The magnate was Ard of Naxos, a name known among the silversmiths, jewelers and slavers of Nearer Tarsh. By repute, Ard owned half the mines on the northern shore of the Sea of Tarshish.

"Good day," Lod said. "Could I have a word with you?"

The beefy men with whips and black leather jerkins turned at Lod's rough voice. Their thick hands dropped to their hook-knives. Others of their kind poked their heads from a nearby tent. Someone whistled into the tent, and more slavers and guards emerged, hurrying to their master.

"Who are you?" Ard of Naxos demanded.

Lod wore a brown leather vest and pants with boots, and had a sword dangling from his belt. Some of Ard's men were taller. None was thicker or likely weighed as much. None had as baleful a stare, either.

"Excuse me, sir," Joash said, stepping forward. He wore his blue tunic and smiled in a good-natured way. Today, the shine wasn't as apparent, although he seemed hale and healthy beyond the ordinary. He had a knife attached to his belt, but it seemed more ornamental than Lod's clearly utilitarian sword. "We're looking for slaves," Joash said.

"Why talk to me?" Ard demanded coldly. "I'm not a slaver."

"We wish to find a certain *type* of slave," Joash said.

Lod didn't roll his eyes, but he felt like it.

"That doesn't answer my question," Ard said. "Now make your point, young man. I'm busy."

"Of course," Joash said. "Several men you purchased are the type we need. We would like to buy them from you."

Ard's fat-enfolded eyes narrowed in calculation. By this time, his slavers and guards had gathered in large number, six or seven times the number of the Elonites.

"I would gladly pay you extra if you would sell them to us," Joash said.

"I know you," one guard said, pointing at Lod. "He's friends with Lord Uriah of Elon."

Ard gave Lod a harsh study. Perhaps Ard of Naxos disliked Uriah of Elon. His next words proved it. "Sorry," the magnate said, not sounding sorry at all. "None of my slaves are for sale."

"Not even at a profit?" Joash asked.

Ard glared at Joash, fingering his gold chain. "Am I a scrambler for dung like you, that coins fill my dreams?"

"Watch your mouth," Lod growled.

Ard drew himself upright, scowling at Lod. "How dare you threaten me? Why, I could order my men—"

Lod drew his sword with lightning speed. It was more incredible because of the size of his muscles. None built like him should move with cobra-quickness. As he drew his sword, Lod stepped near so the tip tickled Ard's protruding belly.

Ard grew pale as he looked down at the sword and then up into Lod's blazing blue eyes. Did he see the madness barely controlled by Lod's will? Did he realize Lod hated his kind with searing passion? It would have been an easy guess, and Ard of Naxos was not stupid in the slightest.

"Stay back," Ard told his men. Likely, the magnate was an excellent judge of warriors. He had traded in men far too long not to realize the quality of each. The crazy man before him…it would be better to give him what he wanted and get as far away from him as possible. Fate would deal with the crazy man soon enough. There were bold warriors and there were old warriors, but there were no bold old warriors, or so the saying went.

46

"Let me tell you—" Lod said.

"My man," Ard said, forcing a greasy smile onto his lips as he gently pushed the sword tip from his belly. "There is no need for that. If you will allow me…?"

Lod thought about it and he recognized the magnate's wish to get rid of him as fast as possible. Thus, he nodded.

"You may go," Ard told his slavers and guards. "I'll deal with these men on my own."

"Begging your pardon, Lord," one of the guards said.

"Go!" Ard bellowed. "That is an order."

The slavers and guards turned away, a few of them giving Lod evil glances.

The white-haired warrior sheathed his blade, seemingly unconcerned with them.

Joash stepped up, clearing his throat. "Lod is a champion, my lord. He is eager for glory."

"I can see that," Ard said.

"We mean no disrespect," Joash said. "We have pressing needs for a particular type of man. You might even say that we're desperate."

Lod shot Joash a hard glance. He didn't like hearing Joash speak nicely to this rich filth. But he remembered—barely in time—that Joash had convinced the elders of Shur to send hill warriors with Uriah. That had solved many problems for them. Maybe there was a time to use Joash's softer methods. Thus, Lod closed his mouth and held back any hot retorts. Instead, he began watching for a secret attack by the magnate's guards. He was sure it would come in time.

In that, Lod proved wrong. The slavers and guards did not show up again. A few new guards came over later once Joash had selected four stout men. They were short and stocky with dark hair like Joash. One of them had whiter skin on his wrists, indicating that he usually wore a wrist guard of some kind.

The four men Joash chose looked tough. He had each take off his rough-spun slave tunic. Each of them had whip-scarred backs, some of the wounds fresh.

"You've saved me trouble by selecting those four," Ard said at the end of the bargaining.

"I'm sorry Lod drew steel on you," Joash said. "Take this extra gold as a favor to me." The young man held out a small sack of coins.

Ard glanced at Lod before accepting Joash's final and rather large offer for the four foreign slaves. Let the young man have them. What did he need four ex-mammoth riders for anyway? They had proven quarrelsome and would surely perish quickly in the mines.

That night, his chief guard asked permission to ambush the Elonites as they left on the highland road to Elon.

"No," Ard said. "Let them go. The young man paid me generously. There was something about him…" Ard of Naxos shook his head.

"But Lod insulted your honor," the guard said.

Ard thought about how much Joash had paid for the mammoth riders. "My honor is intact," he said. "Now shut up about it. Besides, that man, Lod…I have a feeling he's going to get exactly what he has coming."

8

Lod growled low in his throat as he drove his chariot. He'd known this would happen, had just known. He had excellent vision and employed it now. Emerging from the forest ahead was the gray-streaked Huri tracker that had visited Havilah Holding the other day. Making it a hundred times worse was a Huri war party following the older chief.

Lod had wondered at the time if the Huri had been more than a mere tracker. The man had been too self-confident back in the lodge. Now, Lod understood why. The tracker was really a chieftain. The three red-dyed eagle feathers in the man's hair said as much.

On the main road, Joash drove the lead chariot, with his hunting pack trotting behind him. One of the mammoth riders rode with the young man, the one named Thoar. Adah rode in a chariot at the rear of the company.

Lod wasn't going to wait for the war party to start firing their famous bows. By then, it might be too late. He flicked the reins and shouted at his horses. The pair responded beautifully, fairly leaping into a gallop. In a rush, Lod passed the others and then turned off the main road, rolling over bumpy, grassy ground as he charged the war party.

"Get set," he snarled at the warrior hanging onto the railing beside him. "Ready a javelin. Pierce the gray-haired warrior. He's the chieftain, the one with the red feathers."

The Elonite glanced at Lod, nodded sharply and released the railing. The Elonite had splendid balance on the cart's reed-woven matting. The matting was made to absorb some of the shock of a careening chariot. The warrior yanked a slender javelin from the holder to the side.

Lod laughed, his blue eyes shining madly. He counted two dozen or more forest warriors. The gray-streaked chieftain raised both hands as if signaling peace. That didn't fool Lod.

At that point, one of Joash's hunting dogs raced even with the chariot.

"Hi-ya!" Lod roared at the beast. "There's a good boy. You want some Huri meat, do you?"

The shaggy hound surged ahead of the chariot, running faster than Lod had ever seen a dog do. Then, the hound did something insane, darting to the right, racing in front of the horses.

"Whoa!" Lod shouted, yanking on the reins, checking the horses barely enough. The hound raced from under flashing hooves just in time, streaking onto the other side of the chariot.

Lod's hard motion must have caught his fellow warrior by surprise. The man shouted, released his javelin and might have toppled over the front railing. Lod grabbed the back of his jerkin, hauling the man back into the cart.

"Look!" the pale warrior shouted. "Joash is signaling us."

Lod glanced back. Joash spoke to his horses, and they raced like the wind, gaining on him. To Lod's chagrin, he saw that Joash's warrior had leapt off the cart. The young seraph was alone. What was Joash thinking?

The young man's shout drifted to him, "Stop, Lod. Don't attack."

Lod hesitated only a moment. He drew the reins again, turning his team.

Joash's team responded perfectly until they pulled even with Lod. The two chariots no longer aimed at the forest but moved parallel with the tree line and the road.

"What are you doing?" Joash shouted.

"Attacking the ambushers."

"They're not ambushing us. They must have come because the chief spotted more mammoths for me. He told me about a small herd some of his people had seen. I told him we would likely be passing this way."

"Lad," Lod said. "That was foolish. This is a Huri ambush. It's what they do."

"I don't think so. Let's parley with them and be certain."

By the way Joash looked at him, it occurred to Lod he might have misjudged the moment. If Joash had been Lord Uriah, the old man would have openly rebuked him. Joash did it like this. Once Lod realized the truth, he blushed, embarrassed that he had almost started a needless fight.

"Lad," he said, the word sticking in his throat.

Joash smiled. "You showed them Elonite courage and battle-readiness. They won't soon forget that, I warrant. I appreciate your keenness, Lod. There is none like you."

"Lad," the warrior said thickly. "There is none like Joash. Yes. We will parlay. You can lead it."

"Nay, Lod. You will lead it. I'm but a young man."

"Fine. I'll lead us there. Let's go see what they have to say."

***

Joash was right. The chieftain had learned that a small mammoth herd was close. The chieftain had brought along a man that could show them the way.

The great beasts roamed this part of the Elon plain, seldom entering the gloomy forests of Huri Land. There were greater herds upon the Kragehul Steppes—also known as Giant Land. But neither Joash nor Lod had any desire to cross the Suttung Sea and try their luck there. The smaller mammoths in Elon had been enough so far. Maybe this herd had a few bigger bulls they could use.

There were two Mammoth Men cousins with the company, Thoar and Boar. The other two had been tenders, not actually mammoth riders, meaning not official Mammoth Men.

Soon, Lod and the others parked their chariots at the bottom of a rocky hill. They were several miles already from the forest.

"Better a few of us go than many," Thoar said, speaking to Joash.

The young man studied the Mammoth Man, nodding shortly. He pointed at Thoar, Boar, Lod and the Huri who had spotted the herd earlier.

Lod brought up the rear so he could keep an eye on the two Mammoth Men. Boar was older and deeper-chested with a scar running across his broad face. He claimed to have gotten it in battle. Thoar was taller, handsome and had an easier way about him. Both

51

Mammoth Men were dark-haired and stout, shorter than Lod would have guessed from the legends he'd heard about them.

Mammoth Men were plains people from across the Great Sea. They lived far west of the Jogli Steppes and west of the city of Iddo. That city hired mercenary mammoth riders sometimes. Thoar and Boar had fought Jogli nomads on several occasions for Iddo, having been captured the last time and sold to a slave-trader on the shore of the Great Sea. The trader's ship had wrecked to the north, and the slavers had trekked overland to Nearer Tarsh with their cargo of chained slaves.

According to Thoar, Boar had traveled abroad in his youth, having the wanderlust in him. Of the two, Thoar was pleasanter and more sociable. Of the two, Boar knew more about taming and training mammoths.

The five men trudged up the stony hill, with the Huri leading. The forest man threw himself onto his stomach, crawling to the top. Joash did likewise. After a moment, Thoar and Boar followed the example.

Lod hung back, watching the Mammoth Men. Neither of them had a weapon, not even a knife. If one of them should loft a stone to crash upon the back of Joash's head—

Lod growled to himself. What was wrong with him? Why did he suspect everyone and everything? He hadn't been this paranoid in the past. Had Lord Uriah's charge to keep Joash safe unhinged his thinking?

Lod charged up the hill, barely remembering to throw himself onto his stomach and crawl the last part. He joined the others, who hid behind boulders as they peered down the hill at the valley below.

Lod saw what had the others enraptured. A dozen mammoths grazed at the bottom of the hill, so close he could have heaved a spear that far if he had a running start. The bull of the herd was bigger than any mammoth Lod had ever seen before, at least twice as high as a tall man. The bull had a thick coat of shaggy hair and two impressive curling tusks. For his size, the bull had beady little eyes. Did he sense them?

The bull had halted and raised his trunk in the air, sniffing perhaps.

"He's big," Boar said in a terse voice. "If captured young, he would have made a fine mount. Now…" He shook his head.

52

There were cows and young, and two other bulls, not nearly as big as the old one.

Joash turned bright eyes upon Lod. "We should take them with us."

The bull would be a good addition, Lod thought. But he didn't know if capturing the others would be worth the extra time it would take getting back to Havilah Holding.

Lod noticed Boar staring at Joash. "What's wrong with you?" he demanded.

"You can't possibly capture the mammoths," Boar said.

"Why not?" said Lod.

"You need *trained* mammoths to capture wild ones in the open. See those younger bulls? The old one is going to drive them from the herd in a couple of weeks. That means he's fired up, ready to fight. We have to be careful and not let him see us. If he does, he might charge and attempt to trample us."

Joash clapped Boar on the shoulder. "Don't worry. I'll settle the old one." With that, Joash climbed to his feet.

"No," Boar said. "Are you mad?" And he grabbed at Joash.

Lod scrambled on all fours, reaching Boar like a stoat. He crashed upon the man and tore him from Joash.

"Leave me," Boar said, who started to struggle.

Lod wrenched one of Boar's arms behind his back, and he noticed Thoar climbing to his feet with a stone in his hands. Laughing mirthlessly, Lod surged to his feet, dragging Boar upright in front of him. Thoar checked his rush.

At the bottom of the hill, the bull mammoth trumpeted.

Thoar, Boar and Lod turned to look down the hill. Joash was already halfway to the bull.

The old one watched with beady mammoth eyes as the two-legs approached, and the bull's posture of spread ears and intensity showed he meant to charge and possibly trample as Boar had suggested.

"It's too late," Boar said. "He's a dead man. We must flee or the bull will trample us, too."

Lod flung the Mammoth Man from him, drew his sword and started down the hill. "Joash!" he shouted.

In an instant, the bull switched his target, staring at the white-haired warrior and his bright metal tooth.

"Lod, stop!" shouted Joash. "You're making him angry."

The words penetrated, and Lod remembered who Joash was. The Mammoth Man might know his creatures. Boar wouldn't know a seraph touched by Elohim, though.

Lod skidded to a halt.

The bull snorted and pawed the earth.

Finding it difficult to do, Lod sheathed his sword and forced himself to sit on the side of the hill.

"Good," Joash said.

The young man faced the bull and continued downhill. He raised both hands palm forward. At that moment, an eerie radiance shined from Joash's face. He smiled, and he seemed to communicate peace to the shaggy monster.

The rest of the herd watched Joash intently.

"Mammoths are a gift from Elohim," Joash said in a singsong voice. "Where the Nephilim live, there mammoths will not abide."

The bull lowered his trunk and stopped pawing the soil. His demeanor changed the closer Joash approached. Finally, the young man was only a few feet away. The trunk snaked out and gently touched Joash on the shoulder.

Joash laughed, patting the trunk good-naturedly.

At that point, the rest of the herd, including the cows and their young, began moving toward the two-legs. When the mammoths reached Joash, each gently patted his shoulder with its trunk.

Boar and Thoar stumbled down the hill to Lod. The Mammoth Men looked stunned.

"W-What…what is this?" Boar asked hoarsely. "Sorcery?"

Lod scowled. "This is the touch of Eden in Joash's soul. In some ways, he is like Adam in the beginning. He can commune with animals."

"I-I would never believe this if I hadn't seen it," Boar said. "Why do you need us if you can do that?"

"Joash can tame them," Lod said. "But others will ride the mammoths into battle. We need to know how that is best done."

"Ah," Boar said, nodding. "Yes. We can teach you that—for a price."

Lod eyed the older Mammoth Man, and for once, the blade of Elohim smiled.

Boar must not have liked the smile, because he dropped his gaze. "On second thought, you have already paid us by buying us from the silver miner. It is our honor to teach you Mammoth Men secrets."

"Joash will treat you better than you deserve," Lod said. "But that is for the future. For now, start thinking about the best way to move the herd to Havilah Holding."

Boar and Thoar traded glances.

And Lod decided that Boar would still bear close watching. There was something about Boar that struck him wrong. This time, however, he would not act too soon, but wait for the right moment.

-9-

Cain's gut seethed, although nothing showed on his face. This was reckless and certainly shouldn't fool anyone.

He wore an oversized cloak to try to hide the massiveness of his limbs. He'd also dyed his hair and beard black. He had been hefting barrels of beer for a merchant, carrying them to a location an Elonite had pointed out. From the chuck wagons where cooks slopped beans and laid thick slices of roast pork onto clay plates, Cain could see some of the mammoths cordoned off near the hay wagons.

It was late afternoon, and the host of Elonite charioteers, mammoth riders and spearmen were setting up camp for the night.

Cain, Neret, Ceto and the sea-saurians had crossed the length of the Suttung Sea without incident. There had been a rocky cove along the eastern Elon coast, north of Farther Tarsh, where Cain had stowed the launch.

"It may be several weeks before we're back," Cain had told Ceto.

"No problem," she said.

"Make sure no one spots your…pets."

"I'll have to go farther out then, and there are always fishing boats. Should I sink any if I think the fishermen have seen us?"

"Sink the boats without hesitation and have your beasts eat the fishermen. We're never going to pull this off without perfect secrecy."

Ceto had swum out to sea with her beasts, promising to keep an eye on shore for Cain's signal. He would use a flashing mirror.

Cain and Neret had trudged inland afterward, the spymaster wearing a normal shirt, breeches and boots. He still looked sinister, so Cain had him wrap one of his feet and use a crutch. People gave greater allowances for the injured.

There were few cities in Elon. Most of the cities like Farther Tarsh were on the Suttung coast. The last time Cain had been in this part of the world—several hundred years ago—the plains had swarmed with animals and almost no people. Uriah's coming had changed that.

With the crutch, it had taken longer reaching an Elonite holding, a log-walled stockade. The logs must have come from a Huri forest, gained through barter. The Elonites in the holding housed and fed them when Cain said they were on their way to Nearer Tarsh to meet a cousin of his.

Two days later, on the road to Havilah Holding, a large merchant caravan from Farther Tarsh had overtaken them. Cain and Neret paid to ride on a wagon. A day after that, Neret had sniffed out a trader who had been to the Oracle years earlier. Neret practiced necromancy that night. When Cain approached the selected trader the next morning, the man had eagerly agreed to help. He had been shaking and exhaling a foul green mist. It had terrified him, and he complained of awful stomach cramps.

"Tell Gog I remember my oath," the trader pleaded with Cain.

Afterward, Cain and Neret had laid their plans, discovering that a new crusading host was marching overland to Dishon. What was more, this host had mammoths and riders.

It had been easy enough reaching the host, as Lod accepted merchants and their goods, paying coin for supplies. Naturally, Elonite guards inspected all the wagons, but Neret knew his spy trade inside and out.

Now, as Cain and Neret relaxed by the chuck wagons, sitting on stools with food on their laps, the spymaster said softly, "That one. He's been to the Oracle."

Neret didn't point, so Cain didn't know exactly—

"Do you see the four Mammoth Men," Neret asked.

"Only two are Mammoth Men. The other two are mammoth tenders."

"How do you know?"

"I've been among Mammoth Men before. What are they doing here?"

"Helping the Elonites train mammoths," Neret said, although he managed to avoid saying, "Obviously."

"That's not the question. Did Uriah send men to the southern steppes to hire them?"

"Wouldn't more have come, then?"

Cain nodded as he ate a forkful of beans. "Which one has been to the Oracle?"

"The older one," Neret said, "the one wearing bronze wrist guards."

Cain saw him, and he eyed the man's face. That Mammoth Man did not look happy. He wondered why.

"Same procedure as before?" asked Cain.

Neret set his plate of pork and beans on the grass, slyly eyeing the man. "I don't think so." He stood.

"Where are you going?"

"To talk," Neret said. "Don't worry. I'll be discreet."

With another, Cain might have worried, especially in the midst of their enemies. But Neret knew his trade. He was a lousy oarsman and an indifferent sailor, but as a thief and a spy, he had few equals.

Cain said no more but ate his food. A few minutes later, he glanced over. Neret and the Mammoth Man spoke together. Finally, Neret nodded and scraped low in a fawning manner as if frightened by the exalted rank of the other.

Soon, Neret hobbled to his stool, sat, picked up his plate and almost began to continue eating as if nothing had happened. Cain saw that's what the man wanted to do, but Neret had wisely learned to fear him.

"He's ready," Neret said. "It will happen tonight."

Cain did not scowl, although no one could make a plan that fast or agree so readily. "Speak sense," he said flatly.

Neret scarfed down some beans before looking up and grinning. With his lean features, it seemed he must have stolen a baby from its mother. Nothing else would make him so happy. How could anyone trust a face like that?

"Boar hates Lod, but he especially hates Joash," Neret said. "He begged me to kidnap Joash and take him with us when we leave."

"Does he mean the same Joash men say really leads the host?"

Neret nodded. "Joash is a strange man, if the rumors are true. He can control mammoths the way Sagoth does his great apes or Ceto the sea-saurians."

"I don't believe it. These are Elohim worshipers, not children of the *bene elohim*."

At the mention of Elohim's name, Neret hunched his shoulders and winced as if someone had spat on him. "Please, Lord," he whined. "Don't say that name. It's…" The spymaster shook his head like a cat shaking water from its paw.

"Enough of your games," Cain said. "Whatever else they are, Elonites aren't beastmasters."

"Agreed," Neret whispered. "I'm merely passing along the Mammoth Man's belief. He seethes with hatred against Joash because Joash can control mammoths better than any man alive."

Cain grunted, thinking about it. "Boar is envious of Joash."

"Such is clear," Neret said.

"This Joash must have learned Mammoth Man secrets and applied them."

"Boar seems unhinged on the subject."

"Can we trust him, then?"

"Except on the subject of Joash, I think so."

"Well…" Cain said, thinking. "We're not going to kidnap Joash. He's the real leader of the host from what I hear."

"Others say Lod leads."

Cain grinned humorlessly. "I know this Lord Uriah. I met him in his youth. It's taken me time to remember the incident…but that's unimportant. Uriah is clever like a spymaster. I imagine Lod thinks he's in charge, but it's to confuse assassins like you."

"Uriah raised up Lod as the target?"

"What better target? The man's an incredible warrior. Plus, he's suspicious and quick to act."

"Can you…subdue Lod?" Neret asked.

"There's not a man alive I can't best. What's your plan?"

Neret told it to Cain in whispers.

"Boar actually thinks this insanity will work?" Cain asked, sounding dubious.

"More importantly, *I* think it's our best chance to pull this off."

Cain eyed the spymaster, and he realized the longer they stayed among the Elonites, the greater the likelihood someone would discover their real identity. Could he subdue Lod in time? Neret had set it up that he should be able to use one of his unique talents. This was a risk, but despite the boldness of the plan, the odds seemed good. If Neret and he could pull this off…he, Cain, would have the sacrifice Gog needed in order to read his future.

For the first time in ages, Cain was excited about what was going to happen. It was odd to feel this nervous but delightful tension, the anticipation of a thing…

Neret shivered in dread and looked away.

Cain tilted his head…until he understood that Neret had seen something on his face to frighten him. At that point, Cain forced himself to sit blandly so he didn't give anything else away.

-10-

The chaotic night erupted with trumpet blasts and hoarse shouting. Fires blazed from hay piles, and mammoths stampeded in all directions. The mammoths had already been fleeing. The Elonite reaction and the sabotage from certain quarters caused the great beasts to vent in fear, speeding and trumpeting louder.

Cain tossed an oily torch aside and sprinted past hay wagons, roped-off areas and camp tents to a waiting chariot. The horses neighed in fear, stamping the ground, and might have joined the stampede. Neret was aboard, trying to control them and was proving next to useless at it.

Cain jumped in the chariot box and took the reins from Neret. He spoke to the horses and pulled the reins, showing them who was in control.

The spymaster had torn off his bandage and tossed away his crutch. He had a bag of sinister skulls tied to his belt and wore a hood, his dark eyes shining evilly on the released skull magic.

Cain no longer wore the cloak, but leathers and boots as of old. He wanted freedom of movement tonight.

The camp was a seething mass of confusion, fires, shouting men, rampaging horses, barking dogs and trumpet peals. Chaos begat chaos, and those that attempted to bring order only seemed to add to the madness.

"That way," Neret said in a strange voice, pointing into the darkness.

Cain flicked the reins, and the horses trotted in that direction. Horses could see better in the dark than men could, but it was doubtful the horses could see in the dark as well as Cain did. He guided them around obstacles in the plains. In the distance, Cain spied huge shadowy shapes, running mammoths that Neret had goaded through his spells.

He glanced back at the blaze of fires, some of them with men desperately trying to beat them out. The Elonite camp wasn't quite like an overturned anthill. Joash or Lod had organized the host better than that. People continued to run pell-mell, shouting orders or screaming for someone to tell them what to do.

"West," Neret said in a choked voice. He looked in that direction, and his black eyes glowed like hellish pits. He almost seemed blind. Did he see on a different plane of reality?

Cain felt necromantic heat radiating from the spymaster. Pinches against his skin felt like ants biting. Maybe that's what made the horses so nervous. He turned the anxious team, heading toward the nighttime west. "Where exactly are—?"

"This isn't an exact science," Neret snarled. A moment later, he said in a quieter voice, "Boar..." The spymaster panted as sweat dripped from his wan skin. "Sorry," he said, frowning. "I'm—"

"Forget it," Cain said.

Neret dipped his head. "Boar must do his part. We're counting on him. But yes, keep going west."

Cain didn't know how Neret sensed the Mammoth Man's location, but the spymaster had proven right so far. Cain glanced at Neret, at the sack of skulls tied to his waist. There were fewer than when they'd started the sea voyage. Each specially prepared necromancer's skull contained the concentrated agony of tormented prisoners, some of the soul energy that had leaked from them as the practitioner tortured them to death. That's what it meant that Neret was Flay Rank in the Order of Gog. Each time Neret cast a spell, he used up some of the concentrated "soul energy" in a skull until it simply flaked away into nothingness.

"Ahead," Neret hissed. "I sense Elonites ahead."

Cain squinted into the darkness. Dark blots turned into a small band of warriors. The warriors were running west. He could hear them now and saw a flickering torch.

"I see the bull," a man shouted from the group.

"Wait," Neret hissed at Cain.

62

Cain drew rein. The horses stopped and stamped the ground nervously. Twisting back, Cain could see that they had already covered a lot of territory. The camp was small and distant from here.

"Boar is guiding them," Neret said. "He told me he would bring Lod this way."

"He brought more than just Lod," Cain snapped.

Neret turned to him. "Can you slay the others first?"

Cain nodded slowly. A sneaky bastard always needed a warrior to pull his chestnuts out of a fire for him. Just then, Cain decided that Neret was standing too close. The necromancer stank of death and corruption. Cain jumped off the chariot as if Neret were a plague carrier.

"Wait here," Cain said. "When you hear me hoot like an owl, bring the team."

"I promised Boar we would take him with us."

"Fine," Cain said, not caring what Neret had promised the treacherous Mammoth Man. He took a spear from the chariot and headed after the others.

In the darkness, Cain ran smoothly and surely, seeing enough of the nightscape that he avoided uneven ground. He could see so much better in the dark than a regular man could that it gave him an unfair advantage. He soon caught up with the back of the band of Elonites. They were strung out, with two in the lead, one of those lofting a torch. That one was huge and had white hair. It was Lod! Beside him jogged a Mammoth Man, Boar, no doubt.

Cain gripped the spear with one hand, tightening his hold as he took a deep breath. He could hear other men shouting from all around in the darkness as the Elonites tried to find the fleeing mammoths. They would be wiser to do so in the morning. It might cost them a day or two of travel, but that would be better than the confusion this was causing.

Cain ran noiselessly, coming upon the first stumbling, panting Elonite. The man carried a spear, but he had no idea—

Cain stabbed the man in the back. The Elonite arched in agony. With a cutting swipe of his sword, Cain decapitated the Elonite. The corpse's body and head thudded onto the ground at the same time.

Cain sidestepped the blood, becoming like a hound of Death, soundlessly baying at his enemy's heels. Soon, two more dead

Elonites thudded onto the ground. Two others were still ahead, although behind Lod and Boar.

Lod and Boar had stopped and were standing on a rise of ground.

"I see the bull," Boar said.

"You're lying," Lod said, who peered into the night. "I can't see anything."

Cain reached the next warrior, stabbing him expertly in the back. The man cried out, however, and twisted, wrenching the spear from Cain's grasp. The massive man swerved as the Elonite fell to the ground.

"Look out!" Lod shouted, turning, raising his torch high, trying to pierce the darkness to the rear.

The last Elonite in the group turned just as Cain reached him. "Who's there?" the warrior asked, squinting into the dark.

Cain shoved his sword into the man's stomach, twisting the blade so the man screamed. Cain wrenched the blade free, smashing against the man, knocking him to the ground.

From ahead on the rise, Boar said, "Let me hold the torch for you."

"What are you doing?" Lod said, who kept hold of the torch as Boar tried to take it away from him. "Let go of it, I say."

"No," Boar said, using two hands. "If I hold it up high—"

Something must have given Boar away. He stared at Lod in fear, and the Mammoth Man let go of the torch and jumped away, kneeling, prying at a stone in the ground.

"Treachery," Lod said, and he thrust the torch in Boar's face.

The Mammoth Man roared in pain and fell backward onto the ground.

Lod thrust the torch at Boar again, but the blade of Elohim must have heard something to alert him. He whirled around, and his blue eyes widened in amazement.

"Who are you?" Lod demanded.

Cain panted as he approached Lod. The massive man kept his bloody sword down low, and he walked in a controlled manner, perhaps trying to fool Lod.

"I asked you a question," Lod said.

Cain still said nothing, and he expected Lod to ask again, more angrily this time. Cain was counting on that, as he would attack once he was near enough to lunge.

Lod did not do his part, however. The white-haired warrior was massive with oak-like muscles piled upon his frame. Lod jumped back and looked at Boar. The other was kneeling, ready to climb to his feet. Did the white-haired warrior see the Mammoth Man grin crazily up at him? Lod must have. Without hesitation, Lod twisted to the side and thrust his sword against Boar's face, the blade smashing teeth and going deep into the traitor's mouth and out the neck.

Lod jerked the blade free. Boar gurgled in agony as he toppled sideways onto the ground.

Cain noted the man's speed. He noted the swiftness of decision. Lod showed no hesitation. That was impressive. It was time to use some swiftness himself—

Cain charged silently. Lod snarled and took up a fighter's crouch, holding the sword with one hand and the torch with the other. At the last minute, as Cain neared, Lod leapt to the attack. Their swords clashed against each other, throwing off sparks. Cain was stunned to feel the strength of the other's blow. It nearly numbed his arm.

"You're not a man," Lod snarled, "but a Nephilim. I've felt your spells tonight. So did the mammoths."

"I'm a man just like you," Cain said.

They circled each other warily, feinting, testing, probing, tapping each other's blade—looking for weaknesses. It also seemed as if each decided to attack at the same time. Their blades clashed once, twice, thrice—

Cain saw a flicker of movement behind Lod. It was a second of distraction. But it was enough that Lod's blade passed over his and slashed a shoulder.

"First blood," Lod said flatly.

"Only the last one counts," Cain said.

Lod must have heard a noise behind him. He tried to leap away, but it wasn't fast enough. Boar stood behind him, with blood covering his face. Boar the Mammoth Man had crazed, hateful eyes, and he raised a rock high and brought it down with sickening fury. Lod dodged, but the rock grazed him nonetheless. He staggered sideways, the torch falling onto the ground.

Boar collapsed a last time, with a gruesome smile on his ruined mouth.

Cain stepped up.

Lod roared, throwing up his sword in defense.

Cain hit it expertly, causing the sword to spin out of Lod's weakened grasp. Cain stepped up closer and grabbed Lod in a one-armed wrestling hold. The white-haired warrior strained against him, and Cain was stunned at the man's strength. Cain brought the pommel of his sword hard against Lod's head several times.

Lod groaned, and he toppled onto the ground. Even then, though, he tried to crawl away. This Lod had incredible vitality.

Cain kicked the man in the head. At that, Lod thudded unconscious.

Cain found himself panting, admiring the warrior. No wonder Gog hated Lod so much. Cain ran a hand through his hair and blinked sweat out of his eyes. He didn't have time for this. He had captured the seraph. Now, he had to race to the coast and haul Lod into the launch.

Cain turned and began making the hooting call, hoping that Neret knew enough about chariotry to drive the cart here in the dark.

-11-

Cain and Neret lifted together, stashing the heavy Lod, bound and gagged, into the chariot. Cain double-checked, making sure the warrior could breathe. If Lod died, all of this would be for naught.

"What about Boar?" Neret asked.

"He's dead."

Cain studied the prisoner, a veritable mass of muscles and raw-boned strength. It was possible Lod weighed just as much as he did. Two horses weren't going to pull Lod, Neret and him across endless leagues and stay ahead of those who would come hunting.

"You're driving," Cain told Neret.

"What are you going to do?"

"If you have to, wrap the reins on the tag. You're going to use more of your spells tonight to discourage the Elonites from closing too near."

"Casting more spells is dangerous. I'm already too tired—"

Cain hopped onto the chariot and peered down into Neret's thin face. "Tired? You claim you're tired? Oh no, this is just the beginning. Do exactly as I say, and I might not kill you and leave for their hounds to gnaw."

Neret bowed his head.

That didn't fool Cain. He saw the necromancer bunch his fists at his sides. Cain almost began slapping the necromancer across the head. Maybe the balled fists were for the best, though. An angry man worked harder, and he was going to need the necromancer at peak efficiency if they were going to pull this off.

Without another word, Cain stepped off the chariot and went to the horses. He slipped his thick fingers around a bridle strap. He tugged gently, and thus began the grueling race to the launch, days away on the coast.

Cain ran throughout the night, guiding the team across the least bumpy ground. They reached the main road to the coast an hour later. That kept Neret from falling out of the chariot and made Cain's run smoother.

It was some time during the third hour of the race that Cain heard rattling chariots behind them. He dared glance back, flinging sweat from his face. He saw blazing torches held by men riding in chariots. For a moment, he glimpsed angry, hardened faces. The Elonites must have found the dead men and discerned that Lod had been taken.

"Neret," Cain panted.

The necromancer did not answer, although the man moved upon the matted weaving of the chariot floorboard. Luckily, before he moved around, he'd remembered to tie the end of the reins to the tag on the railing. That was all Cain had time to see. What he felt was different, a wash of heat against him, a prickling against his neck. That meant Neret must have untied his skull bag. Neret began chanting dire words.

The horses neighed in fright, and Cain's horse pulled against him.

He used his strength, keeping the animal in line and trotting upon the road. Now, Cain could feel the blast of death-magic against his back. It made his skin crawl as he became physically nauseous. What kind of spell was Neret casting? An oily sensation descended upon Cain. It was vile, and he felt his thoughts slipping from his control. He considered stopping, taking his blade and carving Neret's flesh until the other howled for mercy. Cain didn't know it, but he was grinning madly and began to chuckle evilly.

Then, Neret's chant broke through the madness that was turning Cain's thoughts.

Grimly, Cain realized he must have felt the edge of the spell—a spell of madness for their enemies. Knowing that, he concentrated. He had cast spells of his own in the past. He had studied sorcery and read demonic script. In time, Cain had realized that practicing magic was changing him in ways he did not like. Thus, he had sworn off sorcery and its vile cousin necromancy. But he understood the fundamentals. Knowing what he faced helped him seal off portions of his mind and more importantly, his soul. Did it make a difference that he was from the original pair? Did it matter that he had seen the East Gate of Eden? Adam, Abel and he used to sacrifice there.

Cain frowned as an ancient memory surfaced, one he forbade himself to dwell upon. Long ago, in the beginning, Elohim had rejected his sacrifice at the East Gate. The One Above had instructed Adam to sacrifice an animal to Him, to shed blood—life—as a token payment for their sins. Instead, Cain had brought the product of his toil, fruits and grains, the best of his hard work.

It was incredible to believe that he had been a farmer in the beginning. That had been so long ago. Elohim had reprimanded him for the grain offering, had told him that the work of his hands was not good enough for the token payment of his sins. Elohim had suggested he be like his brother, and bring an animal for a blood sacrifice.

Would he have gone to Abel and begged for a lamb? Surely, Elohim had known that would degrade him in his brother's eyes. Cain was first born. He would not go to Abel and beg for an animal. If Elohim rejected his hard work, his good crops—

Cain roared in the darkness, and he realized he was not young again near Eden, but that he was gripping a bridle, leading a team of horses on the road to the coast. Neret's spell—

Cain's head snapped up. He did not hear rattling chariots behind him. He twisted back and no longer saw torches. What had happened to the chasing Elonites?

Cain shuddered. Why had he remembered that which he never thought about anymore? Then, he realized…Neret's spell had been one of madness. He had fought the madness, and that must have driven him to remember the terrible time before he'd persuaded his bother to go out into the field with him. Why would fighting madness cause him to think about *that?* Was it sanity to remember his sin—?

"No sin!" Cain snarled. "I am my own man. I reject Elohim and His ways. I do as I will. That is the whole of the law."

A harsh laugh escaped Cain. He remembered now. He remembered hearing screaming and shouting, he heard chariot crashes and soon thereafter the clash of steel. Neret's spell had worked, causing madness to descend upon the hunters.

"Good work," Cain said over his shoulder.

There was no answer.

"Neret?" called Cain, as he kept running.

There was still no answer.

Despite the long chase, Cain had reached a rhythm. It was difficult to break that now and slow down until the lathered horses panted on the road. Cain opened his fist. His fingers were stiff. On wooden legs, Cain approached the chariot box.

Lod was still tied down, but of Neret, there was no sign. Cain frowned. Did he recall… He had heard a thump earlier. Could that have been Neret falling out of the chariot? Had the spell overcome the necromancer? Had Neret been right earlier when he'd said he was too tired to practice more necromancy?

Well, if Neret had died or swooned and fallen off, at least the sneaky bastard had kept the others from reaching him. But if Neret was gone…should he go back and see if he could find the man?

"Good riddance to him," Cain said with a sneer. "I never liked him. Besides, I don't need him. This will keep the horses fresher because they have less to carry."

Half-drunk with fatigue and still touched by madness, Cain tottered to the horses. There, he wriggled his fingers under the bridle of the lead animal until he clutched the leather strap again.

He was Cain. There wasn't a man on Earth like him. He had the primordial strength of the First Ones because he was a first one. He had stamina like no other. He would run all the way to the coast if he had to, so he might as well get started.

"You and me, Lod," Cain whispered. Then, in a display of willpower, Cain tugged the reluctant horses and continued to race to the coast.

-12-

In daylight, Joash walked around the bruised bound man. Aran had found him on the road, a ways ahead of crashed chariots and butchered Elonites. It looked as if the Elonites had attacked each other. That implied dark magic.

The man was lean with sinister eyes. He obviously had Nephilim blood in his veins, even if it was diluted. The man gibbered when asked a question, and his eyes rolled in his head.

Joash and the part-Nephilim were on the edge of a field beside the main road to Farther Tarsh on the Suttung coast. Chariots, hounds and warriors waited several hundred feet back.

The man was presently tied with ropes and propped upright. He had been crawling along the road, mewling and crying out. Some of the warriors had wanted to kill him, but Aran had said no. The young swordsman had grit and ability. Joash liked him, had learned to trust him. Aran had been there when Lod had freed him from the Nephilim two years ago, when Lod had a smith remove the bronze mask welded around his head. Joash did not like to remember that captivity, as it had been much worse than his time with the giants.

The young seraph inhaled through his nostrils, enjoying the morning smell. Someone had captured Lod. Someone had slain Boar. Someone had started the mammoth stampede last night. Thoar was back at camp, rounding up the mammoths. Joash had decided to lead the hunt for Lod. The others with Lod must be getting farther away, but Joash was going to question the tied madman in order to figure things out better.

Joash squatted before the bound man. "Who are you?" he asked.

71

The man's black eyes did not focus. His narrow face twisted with sick laughter.

Joash stood, stepped beside the man and squatted again. He did not like the laughter. It was…demonic. He reached out and put a hand on one of the man's shoulders.

"No!" the man shouted, wrenching himself away from Joash. "Don't touch me!" he screamed at the top of his lungs.

Joash studied the other, who was now weeping. "Who are you?" he asked again.

Without looking up, the man wildly shook his head.

Joash made to touch him.

"No!" the man said, wriggling away on his back. "Don't you dare touch me!"

Joash did more than that, he pounced like a cat, leaping at the man and clutching him.

The man screamed insanely and wriggled wildly.

"In Elohim's Name," Joash said, "I drive you out, dark spirit. You must release his mind and leave the man."

"No!" the bound man howled. "No, no, no, no, I won't leave."

"I pray thee, Elohim," Joash said, closing his eyes. He still kept hold of the man. "I beg thee, Elohim, the Creator of the world and Maker of men. Drive this evil spirit from the man. Return the man's sanity to him."

"No, no, no, no, no!" the man shrieked, higher with each word. "Leave me alone. What have I to do with you, Joash the Seraph?"

Joash's eyes snapped open. The young man's face shined as sweat pooled on his features. He breathed heavily, shook sweat from his face and bowed his head once more. "Elohim, O Elohim, I ask thee to hear me. They have taken Lod. They have practiced foul sorcery in your land. Now, a demon-possessed man is tormented—"

"Stop!" the man screamed, lifting his head as his face turned beet red. "Stop, stop—" The words suddenly choked off, and the man began shaking violently. A second later, the shaking stopped, and the man raised his head again, staring at Joash. "I know you, Joash the Seraph," he said in a tortured voice.

"I know Elohim," Joash said. "He is my strength and my shield. In Him I trust and no other, certainly not in my own puny strength."

The man's mouth opened, but no sounds issued. He shivered once more, and then he gasped, collapsing to the ground.

Joash released the man as he sobbed with effort.

"Are you well, Lord?"

Joash looked up at Aran, a well-built young man with bright eyes and short hair. Worry creased Aran's face as he kept his sword-hand on the hilt of his belted weapon.

"Help me stand," Joash said in a tired voice.

Aran reached down and helped, steadying him a moment later.

The tied one opened bleary eyes. He seemed confused. Then, he focused on Joash, and groaned dismally.

"An evil spirit indwelled you," Joash informed the man.

"You might as well kill me."

"Why should I?" Joash asked, genuinely surprised by the statement.

The man sneered. "You don't fool me. You might fool others, but I know you're a power hungry—"

"That's enough," Aran said, stepping near and kicking the man in the side.

The man grunted and twisted in pain, although he smiled afterward.

"No more of that," Joash said, putting a hand on Aran's arm.

"I'm sorry, Lord," Aran said sheepishly.

Joash shook his head. Aran fell silent, stepping back. Joash squatted beside the bound man and put a hand on his shoulder.

He twisted away as before.

"Why do you do that?" Joash asked.

"Your touch burns."

Joash raised his eyebrows. Experimentally, he touched the man again.

The same thing happened, but this time, the man began to pant. "Please," he said. "Don't touch me."

"What's your name?"

"Neret."

"That's it?"

A sly look entered Neret's eyes.

Joash reached out.

"No, wait. I'll talk. I'm Neret of Shamgar. I belong to the Order of Gog."

"You piece of filth!" Aran hissed.

Joash looked back at the young man.

73

"I won't speak again," Aran said.

Joash recognized the look. Aran was wise beyond his years. He believed Aran, that he would not speak out of turn again.

"What were you doing in Elon?" Joash asked.

Neret licked his lips, and he nodded. "I know you'll torture me if I don't talk. Thus, I want to bargain with you. If I tell you the truth, don't kill or maim me."

"That's it? You don't want us to let you go?"

"I do, but I don't think you'll swear to that."

"I'll swear to nothing. My yes is yes, and my no is no."

Neret didn't reply, but it looked like he wanted to.

"If you tell me the truth, the whole truth, I will not maim or kill you."

"You swear?"

"I have spoken," Joash said.

Neret inhaled through his thin nostrils, and then he began to speak. He told Joash everything. Cain had deserted him last night. An evil spirit had indwelled him because he'd been so tired from using the skull magic and had made a dreadful mistake. He owed his side nothing because they were giving him nothing. If he told enough, he might cause Joash to give him more liberty than he should. At that point, Neret would make his escape. He couldn't go back to Shamgar, though. Gog would surely learn about his treachery.

Finally, Joash stopped asking questions and stopped listening. He looked up at the clouds as if considering. "Cain has Lod and is taking him to Gog to sacrifice deep below the Temple of the Oracle."

"Grim news, Lord," Aran said.

Joash stared at Neret. "You're sure Cain will cross the Suttung Sea to Shamgar?"

"Of course," Neret said. "Ceto's Nidhogg spawn will make sure the launch reaches home."

Joash put his hands on his knees and pushed up to his feet. Cain had Lod. The Nidhogg spawn pulled the launch. There was likely little chance they could catch up with Cain in time. That meant—

Joash smiled and turned to Aran. "I have a task for you. As you love Lod, you must perform it as fast as possible."

"Tell me what it is," Aran said.

Once Joash had revealed his plan, Aran nodded sharply and raced for a chariot. In moments, the young man urged his chariot team to race to Havilah Holding as fast as the horses could gallop.

Joash glanced at a curious Neret. This was probably Lod's only hope, and it was a slender one at that.

***

Too much time had passed since someone slew Boar and Cain and Neret had escaped with a captive Lod. Joash had sent out chariots, seeking information about a yellow-haired man madly whipping a chariot team for the eastern coast. By what Neret had told him, Cain was heading for a hidden cove north of Farther Tarsh.

Joash had heard of a woman glimpsing such a chariot, but the yellow-haired warrior hadn't been whipping the team, but running in the lead.

That puzzled Joash. He knew why he might run in front of a chariot. For many years, Joash had been a chariot runner, fetching tossed javelins and looking after the hounds. Now, though, he was a full ranked chariot warrior, even if he wasn't as good a fighter as someone like Aran.

A shepherd in a different region had reported that the big yellow-haired man had robbed a passing chariot, killing the driver and stealing his team. The ones the killer had cut out of the traces and—

"Why, that's them over there, grazing," the shepherd had said.

Through it all, Joash knew Lod's only hope was the completion of the slender plan. Cain had him, the first Cain, killer Cain, the murderer with the mark of Cain in his eyes. He had been the Earth's first-born human, and Cain was taking Lod to Gog, there to sacrifice him on the Oracle's altar.

The idea sickened Joash. Lod deserved better than that. Lod had started in Shamgar as rat bait. Years later, Lod had been buried alive in the Catacombs and would still be there but for Keros the Warrior and Tamar, a female rat hunter of the canals.

Both Keros and Tamar were with Lord Uriah with the crusading host, presently in Pildash territory. Uriah had asked for reinforcements so they could crush Shamgar's Army, storm Pildash and march on the swamp city for its final destruction.

Thoar helped guide the mammoths of the reinforcement host. Joash would rejoin them as soon as he performed one last task for Lod. Soon, now, soon indeed—

"Lord," Aran shouted beside him in the chariot. "There it is! The sea! The sea!"

Joash nodded wearily. He could just imagine how Cain and Lod must feel. How far behind those two were they?

Joash drove the team to the edge of the Suttung Sea. Gulls cried overhead while the surf washed seaweed and a piece of driftwood onto the rocks. The sound was all too familiar to Joash. Once, he had been adrift in the sea. That had been after Nidhogg smashed their ships. What an awful yet exhilarating time that had been. It seemed like a lifetime ago now.

"Should we wait for the others to catch up?" Aran asked.

"No," Joash said, as he picked up a long, wrapped instrument from the chariot. Several days ago, Aran had fetched it for him from Havilah Holding. The instrument was heavy, and it was ancient. Joash carried it with both hands as he tried to balance his way across the rocks.

"The rocks are slippery here, Lord," Aran said, hurrying near, grabbing one of Joash's elbows.

Together, the two young men worked to the edge of the sea, where foam and spray hit them every time a wave came in.

Reverently, Joash unwrapped the cloth from around a long silver trumpet. Joash knew that a Shining One from Above had crafted this trumpet during the terrible Accursed War. In those grim days, the Shining Ones had captured the *bene elohim* that had come down to Earth, Abaddon the Destroyer, Moloch the Hammer and Magog the Accursed among others. Prophets said the Shining Ones had taken and imprisoned the divine rebels in Tartarus, a place deep in Sheol or Hell. Those fallen angels would not leave their prisons until the Great Day of Judgment at the end of Time.

"It's too bright to look at," Aran said, who used a hand to shield his eyes from the reflected light.

That was funny, Joash thought, as he could look at the trumpet just fine. It was so heavy, though. He wasn't sure that he had the lungs to blow such an instrument.

Steeling himself, Joash inched the last distance, his left foot almost flying out from under him on a slick rock. He saw crabs scuttle away underwater.

Joash lowered the horn until the curved front was in the water. Joash inhaled, put his lips to the piece and blew hard.

Bubbles blew up out of the water, but there was no noise.

Joash inhaled again, and blew again as strength flowed from him. The process intensely wearied him, but that was good. It meant the Leviathan Horn was doing its proper task.

One more time, Joash blew the horn. Finally, exhausted, he abruptly sat back on the rocks, almost losing hold of the horn.

"Aran," he whispered.

"I'm here, Lord," the warrior said from behind.

"Take the horn, Aran."

"Will it slay me if I touch it?"

Joash couldn't look back. He was too tired. Instead, he waited.

Finally, Aran used the cloth to grab the horn. He grunted with effort as he took it from Joash. He replaced the wrapping and staggered as he negotiated the rocks, placing the horn back in the chariot.

Others had arrived in chariots. None of them came out to Joash.

Joash sat alone, and he might have dozed.

"Lord, Lord," Aran shouted from a distance.

Joash blinked and raised his head. Had he fallen asleep? His head snapped up the rest of the way, and he scrambled to his feet.

That was too much. He slipped, but instead of falling backward, Joash leapt forward, belly-flopping into the tidal pool. Even though he was wearing his tunic, he swam out strongly to the leviathan that had broken the surface.

By the height of the sun, he must have dozed for hours. He must have been more tired than he'd realized.

A leviathan had saved Joash's life before. He swam out strongly toward the monstrous sea-creature with its great snout like a giant crocodile. It had an armored hide and incredible size, bigger by far than any mammoth

"Joash," someone yelled from shore.

The young seraph paid no heed. Lod's life depended on him. He swam to the waiting monster that dwarfed him. The leviathan had heeded the call.

"Leviathan," Joash shouted.

The great monster of the deep swam closer and then was beside him. An eye peered down at Joash. How knowing was the creature? Joash had little idea. Even so, he surged forward and slapped a hand on the armored snout.

The leviathan did not lurch away. It seemed very careful to move little so as not to drown Joash.

"You must save Lod," Joash shouted. "Five sea-saurians—spawn of Nidhogg—are pulling a launch. Destroy the launch and carry Lod to safety. You must do this. You must. You must."

Joash's face began to shine, and the leviathan held itself exceedingly still.

"You have to understand me," Joash said. "This is dreadfully important. Kill the Nidhogg spawn, wreck the launch and bring Lod to safety. Do you understand?"

Joash wasn't sure, but he had a sense the great sea monster understood him.

"Go," Joash said. "Go now and save Lod."

The leviathan backed away slowly. Once it was far enough away, the great creature turned and dove underwater.

Joash kicked to stay above water. He waited, watching, and later, he saw the leviathan surface. It was moving fast, and it was heading east. Would it arrive in time to save Lod?

"Please, Elohim," Joash prayed. "Save Lod from Cain and Gog. Let Lod shatter teeth and break bones in Shamgar as he hunts for the First Born of Magog the Accursed. Amen."

Now, Joash was truly exhausted. He turned slowly, and his head went under. Water shot up his nose. He struggled, barely breaking the surface. Aran swam to him and helped Joash stay afloat as he kicked for the two of them, heading back to the rocky shore and the chariots beyond.

-13-

Lod had no idea how long he'd been in a daze. His head throbbed, and his eyesight had been dim. He'd been unable to eat and had drunk barely enough water so he didn't dehydrate. Now, finally, his head didn't throb all the time. His eyesight was blurry, but that was better than being dim, almost dark. The sun beat down on him, feeling good.

Lod stirred—

A shadow blocked the sun. Even though it hurt Lod's head, he concentrated. Slowly, two oil-black eyes came into focus, staring down at him. The eyes were cold and mocking, the face surrounding them hard and brutal, yellow-bearded.

"It's about time," the killer said. "I was beginning to wonder if we'd hit you so hard that you'd turned into an idiot. I thought you were supposed to have a thicker skull than that."

Despite his weakness, Lod scowled. Who had hit him? Who was this ruffian with the sinister eyes of a killer? Why was it so bumpy here with spray settling on him at times?

"Who are you?" Lod slurred.

Bright, strong teeth showed in the yellow beard. "You can call me Cain."

"Cain of what?"

Something happened in those eyes, a recklessness, a wild disregard swirling like a whirlwind.

"The East Gate of Eden," Cain said.

Lod frowned, but that small emotional reaction made his head throb again. He couldn't afford that just now. He was too weak as it was. He let go of his anger, of anything upsetting, and struggled to remain calm, relaxed.

"Where is this place?" Lod asked.

"The Suttung Sea."

Lod tried to rise, but he was too feeble, gasping as he collapsed. That made his heart pound and his head throbbed even more. He let every muscle relax. As his heart began beating normally, he started to remember...

Lod turned to the killer, to Cain. The man was massively built, maybe even bigger than he was. He should remember someone like this, and he realized he did.

"I fought you last night."

"It was longer ago than that. That should tell you how badly you lost."

Lod had fought, at night—the mammoths! The mammoths had stampeded as fires raged in camp. He had— "Boar," Lod said. "Boar treacherously bashed me on the head with a rock. He did it from behind."

"You would have lost to me anyway."

The gibes didn't bother Lod. Boar had indeed hit him on the back of the head with a rock. He would have taken care of this one otherwise. Lod had killed better warriors than Cain.

"What happened to Boar?" asked Lod.

"He's dead."

"Yes...that's right. I killed him, the traitor. There was someone else with you, too."

"He's gone," Cain said, and a shadow crossed his features.

"Did you kill him?"

Cain brooded, finally looking away as he shrugged. "Neret is gone."

"Neret?" asked Lod. "That means vulture in the old tongue."

Cain turned to him in surprise as mockery shined in his eyes. "Don't tell me Lod has book learning."

"Neret...vulture—he must have been a necromancer."

"That's a shrewd guess," Cain said. "It seems you're more than just a lump of twisted muscles."

Lod's eyesight and head—his mind—had gotten better as they'd spoken. What had the man said before? He was of the East Gate of Eden. Sudden understanding blazed into life.

"You claim to be *that* Cain?"

"What if I am?"

Lod grunted as he heaved up to a sitting position. He swayed, turning pale. He fought off the weakness this time, refusing to surrender to it. He was getting his bearings. Looking around, he saw the green sea in all directions. This was the Suttung Sea without any shores in evidence. An even direr sight made him blanch. Three Nidhogg spawn pulled three different ropes attached to the launch. The wooden boat fairly bumped along the sea, faster than Lod had ever traveled before. The worst sight was a naked waif laughing as she clung to the middle spawn's long neck.

"She's Nephilim," Lod spat with understanding.

Cain glanced at Ceto. "Whatever she is, she's useful out here."

Lod studied the huge warrior. If he was the original Cain, the first murderer—Elohim had put the mark of Cain on him and had made a promise concerning him. The one who slew the murderer would receive a curse. That meant—Lod might have defeated Cain that night. But in killing the warrior, would he have received the curse? No... If one slew Cain in vengeance, then the curse would come into effect. Surely, one could defend himself against Cain, including killing him in battle, without enacting Elohim's ancient curse.

Ancient—

"How old are you?" asked Lod.

"Turn around and put your hands behind your back."

"That's no answer."

"I'll knock you over the head if you don't hurry. The blow might turn you into an idiot. But Gog didn't say anything about that. Just that you were still breathing when I brought you in."

Lod's jaw did not drop, nor did he feel a thrill of terror at the mention of Gog. He was in a boat in the Suttung Sea obviously heading for Shamgar. Nidhogg spawn towed the boat. The Earth's first killer had kidnapped him. There was a half-Nephilim guiding the sea monsters. Of course, this had to do with Gog.

"How much is Gog paying you?"

"Turn around and put your hands behind your back. I'm not going to ask you a third time."

Lod turned around and put his hands behind his back. Now wasn't the moment to challenge Cain. He needed his strength.

Besides, ropes—he would pray to Elohim for strength when the time came and tear the cords asunder and battle to the death against the killer from the East Gate.

Cain tied the ropes tight and feeling soon left Lod's hands.

"Do you fear me so much that you tie me as if I'm a wild beast?"

"If you don't watch your mouth, I'm going to slap you across the face. That might knock some of your teeth loose. Better decide how many teeth you want left by the end of the voyage."

Lod bent his head so his hair hid his face from Cain. He was getting angry, and that wouldn't do—yet. He had to bide his time. He had bided his time for years as rat bait in the canals. If anyone knew how to wait... Lod ground his teeth together. The trip to Shamgar would not take long, not with the sea-spawn pulling so hard. How could he slow them down? How near were they to Shamgar?

"How long have we been traveling?"

"You tell me," Cain said, amused.

Lod craned his neck, studying the water. He couldn't tell by the color of the sea or various currents or other methods seamen used to gauge their position. Well, he needed to get strong. That was something he could do.

Lod raised his head. "I'm thirsty."

With the toe of a boot, Cain indicated a bucket. "Drink from that if you want."

Lod edged toward the bucket, sliding carefully due to the speed of the launch and the spray kicking back. Cain picked up a jug, uncorking it and pouring water into the bucket.

Lod bent low like an animal, putting his lips to the water and drinking greedily. He wasn't too proud to drink like this. He'd had to do worse as a galley slave of Poseidonis. Despite upsetting his stomach, Lod drank as much as he could stand. Provided he didn't vomit the water, this was the fastest way to healing.

Lod sat up as water dribbled through his beard. "Got anything to eat?"

"Dried herring," Cain said. "Do you think you can keep it down?"

"Yes."

Cain found a packet, cut some herring from it and tossed the pieces to the bottom of the launch.

Unconcerned, Lod knelt and then bent forward, eating each piece and relishing the food. He didn't vomit the herring up, either.

"You're a practiced slave," Cain said.

Heat rose in Lod, but he pushed it aside. Despite having his hands tied behind him, he lay down on his back, found that uncomfortable and rolled onto his side.

"There's no escape for you," Cain said.

"I know."

"You're not fooling anyone with your act."

"Would you rather have me rage at you?"

"I've seen your kind a thousand times, ten thousand, maybe one hundred thousand times. You consider yourself clever and you've faced trials and won through. That makes you think you're special. But you're not. You're just one more man in the long line of men that march through history. Gog hates you, so maybe you're a little tougher than most, but this subterfuge of yours...it won't last."

Lod sat back up as he regarded Cain. The moment felt surreal. They sped across the Suttung Sea, moving faster than anyone had done throughout time. They headed to Shamgar—

"Why does the first-born of men serve a vile First Born of the *bene elohim?*"

"Better get this straight. I serve Cain and no one else."

"Are you saying that you don't fear Gog's wrath?"

"What did I tell you about asking stupid questions? I can still knock out all your teeth."

"You were at the East Gate," Lod said undaunted. "Surely, you saw the guardian Cherub there."

Cain stared at Lod, stared longer, finally saying, "I saw him and his flaming sword."

"Elohim drove your parents from the Garden of Eden. He drove them out because they had—"

"Listen to me," Cain said in a low voice, interrupting. "I don't need a history lesson from a zealot. I heard the story from the horse's mouth, you could say."

"That's my point. Your father must have taught you the truth, and you saw the guardian with his sword. You saw direct evidence of Elohim's power. According to the tales I've heard, you actually spoke to Elohim."

"What of it?"

83

"You spoke to the Creator. How can you dare to resist Him knowing all you do?"

The yellow-haired warrior slapped his chest. "I'm Cain. I'm my own man. I do as I please, when and how I please. I serve no one but me."

"And has this brought you satisfaction?"

"Yes!"

"Why are you taking me to Gog?"

Cain sneered. "Are you afraid of your coming death?"

Lod shook his head. "Of course, I do not look forward to dying. I do not look forward to having Gog cradle me in his tentacles. I blinded him, by Elohim's grace."

"*You* blinded him. Elohim had nothing to do with it."

"You're wrong."

"Maybe it's time you shut your face."

"I have known great satisfaction in serving Elohim. He has brought me my greatest desires."

"What's that?" Cain sneered

"Slaying His foes," Lod said, as his blue eyes began to shine like a prophet on the verge of divination. "I was rat bait, Cain. I was but a boy with a rope around my neck. I swam in the canals, luring the giant canal rats in range of my master's tridents. The Temple priests paid him a copper coin for each rodent. In time, I slew my master, and I slew an Enforcer—"

Lod shook his head.

"Pretty damn proud of your accomplishments, are you?" asked Cain.

Lod looked up. "I'm proud that Elohim chose me to be His instrument. I have slain many of the evil ones." Lod stared at Cain as knowledge shone in his fiery eyes. "I am not destined to slay you. But I will help bring the downfall of Gog and Shamgar."

Cain snarled as his eyes blazed with murder-lust. He jumped up and struck Lod a stunning blow across the face.

Lod tumbled back, but the white-haired madman seemed not to notice. His eyes radiated something terrible as a smile stretched across his face. He saw elsewhere as a feeling of ecstasy filled him with wonder.

"You will not take me to Shamgar," Lod intoned. "You will try, but you will fail."

"Silence!" Cain said, standing over him, shaking a fist at the crazy prophet.

"Abel's blood cries out from the ground. That is what haunts you throughout Time. You slew your brother—"

"I said silence," Cain thundered, and he kicked Lod twice in the side.

That did it. Lod groaned as he curled up in a fetal ball, with his hands still tied behind him. His eyes still shone with visions, but the waking visions changed. He saw himself striding with a sword and torch through the streets of Shamgar. There were warriors following him. He strode through the streets and over the canals, breaking teeth and shattering bones as he raced for the Temple of the Oracle so he could slay Gog, the First Born of Magog the Accursed.

-14-

Dusk found the launch bouncing and bumping across the sea. The wooden boat had sledded for endless hours. The only interruption had been a changing of the sea-saurians as two fresh ones took the place of the two rope-yoked Nidhogg spawn.

Lod and Cain hadn't spoken since the killer kicked him in the side. Cain sat at the tiller, moodily wrapped in a flapping blue cloak.

Lod had asked for a cloak. Cain had ignored him. Lod had asked for more food and drink. Cain had continued to ignore him.

Lod knew better than to argue. He'd touched a nerve earlier. Besides, he was exhausted by his visions. His shoulders ached because they were twisted back, and his fingers felt puffy. Cain would not ease his bonds. If he came to Gog maimed—

Lod sat on a thwart, trying to think. The bloated sun sank into the western horizon. They were much closer to Shamgar than hours ago. He had to delay them. There was only one way he could see to do that. Lod had debated it for some time. Cain might beat him mercilessly for this. He didn't want more headaches and agony, but those were better than dying.

Lod stood up in the launch.

"Sit down," Cain said from the tiller.

Lod turned to face Cain. As he did, he felt something. Was it a spark of hope? Did Elohim call to him?

"I said, *sit down.*"

Lod sat abruptly.

Cain laughed in a low-throated way.

Lod bent his head. He did not do so in shame because of Cain's mockery. Rather, he'd felt an otherworldly compulsion to sit. He had felt such compulsions on occasion.

Suddenly, webbed hands latched onto a gunwale. The naked waif hauled herself aboard.

Lod saw her misshapen form and the scales outlined on her skin. With her in here, the Nidhogg spawn slackened their headlong pace so the launch slowed.

"Trouble?" asked Cain.

The Nephilim-creature scuttled across the launch, passing Lod. She did look up at him, but cringed as she passed.

"The spawn are frightened," Ceto said in a weird voice.

"Sharks?" asked Cain.

"Something worse, much worse."

"How far are we from Shamgar?"

"Another hour at most."

Lod's heart raced hearing that. He would have to jump overboard any minute. But that seemed more than useless. The excess spawn would capture him in minutes, maybe less. The sea-saurians were many times more dangerous than canal rats. Besides, he still had his hands tied.

"Lod," Cain said.

Lod started at his name, but stilled his nervousness as he turned around to face the two.

"Do you see that?" Ceto asked Cain, pointing into the distance.

Cain did not answer her, as the killer eyed Lod in the deepening gloom. "What's chasing us?"

Lod shrugged.

"No games now. Ceto says something comes."

A spawn cried shrilly in fear.

"It's here!" Ceto shouted. "Look!" she said in horror. "Do you see? Do you see?"

Cain twisted around. "See what?" he asked. "I don't see anything."

Once more, a spawn wailed, and now the launch jerked as the three rope-yoked sea-saurians fled faster than they had traveled so far.

"I'll see you later, Cain," Lod shouted.

"Grab him," Cain shouted, as he lunged across the boat.

Lod ran, slipping as the boat hit a wave, but he righted himself long enough to jump and dive headfirst overboard. He hit the water at speed, skipping across the surface before slowing and finally sinking. He gulped a mouthful of briny seawater and kicked to keep his head above the surface.

Cain was shouting in the launch. Ceto cupped her hands and made strange sounds to her spawn. They did not appear to heed her, but raced away, the other two unbound sea-saurians were nowhere in evidence.

Then, Lod saw a great stirring in the water. A sea monster was heading toward them. For a moment, a long, armored snout broke the surface.

"Leviathan," Lod whispered. A leviathan was coming. Had Elohim sent the sea monster to save him?

"Thank you, Elohim," Lod said. "Thank you, thank you." Only then did Lod admit to himself the dread he had been feeling heading for Shamgar and Gog. He had been in the Catacombs before and feared entombment alive.

Lod kept kicking. He had a ringside seat for an awesome spectacle. The leviathan surfaced as it increased speed, chasing the launch. The sea monster passed Lod.

The bound warrior kicked and kicked even as he lost sight of the launch and lost sight of the leviathan. In time, as he strained, he heard splintering wood and the gratifying screams of dying Nidhogg spawn.

Lod laughed and sang, and he continued to kick to keep his head above water. After a time, after the sounds had died away, Lod realized he would have to swim to shore. How was he going to do that with his hands tied behind his back?

"Elohim," he prayed. "Give me the strength to break these bonds."

Then Lod roared and twisted his hands, but the rope did not part. Soon, agony in his shoulders forced him to stop. Lod panted, defeated but not vanquished.

"So be it," he said. "I'll swim the best I can." And Lod tried. He did not get far.

Suddenly, he felt water stir around him. He looked over his shoulder and saw the leviathan staring down at him. A shudder ran down Lod's spine. In the gloom, the beast was ominous. Was that blood on its teeth?

"Did Elohim send you?" Lod managed to ask.

The leviathan opened its massive jaws and reached for him.

"Praise Elohim!" Lod shouted, certain the leviathan was about to eat him.

Instead, the sea monster gently took the end of his garment just below his neck and raised him out of the water. Like a cat with a kitten in its mouth, the leviathan began to swim strongly.

Lod cried out in wonder and once again gave thanks to Elohim. It was happening, but not in the way he had envisioned it.

Later, the leviathan raced toward a dark shore. Lod saw torchlights, lantern lights. He recognized Carthalo's mighty mountain city. Long ago, legend held, the Shining Ones had used an offshore mountain, hollowing it out to make a city. A vast bridge connected it to the mainland. The many lights moved upon the flat upper mountain ring-ridge, making it like a great hollow volcano.

The leviathan swam toward an entrance chiseled into the mountain city. Through the arch was one of the greatest ports on the Suttung Sea. Surely, soldiers and merchants were seeing this sight.

Lod laughed as the sea monster swam through the arch and past the Muthul Fortress guarding the great Circa Harbor. Lod saw hundreds of moored ships, and he spied people pointing at the leviathan.

The sea monster took him near a circular stone dock, waiting until people pointed and shouted in amazement. The leviathan released Lod then, dropping him into the water. The sea beast roared, turned and sped away for the exit.

Lod floundered in the water. In the torchlight, a few brave souls dived into the water to fetch Lod. He had made it. He was safe.

***

Many leagues away, in the swamp around Shamgar, a black, rubbery-skinned Nidhogg spawn carried a big man in his needle-toothed jaws. The teeth sank into flesh so the spawn could grip the unconscious warrior. Ceto rode another spawn beside this one.

She clicked to it, coaxing it to carry Cain just a little farther. She had saved the warrior from the wreckage after the leviathan had smashed the launch by landing on it from the air. All but two of her spawn had fled. Those two had circled, waiting for the leviathan to leave. Once it did, they raced to Ceto.

She had bid them find Cain.

Now, the two Nidhogg spawn reached the city canals, heading for the great acropolis that held the Temple of the Oracle. She would take Cain to Gog, and he could explain their failure to the First Born. Ceto feared for Cain, and she almost hadn't brought him to Shamgar. But as much as she admired and liked the man that had treated her so well, she feared Gog more.

What was Gog going to do now that Cain had failed? Ceto wondered if she would ever know, if anyone would ever know.

Soon, the sea-saurian set Cain on the dock by the temple. It shook its head so the bloody flesh slid free of its teeth. Then, the two spawn and Ceto fled the Temple area as they headed for the river that would take them back to the Suttung Sea.

-15-

Cain raved for days as a fever leeched his strength. The spawn bite around his right shoulder festered, swelled and came close to claiming the warrior's life.

He was in a small cell deep underground, with a bowl of gruel and a water jug delivered every morning. He had another pail for relieving himself. The only light came from a torch outside his cell, flickering through the tiny grate in the oak door.

The stench steadily grew worse, and maybe the festering would have killed Cain. But he clawed at the wound until he opened and drained it. In his delirium, he crashed off the cot onto the moldy, straw-littered floor. He crawled to and used the jug of water, bathing the raw wound, clawing and pressing it and washing it again. He did this at various times for three days until the wound bled fresh—clean—blood.

He no longer raved, no longer dreamed of olden times and old choices. He slept, paced when he woke and ate the gruel and chugged the water. He had lost weight and strength, but the fever hadn't killed him. He remembered the leviathan, and he pondered its appearance. Would he have drowned if a sea-saurian hadn't carried him to Shamgar?

Cain didn't know the answer. But he realized one day where the prison cell was—under the Temple of the Oracle. Gog had him. Why hadn't Gog sent a healer to tend him?

In time, Cain did pushups and other exercises in order to regain fitness. He found fatty lumps of meat in his gruel, and ate it all.

Finally, he heard yipping, footsteps and the jangling of keys. By the smell, hyenas approached.

Cain swung his feet off the cot. Was the jailor coming to feed him to the hyenas? He was weaponless, but he would do no worse than Lod had done while his prisoner.

Keys rattled, and the heavy oak door swung open. A crooked-backed jailor shuffled in, raising a lantern the better to peer at him. Behind the jailor whined huge cave hyenas.

"You're alive," the jailor said. He wore leathers and had a scruffy, bearded face with sores on his skin.

Cain waited as he sat on the cot. He couldn't tell anything from the one-eyed, smelly jailor.

"You want out of here?" the jailor asked.

"I do."

"Follow me, then, if you can stand. If you make it, you're free of this place. If not, my pets will dine on your flesh."

Cain grunted as he heaved onto his feet. "I'll make it."

"We'll see, we'll see." The jailor turned away and made a shooing motion. The cave hyenas jostled one another as they leaped out of the man's way.

Cain took several lurching practice steps, following the man into a low-ceilinged corridor. Water dripped from the stones overhead. Just how far down were they?

He didn't ask, he just kept walking. The jailor was crooked-backed, but there was something about the man that the cave hyenas feared. The man was broader than Cain had suspected at first, and a sense of strength radiated from him.

The jailor must be part Nephilim.

The one-eyed man shuffled in his odd gait for longer than Cain was healthy enough to go. Cain found himself reeling and crashing against the corridor sides. He began to shiver as the fever tried to reclaim him.

Cain refused to go down. Lod had struggled to the end. He would struggle to the end, as well, and kill the white-haired zealot before he was through with this part of the world. Maybe Lod had nothing to do with the leviathan, but the zealot's preachy certainty had grated against Cain. Besides, Lod must have had something to do with the sea monster. Such things didn't just happen.

"You're not going to defeat me," Cain whispered.

"What's that?" the jailor asked, half turning. "You talking to me?"

"Did you hear me say your name?"

"I did not."

"Then I ain't talking to you."

"Mouthy bastard, aren't you?" The jailor shook his misshapen head. "That's stupid. I want to, I can trip you and maybe knock you on the head—it's all over for the tall straight man then. You'll die down here. You would rot, and Gog would use your bones for necromantic powder."

Cain squeezed his eyes shut and opened them wide. His mouth was dry, and he was about to faint. He yearned to charge the jailor and break his back. Those hyenas would fight, though. Maybe the jailor would fight, too.

"Tough guy," the jailor said with a shrug. "Well, come on, then. We don't got all night...if you can makes it."

"Get on with it," Cain muttered.

"Oh, aye, I'll do that. Just make sure you don't fall, straight man. Otherwise these boys will crack your bones, they will."

The cave hyenas whined with anticipation.

Cain barely saw them as he swayed back and forth.

The jailor watched with anticipation, finally shrugging again when he realized Cain wasn't going down yet.

The underground trek continued.

Cain soon found the going more difficult and wondered why. He trudged up and up.

"Up?" he whispered.

Elation filled him. He staggered up a ramp, leaving the bottom dwelling and reaching a dryer place, one that didn't stink like a sewer. How could Gog live down here year after year? Had the First Born gotten used to the stench?

Cain cried out as sunlight shined in his eyes. He threw his hands up and winced at the brightness. "I thought you said it was night."

"Did I?"

Cain didn't reply. He staggered toward the light. A huge shape stepped before him, partially blocking the brilliance.

"Where do you think you're going?" the silhouetted shape asked.

Cain halted, squinting ahead, realizing someone bigger than him blocked his path. The man—the Nephilim or half-Nephilim—was seven feet tall, square-shaped and wore black leather armor. He had a trident tattoo on his broad forehead and dark glittering eyes.

"Think you can fight past me?" the half-Nephilim asked.

Cain did not reply.

The half-Nephilim drew a heavy short sword with a roaring lion head for its pommel. "This is Bolverk-forged. Do you know what means?"

Cain did indeed, but said nothing. Bolverk was a Nephilim giant, a son of the First Born Jotnar of Giants. Bolverk was a smith and had a unique gift with iron, able to fashion the best weapons.

"I'm Minos," the half-Nephilim said, "Captain of Shamgar's guard. If you can kill me, you can walk out of the city and be on your way."

"I'm not leaving."

"Course you're not," Minos said, "because you can't kill me."

"I promised Gog a service. Until I perform that service, I have no intention of going anywhere."

"You're on Gog's shit list, buddy boy. So, don't talk to me high and mighty-like. He was going to let you die, but you pulled through. Now…now Gog is considering what to do with you."

"I want an audience with Gog."

"I don't think you do."

"I have a proposal for him."

"Gog wants to rip you apart. He wants to pulp your flesh and crack your bones."

"Much better for him if he hears my proposal."

"It's time to shut up," Minos said, and he advanced.

Cain looked around, and he realized that the crooked-backed jailor and the cave hyenas had left some time ago. When he faced the half-Nephilim, the tip of the short sword jabbed at his stomach.

Cain skipped back, tripped over his own feet and went down onto his back.

Minos laughed. "The 'Mighty Cain,' are you?"

Cain climbed to his feet and found that he was shaking. The legacy of the fever was betraying him.

"Turn around, Cain, and duck your head. If you can recover— well, we'll see what will happen."

Cain turned, saw the open door into another cell, and decided now wasn't the moment to make his move. He had to get better first.

He staggered through the cell door, realizing this place was bigger and cleaner than where he had been.

The door clanged shut behind him, and Minos peered through the tiny grate. "Are you a praying man, Cain?"

Cain shook his head.

"You too tough for that?" asked Minos.

"Who do you pray to?"

"Gog."

"The First Born is a god?"

"If he ain't, he's going to be. Almost become one a few years ago." Minos grew silent before he added, "Gog is our lord and master. We serve him, and if we're wise, we worship him. There's a new day coming...but I don't know if you're gonna be alive to see it."

Cain shuffled to a bench, sitting down. He had come so close to bringing Lod to Shamgar. Another hour or two would have seen it done. Now...now it was time to wait and see what happened next.

PART TWO
THE BATTLE

-1-

Lord Uriah trained freshly levied spearmen from Carthalo, who had joined the host after witnessing Lod's arrival at the city via leviathan.

Uriah trained the spearmen in the newly evolved techniques he had perfected in Elon during the last several years. He trained the new spearmen as he waited for Joash's reinforcements to swell their ranks. The summer had seen more Shurite defections, increased raiding from Nebo tribesmen and more attacks by monster beasts that had been altered deep in the dungeons of Shamgar.

By the reports, Joash and the mammoths moved slowly, as it was the nature of the great mammals to meander. By message scroll, Joash explained that he didn't want to push the mammoths too hard or his ascendancy over them might weaken. That could prove disastrous on the battlefield. He added that the Mammoth Man Thoar had been training a select band of Elonites to fight from the beasts' backs.

"You should instruct Joash to send the chariots and spearmen ahead," Herrek suggested one day outside coastal Dishon. "We could use them while the weather still holds."

"That's just it," Uriah said. "If the chariots and spearmen arrive, men will demand we march on Pildash. That means Gog's army will likely try to check us. To face that army, we need the mammoths."

"I don't see why," Herrek said. "You heard what happened when Cain and Neret began the night fires. The mammoths bolted into the night. I know mammoths look impressive, but they're actually panicky beasts. How are they going to help us on the battlefield?"

"I told Lod long ago," Uriah said. "Joash is the key to defeating Gog and razing Shamgar to the ground. That still holds true."

"I like and admire Joash greatly," Herrek said, puzzled. "But he's no general or champion at arms."

Uriah smiled at his great-great-grandson. Warriors adored Herrek, following his tall red-haired figure on battlefields as he led them from one victory to another. Herrek was known as the giant slayer because he'd killed a Nephilim hero on the shores of Giant Land several years ago. But the Champion of Teman Clan could not lead the host to victory against an army led by *countless* Nephilim heroes. Men needed something more to defeat such an army.

Uriah had a problem, one he kept to himself. The men wanted to march on Pildash *now*, while the campaigning season was still upon them. But Uriah was certain they needed the mammoths if they hoped to defeat Gog's force. Waiting here could prove problematic, however. Once the men learned Gog's army had swelled with new levies, would they continue to wait or melt away by ones and twos as fear eventually took hold?

Uriah fingered his beard. Had the First Born hired more mercenaries from Arkite Land or places farther afield? Or could Gog's enforcers have impressed the independent city pirates into the army? If that were true, it would leave Shamgar's coastal defense fleet weaker than expected.

Uriah became pensive. The moment of decision was fast approaching. If they lost the next battle, all their hard-earned momentum would vanish and give Gog a reprieve. With Herrek's help, the host had won an impressive initial victory at the Battle of Three Creeks and then a few days later at the land gate of Dishon, capturing the city. Since then, Uriah had done everything he could to keep from throwing those advantages away. If the truth were known, he'd hoped Joash's host would have already arrived. Maybe he should have suggested the men and beasts travel along the southern Suttung coast by ship. Would the barely tamed mammoths have walked peacefully onto converted merchantmen? And remained calm once aboard and underway, with the herd divided amongst a number of ships and only one Joash?

These questions and their answers didn't matter. He hadn't possessed such ships, and the reinforcements had taken the longer land route. Clearly, too much time had passed, giving Gog time to swell his ranks with recruits from…somewhere. That could prove disastrous.

Days passed and turned into weeks, and a small trickle of men slipped away as Uriah feared. Finally, a full month later, just as the autumn rains started, Joash and the reinforcements neared Dishon's hinterland territory.

"This rain…" Herrek said, standing under a tent's awning as drops pelted the leather. "If it continues like this, the rain will turn the ground muddy. That will hurt our mobility, especially if the chariots travel near Nebo territory."

Nebo tribes always chose swampy land as it afforded them protection. Heavy rains would make the swamps impassable for chariots and nearly impossible for a marching host.

"We will pray for a dry autumn," Uriah said, standing beside his great-great-grandson. "But if it does continue raining like this—well, the mammoths might prove even more important than before."

Several hours later, Uriah met with his captains, Herrek and Keros among them. They met in a large tent.

Uriah stepped up onto an overturned wooden box and cleared his throat. "We're about to undertake the great test," he began. "The work of years—" The old seraph choked up. How long ago had he left Caphtor in order to scour the northern lands of Nephilim? He'd settled in wild Elon, building a country for the day he could finish the ancient fight against the evil ones who had come down from above.

Gaining control of his emotions, Uriah stepped off the box and across to a large table in the center of the tent. He untied a big leather scroll, unfurling a map he had painstakingly drawn. The captains bent closer as he showed them what he planned to do.

"For everything to work as you envision," Herrek said, "we'll need a fleet."

The greater idea had come to Uriah after he'd learned Gog's army had taken in fresh levies. The implication was that the First Born had impressed many of the city pirates, even if Gog had hired more mercenaries from elsewhere. Taken as a whole, Uriah knew he had more numbers than Gog and his allies, and the new idea employed that to their advantage.

"The League of Peace is outfitting war-galleys for the operation," Uriah said. The league included the coastal cities of Carthalo, Bomlicar, Farther Tarsh and Thala. The city of Mago had dropped out a year ago, and that might prove troublesome, as the fleet would have fewer biremes and triremes than otherwise.

"Is Admiral Nar Naccara leading the fleet?" asked Herrek.

"The same," Uriah said. "But leave that information in here. I don't want word reaching Gog's spies just yet."

"Autumn storms will hurt the fleet worse than such storms will hurt our land host," Keros said.

Trust the shrewd mountain warrior who had begged as a cripple in Shamgar many years ago to know that.

"We're taking a risk, granted," Uriah told his captains. "But this is the moment to press our advantages, to strike, not to let up and allow Gog to wriggle free. We've never been this close to defeating Gog for good."

Herrek and Keros nodded in agreement. Other captains did not look convinced. Well, at least they didn't openly balk. Uriah could accept that for now, and he soon dismissed the captains to their men.

Two days later, the host that had camped near Dishon all summer, pulled up stakes, rolled up their tents and began to march inland. It soon became apparent that the men had grown fat and lazy from lounging around all summer. The good part was that no one had called on their reserves of strength lately. Even so, the next few days of marching brought endless complaining about tight sandals and blistered feet.

Uriah was reminded yet again that once a host stopped moving, it quickly settled into a sedentary routine that was often difficult to break.

A day later, Joash's newest message arrived via chariot. Although the ground was soggy, the sun shined today, and if the chariot stuck to the right kind of ground, it had no trouble remaining mobile. The message said his mammoths were five leagues away. Three days march should bring them to the main host.

Uriah had other ideas. He'd been feeding off the largess of Bomlicar, Carthalo and Dishon for months, and the stores had almost run dry. If he joined the two hosts too soon, it would be harder to feed everyone through foraging. Marching in smaller, separate groups allowed the foragers to spread out and comb the countryside. If everyone marched together, Uriah would have to tap into his remaining stocks. They would run out of flour to make bread, and deplete their supply of cheese, before they reached coastal Pildash. Once there—if they had to besiege the city while camping outside its walls—he would need as many stores as possible to keep his warriors in one place.

The truth of war was that armchair generals spoke about tactics, while winners worried about logistics—food and water in particular.

Gog's raiders struck the next night, a drizzly one. Lightly armed warriors and savage dire wolves attacked the eastern edge of camp. After slaying over a hundred surprised men, the enemy fled several hours before daylight. When the chariots took to the wet field to chase them, they were long gone.

"Gog is testing us," Uriah said under a dripping cypress tree in the late morning.

For the next three days, Uriah pushed his people into Pildash hinterland territory. There was one extra-soggy neck of land that passed between towering mountains of Arkite Land and a large Nebo swamp. Nebo tribesmen began sniping at the marching formations snaking across the land bridge.

On the third night of that, Keros led a band of Shurites, ambushing over one hundred Nebo warriors. The Shurites cut down half the stone-age tribesmen, the Shurite leather armor and iron weapons proving superior to flint weapons and wooden shields.

Keros maintained his location as Joash's mammoths, chariots and spearmen used the land bridge. The Nebo didn't show up this time.

Since it hadn't rained for several days in a row now, Uriah unleashed Herrek. The Champion of Teman Clan led the main chariot force north through Pildash territory. The charioteers and their runners burned villages and butchered cattle and sheep, driving people toward Pildash on the coast.

The good weather held for two more days, and Herrek led the chariots even farther north. The ground had begun drying out with all this sunlight, giving the bronze-wheeled chariots their normal mobility.

Now, Herrek instructed the runners to begin carrying the autumn harvests they'd taken from the people. The runners were to take sacks of wheat, apricots and beets to Uriah's wagon train, adding to the stored supplies.

The chariots pressed on, raiding several more villages. It began raining several hours before dusk. Herrek called a halt, setting up camp on a flat-topped hill, the chariots parked in one level area and the horses cordoned off in another. The charioteers and their drivers pulled out hooded cloaks, sitting around fires and eating their supper.

Maybe a sudden downpour caused the outer guards to huddle deeper inside their cloaks or cluster together under the few sheltering trees. Whatever the case, they did not see or report a party of Nephilim and dire wolves sneaking up the hillside.

The rain began to slacken as the sun moved from behind a cloud and down into the horizon for the night. There was still hazy light, enough to see to move around without stumbling.

At that point, trumpets pealed with wicked noise, and dire wolves howled—the sounds were almost on top of them. As the men looked up from their fires, huge dire wolves launched at them, while hulking Nephilim raced to engage.

Some of the Elonites still wore their chainmail and belted swords, Herrek among them. The tall prince of Teman Clan shouted his war cry, jumping to his feet as he drew his short sword. A shaggy dire wolf with a spiked collar crashed against him, knocking them both into flames.

The dire wolf whined as the hot flames began singeing its fur. Herrek struck blindly, shoving his steel through the beast's ribs. He scrambled out of the fire, pushing the dead wolf from him.

"To me, to me!" roared Herrek. He ran to a charioteer's aid, cracking a dire wolf's skull, driving the blade deep into gray matter, yanking it out as the beast died at his feet.

Hounds bayed as some unknown youth ran among the brutes, using a knife to slash the ropes tying them in place. The hounds raced at their mortal enemies; the spiked collars proved instrumental in protecting the dire wolves from the hounds' teeth, giving the altered creatures a deadly advantage.

Nephilim struck hard with sword and spear, slaying shocked charioteers, pushing the others back and keeping them confused.

At the same time, a second party of Nephilim struck the cordoned off horses. With spears and lances, they went berserk, killing many of the finely trained equines.

"Grab brands out of the fire!" Herrek shouted. "Find spears and partner up. Fight the Nephilim as you would bears. Team up! Attack!"

The Champion of Teman Clan howled a war cry and rushed a half-Nephilim. The crazed warrior of Gog turned with a snarl, holding the severed head of an Elonite. Herrek struck unerringly, thrusting his sword through a Nephilim eye. The warrior of Gog toppled, dropping the head and his weapons.

Herrek sheathed his bloody sword and picked up a spear. He saw Nephilim among the screaming mounts, and realized the enemy plan.

"Follow me!" Herrek cried.

He led a band, hitting the murderous Nephilim as they butchered the horses.

The fighting proved bloody and costly to the charioteers of Elon. For every Nephilim that went down, ten or more Elonites perished. These were Uriah's elite—the finest warriors any nation could have boasted. And yet, they fell by the handfuls to each enemy hero.

The greatest of the heroes of Gog was an eight-foot Nephilim named Sakard Axe-Slayer. He was a monster of a man with an incredible breadth of shoulders. He wore iron-studded leather armor and had the face of a beast with a splayed nose and grotesquely wide mouth. There were runes tattooed on his cheeks, said to give him sorcerous strength. Sakard had raged among the horses and was now slaying Elonites left and right.

Over twenty-three charioteers lay dead on the wet ground because of him.

Herrek spied him, and he saw Elonites flee as Sakard looked at them. The huge Nephilim roared. It was a deafening sound. The monster man shook his axe, terrifying everyone.

"We will slay you all!" Sakard shouted, his words reverberating with sorcerous power. "Gog will give me the great prize for this victory."

"No," Herrek said grimly, as his heart thumped in his chest. He panted from the fighting, and his limbs quivered with exhaustion and fear of the Nephilim.

"Give me strength, O Elohim," Herrek said. Then, hefting his spear, judging its weight, the champion of Teman Clan ran at Sakard.

As fiery brands blazed light, Herrek hurled the spear. It sped nearly as fast as a Huri-shot arrow. It flew true, piercing the hardened leather armor, lodging in Sakard's massive chest.

The Nephilim hero staggered back, and a pall of silence settled over the flattened hilltop.

"They're mortal!" Herrek roared, his bloodied short sword once again in his right hand. "Watch Sakard Axe-Slayer fall. See that Gog's warriors are flesh and blood just like us."

"Puny man!" roared Sakard. "You are dead."

The eight-foot hero of Gog raised his two-bladed axe high over his head and then behind. With a roar, he hurled the axe two-handed. It spun end-over-end at Herrek, and with sickening fury, the axe split the Champion of Teman Clan's head in two.

Herrek's corpse collapsed onto the bloody ground.

Sakard smiled broadly, exposing great horse-like teeth. He plucked the spear from his chest. The iron tip was bloody, but he ignored the wound as he strained, snapping the shaft in two, tossing the broken spear aside. It was an amazing feat.

That should have been the end of the fight as the Elonites broke and ran, their champion slain. Something else happened as charioteers and drivers of Elon saw their famed prince dead on the ground. They witnessed the mocking Nephilim, and he stood so proudly, so arrogantly. What hope was there for men if heroes of Gog slaughtered mankind's best?

"Herrek!" a charioteer shouted. "The monster has slain Herrek! Kill him! Kill the murderous beast!"

"Herrek! Herrek!" men began to chant.

At that point, Sakard Axe-Slayer took a staggering step forward as a strange expression twisted upon his wide features. His hands flew up to his chest wound, and he staggered, going down to one knee.

"Herrek!" the warriors of Elon screamed.

As one, the remaining charioteers went berserk, bellowing and gnashing their teeth. Herrek had led them for years. Every one of them had a story in which Herrek had helped or saved him. To see the great prince die by the monster man's hand—

The bedraggled warriors of Elon charged the Nephilim, hurling themselves at the raiding party. For a minute, the Nephilim fought back. Three Elonites swarmed a half-Nephilim, the first diving at the hero's legs and grabbing them. The half-Nephilim hacked at the man, but it didn't matter as the other two bowled him over, stabbing with knives until he lay dead. Five men rushed a Nephilim who hacked off three of their heads. The fourth and fifth warriors drove broken spearheads into his chest, screaming their fury.

At that point, the raiding party turned and fled, dashing down the hill as they sprinted into the night.

The berserk fury saved the rest of the chariot horses and likely saved the rest of the warriors. But that night, the warriors mourned the passing of one of the bravest Elonites and many of his fellow warriors, more casualties in the grim war against the sons of the *bene elohim*.

The next morning, the survivors headed south under torrential rain. The ground turned soggy, and in places, the wheels churned endlessly. They left many of the carts as debris of war, pushing the other chariots through mud until they reached stonier ground.

The grubby survivors returned to the main host, saddened and demoralized by their losses. They had lost half their number, fully three hundred warriors and even more trained horses.

Uriah gazed upon his slain great-great-grandson that afternoon, and he drank himself into a drunken stupor that night, collapsing as one dead on his cot.

The rains stopped by mid-morning of the next day, with everything and everyone sodden beyond belief. Men moved listlessly in camp, and rumors abounded saying the host would retreat to Dishon. No one could campaign in the autumn rainy season, and the season was about to enter its worst times.

It looked as if the great campaign against Gog and Shamar was ending.

-2-

Lod arrived that afternoon, squelching through mud as he trekked to Lord Uriah's tent.

A guard stepped out from under the awning and into the rain. He told Lod, "Lord Uriah said no one is to disturb him."

Lod wore a hood, with water dripping from it. He stared as if it took him time to comprehend the guard's words. Finally, he said, "Uriah will see me," and marched toward the flap under the awning.

The guard lowered his spear so it blocked Lod's passage. The second guard hurried out from under the awning and crossed his spear with the first guard's weapon, also blocking Lod.

"Uriah is miserable with the news of Herrek's death and is in mourning," the first guard informed Lod.

"Herrek is dead?"

The guard nodded solemnly. "An eight-foot Nephilim slew him."

"He must have been a Defender of Gog."

"I have heard the same. Men say Herrek wounded him, perhaps unto death."

"Did men see the body fall?"

"Stumble," the head guard said. "The others scoured the battlefield in the morning, but the body was gone. One of the raiders must have carried it off."

"What was the Nephilim's name?"

"Men say it is Sakard Axe-Slayer."

For a moment, Lod had a faraway look. Maybe he was memorizing the name.

He came to a moment later. "Sakard yet lives. But he won't much longer. Now, move aside."

The guard shook his head.

Lod eyed the guards, wondering if he should pluck both spears from their grasps. That might mean he'd have to knock both guards to the ground.

Fortunately, the tent flap opened, and a bleary-eyed Uriah swayed in the entrance. "What's all this noise? Oh?" the patriarch said in a low voice. "Lod." It appeared Uriah had more to say, but he didn't say it.

"Joash is several hours away," Lod said.

"He's too late," Uriah said, shaking his head.

"It's not too late."

Uriah snorted. "Take a good look at the skies, Lod. Rain. I was wrong to advance during the rainy season."

"Get out of my way," Lod said, brushing past the two guards. He stood before Uriah, staring at the drunkard. "This is exactly the time to advance."

"Go away," Uriah said, turning into the tent.

Lod grabbed one of Uriah's arms. "Herrek is dead. Is this how you'll mourn him?"

Others were watching from a distance, including the two guards. "Take him away," Uriah said over his shoulder.

The guards motioned for others to help them. Then, a group converged on Lod.

"Unhand me," Lod said, shrugging them off. He grabbed Uriah's arm again, yanking him close. "Joash is almost here."

"Unhand our lord," a guard shouted.

As one, the others drew their swords, and they closed in around Lod.

"Wait," Uriah said wearily, examining the scene. "I don't want more death on my hands. Let him in. I'll speak to him and explain why our cause is hopeless."

Eying each other, the guards finally retreated.

Scowling, Lod followed Uriah into the tent.

"Herrek was the best among us," Lod said inside the tent. "There's no denying that. But to let his death unman you—"

Uriah spun around, and he seemed a different man.

106

They were alone. The cot was unmade and wine flagons lay scattered on the floor. A main tent pole held up the waterproofed leather, and several campaign chests were arranged as seats around a table, topped with a map and a flickering candle. Several other oil lamps hung from the tent pole.

"Sit down," Uriah said curtly, the defeated, hangdog look disappearing completely from his features.

"What is this?"

"Sit," Uriah said, as he sat himself before the map table. He slid a plate of cheese across to Lod.

The huge warrior picked it up and gnawed off a hunk before sitting on a chest. He kept the cheese, gnawing off more.

"Keep your voice down," Uriah instructed.

Lod kept chewing as he studied the older man.

"I loved Herrek like a son. His death hurts." Uriah looked away before regarding Lod again. "I've sired too many warriors and seen them and their children and their children's children die violently. It never gets easier. Herrek performed prodigies, and his last act of valor saved the bulk of our chariots."

"What good is that, according to you?"

Uriah sighed as he looked up at the tent ceiling. "I've waited all spring and summer for Joash to arrive. He gathered mammoths, maybe too many of them. Fewer gained earlier would likely have been better. But that doesn't matter now. One thing I've learned these past months is that our camp is riddled with spies."

"You mean…" Lod said, working it out. "That was an act?"

"An act to let Gog's commander know I'm sick at heart."

"Won't your act dishearten our men?"

"You're going to fire me up, and you're going to do it openly by giving a speech in two days that will rouse the warriors. We'll have funeral games to celebrate Herrek and all those who have died so far. That's when you'll give the rousing speech."

"I'm glad you still have heart. But what does such trickery accomplish?"

"The one thing we need more than any other, that's what. We have to defeat Gog's main army if we're going to successfully besiege Pildash. The wisest and safest course for Gog is to let us expend ourselves camping all autumn and winter before Pildash. The walls will wear us down, as we dare not spend our warriors trying to storm it as Gog's army waits half a day away to our rear."

Lod considered that as he ate more cheese. He said, "Gog is cunning. He must know this as well as you do."

"I'm sure he does. But an army commander cannot always do the wise thing. There is morale to consider, as well as supplies and other factors. I unleashed our chariots against the hinterland Pildash villages, trying to stampede the people as I gathered their stored supplies for us. Some of that worked as planned until Gog's commander unleashed a larger-than-average raiding party to slaughter my charioteers. I think Herrek saved us from the worst outcome of that maneuver, but it cost him his life."

"Gog's commander succeeded, then."

"Maybe," Uriah said. "We're still going to march on Pildash. I've also had word that Nar Naccara led the Grand League of Peace Fleet before Pildash. Naccara and the fleet are now beached near Pildash. The implication is obvious to all. We're going to storm Pildash by land and sea. The combined attack should succeed. That means Gog's commander must either destroy our reinforced host or march his soldiers into Pildash as defenders. I don't believe Gog would want that, though. If Gog can't keep his army free, he would surely want it in Shamgar. Thus, I'm trying to entice Gog and his commander into making the decision we want."

"Wouldn't our freely storming Pildash by land and sea be even better?"

"No," Uriah said. "Because our real target is to sack Shamgar and kill Gog. But if we're going to do that this year, we need to kill as many of Gog's soldiers as we can now. Those same soldiers behind Shamgar's walls will be many times more dangerous than outside."

Lod considered all that as he finished off the cheese. "You're cunning, but so is Gog. I doubt—"

"Listen," Uriah said, interrupting. "You're right about Gog being cunning, but never forget that he's also a First Born. That means he's incredibly proud and arrogant. He views us as cattle. But we're destroying his kingdom. That sticks in his craw. You're here, and we know Gog hates you above all others. These things combined might be enough to force him to attack our host."

"He must know we have mammoths."

"I'm sure Gog knows that, but does he really understand Joash's power? Frankly, I doubt it. Mammoth Man Thoar has been advising Joash, and now two hundred Elonites dress and ape Mammoth Men behavior. They ride the mammoths everywhere and practice new battle evolutions. Gog will have seen that through pterodactyl eyes, the trained sliths from Poseidonis. He'll also have listened to many reports from his spies."

"I don't understand what you're getting at."

"If Gog believes we've recruited Mammoth Men, he'll believe we use Mammoth Men tactics. That's where he—or his army commander—will make a dreadful mistake. I trust that is so, I should say. Has Joash trained the mammoths as I suggested he do?"

Lod shook his head in wonder. "It's amazing to witness. The mammoths love him. You were right from the beginning. Joash is our great prize. But won't Gog come to realize that?"

"I would think so, yes, but only when it's too late. Even so, I'm giving you a critical task. When we march into battle, you must stick by Joash and defend him from all comers. Once the enemy realizes the mammoths obey Joash, they will surely attempt to swarm and kill him."

"That was my task before, remember? Only it turned out the other way. Joash saved me from Cain, not me saving him."

Uriah frowned. "I've listened to reports, and I find them most incredible. Was he really the original Cain, the son of Adam?"

Lod nodded.

"Oh, that's bad, very bad."

"Why?"

"The original Cain is said to be a fantastic general. If Gog were wise, he would put Cain in command of his army."

"Would a First Born do that?"

"More to the point," Uriah said, "would Nephilim and half-Nephilim warriors submit to a man's command, even a man like Cain?"

Lod snorted, shaking his head. The answer was obvious. Those with the blood of the *bene elohim* looked down upon men.

"Thank Elohim our enemies are so arrogant," Uriah said. "Without such arrogance, they would have conquered the world a long time ago."

"Do you know much about Gog's army?"

"Not yet," Uriah said, "although I've been busy rectifying that. Now, listen, Lod. There's something else I need to tell you."

"I'm listening."

Uriah bent over the map and began to whisper in earnest…

-3-

The funeral games started as the host celebrated the courage of Herrek and the many warriors who had died fighting the evil ones. Then, Lod arose and gave a rousing speech. He said many of the things Uriah had suggested, and he told the listening throng about his visions of Shamgar burning as they marched victoriously through the streets and over the canals.

It rained afterward, lasting all that night and the rest of the next day. That turned the ground even soggier than before and made the wet tents miserable.

The next morning, the great host from Elon, Shur and Huri Land, with thousands of spearmen from Carthalo and Bomlicar, began to march through the mud toward Pildash on the coast.

Wheeling pterodactyls watched from the cloudy skies, screeching cries when thunder boomed in the distance.

The host would not have advanced as fast as it did, but Thoar had shown Joash how to harness mammoths to wagons and carts. The great lumbering beasts pulled the wheeled vehicles through fields of sticky, slurping mud. Horses, donkeys and even oxen would have had a difficult time at best taking the wagons through. The mammoths made it look easy.

Because of that, the host moved faster than anyone could have predicted.

Halfway to Pildash, Shurite scouts ran back during late morning. They reported seeing the van of Gog's army. It marched at the host, and would likely reach their vicinity in half a day.

"We stop here," Uriah declared.

111

"Here" was a large open area, with a burned village half a mile to the west. The area must have been grazing ground for village cattle. To the east were many stone fences holding garden plots. The low stone fences could prove troublesome if the battle took place over and around them, as the fences would hinder both chariots and carefully aligned spear hosts.

Shurite raiders took off running to harass Gog's approaching army.

Meanwhile, Uriah called the battle captains to his tent so it was packed with war-leaders from different lands. Keros of Shur was here, Joash, Lod, Thoar, Lord Hanno from Carthalo, Lord Gisgo from Bomlicar and Chief Hobah from Huri Land. There were others, and those in back craned their necks so they could see more.

"Gog's army is coming," Uriah told them as he stood by the map table.

At that point, the tent flap ripped back and the chief of the Shurite scouts staggered in with a dirt-stained, sweaty face. "Lord Uriah," the lean warrior said in a ringing voice. "I have compiled our present information about the enemy as you requested."

"Come in, come in," Uriah said. "Yes. Stand here beside me. Now take a breath."

The chief of scouts nodded, breathing deeply and accepting a horn of mead. He threw the honeyed contents back, gasping afterward and wiping his lips with a muddy forearm. "A few of our raiders returned. You were right about levies from Pildash joining Gog's army."

Uriah nodded in a knowing manner.

That didn't fool Lod. The patriarch didn't like hearing he was right about that. But at least they knew the truth now.

"Speak up," Uriah told the chief scout. "Tell us more."

The Shurite told the assembled captains what the raiders had discovered about the enemy's composition.

There were thousands of pirates, maybe six thousand all told. The pirates wore a variety of clothes and armor, most having cutlasses, javelins and boat hooks. The pirates did not march as one group, but stayed with their captains. They seemed like hardened fighters, but were likely unused to working together as an army on land. Fighting on heaving, slippery decks was their specialty.

Next, were the spear-armed levies of Pildash. Shurite scouts had counted ten thousand of them. Many wore leather armor or metal chest-plates. All had shields, and their spear-tips glittered in unison whenever the sun peeked out from behind the clouds.

The Arkite mercenaries were tall, proud and fur clad. They carried spears, javelins, bows, and iron and flint-tipped tomahawks. A few had swords. They numbered two thousand.

The Nebo tribesmen were squat with low-sloping foreheads, most of them bow-legged brutes with flint-tipped spears and hatchets. Possibly a thousand marched with Gog's army. Another two thousand lurked in the forests and swamps.

Last was the kernel of the enemy army: fifteen hundred heavily armored and armed men together with mixed Nephilim of the fourth and fifth generations. Maybe one hundred Enforcers or half-Nephilim led those, while fifteen Defenders or full Nephilim heroes would roam the battlefield, slaughtering at will.

"Oh," the chief of scouts said. "I almost forgot."

He told Uriah and his captains about packs of dire wolves, two hundred altogether, with twenty shaggy sabertooths. In the back of the army were covered wagons, and from them terrible beasts roared with rage.

"What sort of creatures are in the wagons?" asked Lord Gisgo of Bomlicar.

The chief of scout shrugged. "None of us knows, but maybe cave bears. Gog has altered and used those in the past."

"I count twenty-two thousand, five hundred enemy soldiers," Uriah said, "with one hundred and fifteen named half-Nephilim and Nephilim heroes and at most, three hundred battle animals."

"The half-Nephilim and Nephilim are *champions,*" Hanno said. He was a tall, dark-haired man, wearing the Carthalo signet ring of command, a heavy gold band with a giant ruby gem.

"We have champions, too," Uriah said.

"One hundred and fifteen *named* heroes?" asked Hanno.

Uriah hesitated.

"There's something else we haven't talked about," Hanno said. "Gog's army will have sorcerers and necromancers. They will cast spells before, during and after the battle. Lord, this does not sound like an even fight to me."

"I hope not," Uriah said promptly.

Hanno did a double take before looking worriedly at Lord Gisgo.

"We have forty-five hundred hardy Elonites," Uriah said, "twenty-five hundred Shurite warriors of note and fifteen hundred Huri archers who can shoot a pear off a man's head at two hundred paces. Combined with that, we have over eighty bull mammoths and two hundred mammoth riders. We have thirty-five hundred spearmen from Bomlicar and four thousand from Carthalo. We would have even more spearmen, but many of the city soldiers garrison Dishon and too many, I'll admit, have fallen sick. Add that up, and we almost have as many men as the enemy."

"Nay, Lord," Hanno said gravely. "I count sixteen thousand warriors fighting on our side. That's sixty-five hundred less than the enemy has."

"We have eighty mammoths," Uriah countered.

"He has one hundred and fifteen heroes and three *hundred* battle beasts."

"Our mammoths will prove greater than their heroes and beasts," Uriah said. "Eighty mammoths and their riders will turn the tide, allowing us to smash Gog's army."

Silence followed his words. Too many of the captains obviously did not believe him.

"Gog's army marches to do battle with us," Uriah said. "I didn't want to say this, but his army is moving onto the wrong ground for them. It's wet here, but not soggy everywhere. Some of this region has rocky soil, the reason I halted. In other words, chariots can maneuver on some of the ground. That maneuverability is going to be critical. Gog's army lacks horses or any other creatures warriors can ride. That limits them to maneuvering only as fast as men can run. We have chariots and mammoths, and the room to maneuver them. Plus, we have thousands of stout-hearted warriors and spearmen to hold the enemy in place. That means this is the time and place where men will finally smash a Nephilim-led army. Perhaps a few sorcerers of theirs will cast spells. What do we care? We have Elohim's chosen—his seraphs—to help us. We have Joash who went to the East Gate of Eden and back, who helped defeated Tarag of Sabertooths and some of the greatest giants on Earth. Joash held a fiery stone that poured even more anti-sorcery power into his body. If that isn't enough, we have Lod. You all know him. Lod has slain countless Nephilim, and he will do so in the coming fight. Lod went

114

into the Catacombs and back, driving out evil spirits even as he blinded Gog with a spear. I have some ability to thwart Nephilim spells as well. Their magic will not help them on the coming battlefield."

Lord Hanno shook his handsome head. "I want to believe you. But how can we defeat the hated enemy when his half-Nephilim and Nephilim are all champions?"

"Ah," Uriah said, who did not feel the same hope that he tried to impart to his captains. "I'll tell you how. The key to every fight is to make the enemy run. Once the Nephilim and their warriors show us their backs, slaying them will merely be a matter of pitching a javelin hard enough to pierce their armor."

"Once an army flees, it is vulnerable," Hanno admitted. "How do you propose making Nephilim flee before the fact?"

Uriah scanned his assembled captains, noting their fearful concentration. "We have mammoths and chariots. On those two arms rest the coming fight—provided our foot soldiers battle long enough to give us time."

"Enough!" Hanno said. "I grow weary of these hints. Tell us the exact plan."

Uriah began the explanation, hoping with all his heart that what he proposed was possible against a Nephilim-led army.

-4-

As a cold morning wind blew over the land, Lod walked behind Joash and Thoar, who watched the mammoth riders leading their shaggy beasts onto the likely battlefield.

Lod wore a coat of mesh-mail with a helmet covering his white hair. Before leaving his tent, he'd belted on a legendary weapon, the sword of Tubal-Cain, who came from the line of Cain. Tubal-Cain had been the world's first bronze smith and this sword his prized creation. Lod had won the sword when he'd slain Tubal-Cain's animated corpse on a strange isle far to the south of here. He'd also slain Naamah the Beautiful, the sister of Tubal-Cain. Naamah was the one who had first lured the *bene elohim* to Earth. She had been ancient when Lod slew her, a dread sorceress who had tended the Yggdrasil Tree.

The sword was finer than other weapons, possibly as good as or better than a Bolverk-forged blade. Its edge did not dull, and Lod had wondered before if it would ever shatter.

Gog's army had moved close yesterday, camping two miles from them for the night. With morning, the army formed and moved toward them as the last morning mist dissipated.

"There!" a scout shouted. "I see Nebo out-runners."

Lod shaded his eyes from the sun. It was cloudy elsewhere, but not above him. It didn't seem as if it would rain today, but that could change with this wind.

As a mammoth moved into position, the beast raised his trunk and trumpeted.

Lod shifted uncomfortably, looking around. Bull mammoths were all around, eighty in all. The cows and calves were back in camp, roped off and well fed with hay.

The eighty bulls had come from the plains of Elon. Among them were two hundred riders, Elonites trained to fight with the newly tamed animals. The riders wore long leather coats, tough enough to turn many arrows and glancing sword blows. The leather coats would not turn Nephilim-hurled spears, however. The other mammoth riders held large shields and carried a supply of javelins on their backs.

Someone had suggested Huri archers ride the mammoths. The Huri had refused. Only the Elonites who had grown up with tales from Lord Uriah had enough faith in Joash to ride the shaggy beasts.

Lod stared into the distance. Gog's army would march slightly downslope, giving them a small advantage. Behind the long plain were trees. Uriah had not wanted the battle to take place there.

It would still be a little time before Gog's army marched through the trees to the top of the rise. Right now, Nebo tribesmen stood there, shouting and waving spears and flint-tipped hatchets.

Joash finally looked up. He'd been praying with a bowed head. The slender young man wore a mammoth rider's long leather coat and leather helmet. He carried a javelin in his right fist, and used it as a pointer. Thoar was beside him and was bigger and dark-haired like Joash. The Mammoth Man eyed the great beasts with obvious delight.

"Gather around me," Joash shouted.

Some of the mammoth riders left their beasts and lurched toward him.

"No," Joash said, "I want the mammoths to gather around me."

That took more time and some coaxing on the part of the riders and Thoar. Finally, the largest bulls moved in, reaching out with their trunks and touching Joash on the head and shoulders. The other mammoths gathered behind the old ones.

Joash did not speak verbally. Instead, he looked up at the mammoths, and his face began to shine with an eerie radiance. He stabbed the javelin in the ground and raised his hands. He began turning in a slow circle so he could see all of them.

The mammoths responded by lifting their trunks. A few blew mighty trumpet sounds. Others stamped their feet.

117

Lod could feel the ground shake and knew a moment of awe.

Joash nodded and smiled, raising his hands as high as they would go.

"Today," the young man shouted, "we will rid the Earth of hated Nephilim. They have despoiled the land with their presence. Today, Elohim has chosen to use the great beasts of the Earth to help men. I, Joash, will be watching you. If you fail, if you run away, the Nephilim will catch and kill me. I need your help, mammoths. You are my chosen ones. You are the great ones that will fight for the beasts of the field. Do not fail, but show your mighty courage and what happens to beings who defy the will of the Creator."

That proved to be too much. All the mammoths began to stamp their feet so the ground shook more, and they trumpeted.

"Quiet!" Joash shouted, although he laughed with delight. "Quiet down. Don't frighten the evil ones too soon. They likely fear you enough as it is. When the time comes to charge, then stamp and trumpet with all your might. You can kill the evil ones and those who fight with them. Remember, men will ride you. Listen to the riders, and let them help you rid the Earth of wickedness."

Lod barely restrained himself from drawing his sword and shouting at the top of his lungs. This had to be the greatest speech he'd ever heard, and it had been for the ears of beasts who understood Joash.

With Thoar's advice, Joash began to place the mammoths in a long line. As he did, the riders began to give each other a leg up onto the mammoths. Then, the ones up there reached down and gave a hand up to their partners.

It took longer than Lod would have believed. When Joash finally set the last mammoth in place, the army of Gog was forming up on the rise.

Lod looked back. Uriah and the captains were marshaling the host of Elon and its coastal city allies. Sunlight glittered off polished spear-points and shined from some shields polished like mirrors. There were countless standards and flapping flags throughout the formations.

In the center, behind the mammoth line, gathered the spear-armed levies of Bomlicar and Carthalo. On the left of the spearmen were the warriors of Shur gathered by clan. Beyond the Shurites were half the chariots of Elon. To the right of the city spear-host were Huri archers. To the right of them were the other half of the Elonite charioteers and runners.

Lod's heart began to race. This was it. He'd waited years to witness this battle, to engage in it. The army of Gog, of Shamgar and its allies, marched to do battle against Lord Uriah's Elonites and allies. He had never dreamed their side would have mammoths to help them fight the Nephilim.

Lod used to wonder how Elohim would give them the victory. Nephilim heroes shone particularly in open conflict. Men could only face them if they had greater numbers and hardy resolve.

Lod swallowed. The enemy had more numbers. They had mammoths—and chariots. Lord Uriah set great store by the diminished chariot arm. Herrek would not lead the charioteers of Elon today. That right went to Lord Uriah. Did they have enough chariots, and would the chariots prove their worth on a soggy, rain-threatening battlefield?

"Gonna find out," Lod muttered to himself.

Time passed in a blur as he waited and observed. Most battlefields were dust-choked slaughterhouses. This one would have next to no dust due to the autumn rains and the correspondingly wet ground.

"Do you see them?" Joash asked.

Thoar stood nearby along with a guard of Elonites in chainmail. They would help Lod keep Joash alive. The young man had refused any other spot.

"The mammoths need to see me and feel my presence," Joash had told Uriah yesterday.

"Do you mean. 'See the enemy?'" asked Lod.

"That's right," Joash said. The young man wore leather armor and carried a spear and shield. Uriah had forbidden him to take an active part in the fight, although he would naturally defend himself if the enemy got close enough.

It was Lod's task to make sure no enemy hero did.

Sliths screeched overhead, while the bigger enemy army marched down the slight rise.

A host of Nebo skirmishers fanned out, screaming insults and pumping their weapons in the air. Behind the chaotic mass of stone-age tribesmen, the pirates marched to the right and the spearmen of Pildash to the left, two giant blocks of warriors. There was no evidence of the Arkite mercenaries. Had the mountain men fled before joining battle? That seemed unlikely. Arkites were fierce warriors, known for their valor. There was also no evidence yet of Shamgar's city guard, the enemy's deadliest formation. Clearly, the guard must be behind the two giant blocks of pirates and spearmen.

A horn pealed in the background, and more horns took up the cry. That was the signal.

Warriors clashed their spears against their shields as the great assembly of Elon and its allies started to march at Gog's army.

"Walk at first," Joash said through cupped hands.

A mammoth rider raised a horn to his lips and blew. The first bull mammoths started in their elephantine shuffle at the enemy.

Now, the entire battlefield was on the move.

Horns and bugle cries drifted from the enemy army.

"What's going on?" Joash asked Lod.

Lod, who was farther ahead than Joash, peered past some shaggy mammoths. It was difficult to make out past the shifting mass of Nebo skirmishers, but—

"The pirates and city spearmen are moving into a tighter and deeper formation."

"I wonder why they're doing that."

Lod scratched his cheek. "Maybe because of the mammoths," he shouted back. "Maybe they figure if they have tighter, deeper ranks, the mammoths can't smash through them."

"Ah-ha!" cried Thoar. "That's their first mistake."

Joash glanced at the Mammoth Man.

"The right idea is to open ranks," Thoar said, "to coax and trick the mammoths to run right through their formation. The warriors over there must have never faced mammoths before. There's another way, as well. To seed the field with caltrops."

"What are those?" asked Joash.

"Mammoth-crippling spikes," Thoar said. "But let's not talk about them. We don't want anyone getting the wrong idea."

Lod had overheard. Was Thoar correct? A tight, deep formation should prove too dense for even mammoths to break. But even if the—

Lod groaned as an oily sensation struck. It was vile and seemed, seemed—his head began to pound and his eyes watered. He felt dizzy, and the ground shimmered. What was wrong with him? The evil sensation became more powerful as if someone was beating a drum, and every time the drummer pounded, Lod's eyesight shifted strangely.

At that point, a *thrum-thrum-thrum* compulsion forced the seraph to look up into the sky. His gaze shifted again as the sliths wheeling up there seemed different than he remembered. Had they gained in size and ferocity? They soared—yes! As the *thrum-thrum-thrum* sensations beat into his brain, the sliths grew stockier, much larger than any slith Lod remembered seeing before. He'd been a galley slave of Poseidonis for twenty long years and had seen countless sliths throughout the years. Never had he seen creatures like those up there.

Thrum-thrum-thrum, an almost audible beat forced thoughts and sensations into Lod. If they did that to him, what did the vile drum beats do to others?

Lod was too transfixed with the horror in the skies to look around at his fellow warriors to find out.

The sliths—the Yorgash-tamed pterodactyls—grew larger as their puny legs lengthened into vicious weapons with sharp gleaming talons like a gigantic eagle. Their triangular-shaped beaks became great slavering jaws that dripped with liquid fire, while the fins on the top of their heads turned into black horns that would gore any mammoth to death.

Thrum-thrum-thrum. Thrum-thrum-thrum.

Lod blinked several times and rubbed his aching forehead. The sliths roared thunderously, more than twenty of them, and they began to circle lower over the Host of Elon.

"Lod! Lod!" a man shouted.

Thrum-thrum-thrum. Thrum-thrum-thrum.

Lod swallowed uneasily. Would those fiery liquid drops burn his flesh?

Thrum-thrum-thrum. Thrum-thrum-thrum. Thrum-thrum—

"Lod!" the man shouted in his face.

Lod blinked again, and the drumming in his mind lessened. His eyesight blurred before focusing once more, and Lod realized that Joash was staring at him.

"What do you see?" Joash shouted.

Lod frowned. What kind of question was that?

Thrum-thrum-thrum. Thrum-thrum—

"I'm speaking to you," Joash said.

"Yes…" Lod said, as he began to understand. "I see great beasts of the air. The sliths…have grown armored hides, and fiery poison drips from their slavering jaws."

"No," Joash said. "That's a lie, an illusion of the evil ones. They're using necromantic-powered sorcery against us."

Lod nodded vaguely.

"I remember the Hills of Kel-Hemen and the cursed gems that Mimir the Wise used to delude Herrek, Elidad and the others. I'm seeing the same possessed look in everyone's eyes around me. We have to break the spell."

"Illusion…" Lod said dully.

"Sorcery," Joash shouted, grabbing Lod and shaking the bigger man. "Lord Hanno said Gog would practice sorcery today. This is it. If we don't defeat the illusion soon, our host will scatter in terror. Look at them, Lod."

The white-haired warrior looked around. Men and beasts gazed skyward. Some men shivered in dread. Others were blank-eyed with their mouths hanging open. A few were simply slack-jawed in terror. Yes, yes, Lod felt the fear billowing from the massed warriors. The mammoths also looked up and were on the verge of breaking, possibly trampling the Host of Elon in the process of running away.

"Give me a bow," Joash shouted.

No one obeyed him, as everyone but Lod looked skyward at the terrifying creatures circling lower and lower.

"A bow," Lod said, as his mind began working again. He knew Joash was more powerful than he was in halting evil spells. But as Lod realized the evil ones had been using him, anger burned in his heart. The anger ignited at the thought that Nephilim sorcerers would have handed the victory to Gog, might still do so unless he acted.

Lod snarled under his breath, and his blue eyes began to burn with hatred against the enemy. He sprinted to a mammoth rider with a bow slung on his torso. "You!" Lod roared up. "Give me your bow."

The trembling rider did as asked, pitching the bow and a quiver of arrows to the ground.

Lod scooped them up and raced back to Joash, thrusting them into the young man's hands.

Joash put an arrow to the string and walked behind the line of mammoths in full view of the Host of Elon. He looked up and spoke in a loud voice:

"Gog comes against us with Nephilim spells, with swords and spears. But I go against Gog in the power of Elohim and His mighty promises. I defy Gog and defy his sorcerers who trick our minds with illusions. Those are but sliths, and I will prove it."

Joash drew the bow until his arms trembled, and he released the arrow so it sped upward. The arrow lost velocity just before it reached a descending flying monster. But as the arrow reached its summit, the great flying beast wavered until a mere pterodactyl soared there.

The pterodactyl screeched, and the arrow began to fall back to earth.

Then, a second and third arrow thudded against the underbelly of the pterodactyl. It screeched again, in pain. At that point, a fourth arrow struck its left wing. Now the pterodactyl plummeted to the earth, striking the ground and flopping about in pain.

Lod rushed up and chopped off its head with the unnaturally sharp sword of Tubal-Cain.

Up in the sky, one after another, the other flying monsters became mere pterodactyls—sliths—once again.

Joash hadn't shot the last three arrows, but Lod had. The big warrior had pulled the string farther and thus shot higher and harder.

Lod now waved his bloodied sword for the Host of Elon to see. Joash raised a javelin and shouted prayers. He ran along the forward line of warriors. Lod did likewise in the other direction, the two seraphs using their inner fire to shield the men of Elon, Shur, Huri Land, Bomlicar and Carthalo from the awful sorcery of the necromancers with their death-skulls.

"Pray to Elohim!" Lod shouted. "There is victory in Him. Trust the Creator as we face the evil ones with their vile magic. We can win this fight. We have the valor, and we wage war under the banner of Elohim!"

The biggest bull mammoth—the one Joash had found after the trip to Nearer Tarsh—trumpeted with peals of mammoth courage. He seemed to understand what was happening, and perhaps among the animals, there were those who trusted the Creator or hated the

Creator's enemies more than others. Two more mammoths took up the great bull's cry.

Then, Lord Uriah wheeled before the host in his chariot but behind the great shaggy beasts of the plains. He shook a lance and shouted, taking up the cry, using his inner seraph fire to douse the spells sent by Gog's sorcerers.

At last, the insidious *thrum-thrum-thrum* departed from the last warrior's mind. In the drumbeats' place welled a knowledge that they fought on the side of righteousness. That knowledge was heightened as a ray of sunlight broke through the cloud cover.

First one warrior and then another took up Joash, Lod and Lord Uriah's cry. Soon, a great rolling chant and cheer thundered from the ranks. It rose in volume as the men cried, "Elohim! Elohim!"

Joash seemed to have an endless supply of vitality. He now sprinted away from the assembled warriors and to the rear of the long line of mammoths. He raised his arms, pumping the javelin in the air, shouting as his face shined with an eerie radiance.

Lod panted, refusing to slow down and waved his shiny sword. Oh, how he had longed for such a day. His heart swelled with anticipation. They were doing it. They were facing a Nephilim-led host with an eager desire to defeat the enemy.

Now, from being on the verge of panic, the great mammoths of the plains raised their trunks in unison with their three bull leaders and trumpeted peals of fighting rage. Their ears stiffened outward and on rigid legs, they charged the Army of Gog before them.

As the mammoths charged, the Host of Elon marched after them.

-5-

The commander of the Army of Gog miscalculated. He threw the Nebo tribesmen forward as skirmishers. They were stone-age warriors and likely no good at formation fighting. Perhaps the enemy commander hoped the tribesmen would hurl showers of javelins and bloody the Host of Elon. Maybe the enemy commander planned for the tribesmen to absorb the initial charge and possibly confuse Gog's enemies.

None of those things happened. Instead, the swamp-bred tribesmen—excellent scouts and raiders—fled in sheer terror at the wall of enraged and trumpeting wooly mammoths racing at them. Some of the Nebo tried to scramble through the pirate and Pildash spearmen blocks. The squat swamp-warriors died on the Pildash shield-wall, while they threw the front-rank pirates into confusion. Finally, the hardened reavers cut down the hairy, sobbing warriors. Other Nebo fled to the sides, scampering from the battlefield as fast as they could sprint.

Perhaps the easy success goaded the mammoths. The ground shook as the huge accelerating beasts neared the dense front ranks of the levies of Pildash and the crowded horde of Shamgar pirates.

As Lod struggled to keep up, he witnessed a spectacle he would never forget. The great beasts literally ran over the front rank of enemy warriors, trampling many to death. As the mammoths did so, the next rank of enemy warriors shrank back from them, causing countless warriors to crash upon the ground as one after another stumbled against the man behind him.

Despite mammoth moral ascendancy, the sheer masses of human flesh meant the mammoths did slow down and even stop. Now, individual animals reached out with their trunks, many a one plucking a screaming man from the ranks, lifting and often killing him by goring the man against a tusk. Another mammoth raised its shouting man high above his heads before hurling the man deep into the enemy formation. Yet another of the beasts set his victim on the ground and deliberately stepped on the man's chest, pressing down until all his ribs shattered. The mammoths did not wade deeper into the sea of humans, but fought along the front edge, pressing the entire enemy formation back.

Yet, despite the terror the mammoths imposed upon the enemy, the pirates and Pildash spearmen did not break and run away. In fact, some of the pirates and the bravest spearmen of Pildash rushed the mammoths, hurling spears or javelins at the riders or beasts and swiping at the trunks with cutlasses or knives.

At the same time, mammoth riders hurled javelins into the packed enemy ranks. Unfortunately, the riders were horribly outnumbered by the sea of enemy soldiers before them, but the awe the enemy held for the murderous beasts kept them from acting logically in great enough numbers...yet.

As the mammoths held the main Army of Gog in position, the city spearmen of Bomlicar and Carthalo marched closer. Soon, only fifty feet separated them from the trumpeting, stamping, killing beasts.

On the right side of the mammoth line, Huri archers ran up and fired volley after volley upon the enemy opposite them. On the other side of the battlefield, Shurites rushed forward, fighting pirates.

A curious thing happened, though. The Army of Gog had tightened up and deepened in order to face the mammoths. That meant their frontal exposure was less than usual, given their numbers. Because of the shortened length of the line, the Shurites began to overlap the enemy front. Soon, they attacked the enemy's left flank.

The pirates on the flank no longer faced forward, but turned to face the howling Shurites heaving javelins into their packed ranks. Some brave Shurites dashed near, using tomahawk or sword to engage pirates. Those contests were brief. Mostly, a pirate groaned or screamed, pitching to the ground. A few times, the Shurite died. If

126

the Shurite lived, he ran back to the mass of howling warriors that continuously hurled javelins at the pirate. No pirate dared to rush forward and single himself out as a target.

The Shurites in back began passing their extra javelins forward, leaving the pirates with nowhere to flee. Often, as a pirate tried to dodge a javelin or tomahawk chop, he jumped back, bumping up against two others, who essentially pinned him in place as a target. That meant many of the pirates on the flanks tried to press deeper into the pirate mass in order to hide from the murderous missiles.

Horns pealed, and on both flanks of the fighting, chariots wheeled around.

The enemy commander must have been waiting for this. Drums beat from the rear of Gog's Army. Handlers rushed forward and unleashed shaggy dire wolves. The Gog-altered beasts raced at the chariots Lord Uriah led on the left flank.

The Elonites in the chariots waited as the dire wolves closed and then hurled a mass of javelins, which sank among the attacking wolves, wounding and killing many and tripping others.

Perhaps the commander of Gog's Army miscalculated, overestimating the terror the dire wolves would produce on the battlefield. These were the charioteers of Elon after all, hunters, most of the time, on the plains. These warriors hunted wolves, sabertooths and lions in order to protect their valuable herds. This was exactly the type of combat they understood best.

Instead of checking the chariot maneuver, the dire wolves boosted Elonite morale as the surviving beasts lost their nerve, tucked their tails between their hind legs and raced away in various directions, some fleeing the battlefield altogether, following the disappeared Nebo.

On the other side, a similar event occurred, with the smaller number of sabertooths charging the chariots. Although the sabertooths were bigger and deadlier than individual dire wolves, because there were so few of the great cats, they went down even faster to Elonite javelins.

The two chariot arms wheeled in against the packed Army of Gog, nearly encircling the entire vast formation.

At the same time—due to hastily shouted orders—some pirates and spearmen of Pildash dared to rush through the line of mammoths. Most made it, even though a few mammoth riders hurled darts down at them. Those pirates and spearmen that made it looked around and raced at Joash. Perhaps their captains had promised great rewards to the soldier who slew the young seraph. These pirates and spearmen were eager, dashing at Joash as warriors sure of their fighting skills.

"Get set, lads," Lod said. He gripped the sword of Tubal-Cain and hefted an iron-rimmed shield with a wicked spike in the center.

Around him, Elonites formed a line, with Joash and Thoar behind them.

A huge, one-eyed pirate chose Lod. The fellow wore a leather jerkin, sported an evil gap-toothed grin, and held a heavy cutlass in each knotted hand. As the pirates and spearmen collided against the Elonites, the huge fellow bellowed.

The pirate was strong, and he not only wielded the two cutlasses skillfully, but with muscle-packed strength. In the first few seconds, Lod used his shield and sword to parry blow after blow, feeling like an anvil as the blows clanged and clashed against him. The pirate did not tire, however, as Lod had hoped. The fellow actually began to sing a pirate chantey, as if hugely enjoying the fight.

An Elonite went down beside Lod with blood pouring from his gashed throat. More pirates made it through the mammoth line, and they ran to help their fellow warriors.

"I am Horst Two Swords," the pirate boasted. "You will soon lie at my feet, muscle man."

Another Elonite groaned as a Pildash spear thrust into his gut. That warrior went down, and the swordsmen protecting Joash had to tighten their line once again.

Lod jumped back, thrust his sword into the wet soil and tore off his helmet, hurling it at Horst Two Swords to back him off.

The pirate used a cutlass to knock the helmet away.

Then, the former rat bait of the canals and galley slave of Poseidonis gnashed his teeth. His eyes blazed with murder-lust as wild fury grew in his heart. Horst Two Swords was keeping him from dominating the fight. If Joash died, all Lod's dreams would die with the seraph that held the mammoths on the battlefield.

Horst frowned as he looked at Lod. Then, the big, one-eyed pirate laughed as more Shamgar pirates joined him and his fellows in the attack.

Lod howled as one demented, with spit flying from his mouth. The hammering of his heart had reached his brain. A blur of red dripped into his gaze. He laughed crazily.

As the berserkergang took hold, Lod charged Horst Two Swords. With the shield, Lod bashed a cutlass. With the sword of Tubal-Cain, he struck as hard as he could. The cutlass shattered into pieces.

"Witchcraft," Horst said.

Lod thrust through the thick neck, and he bashed the shield spike into the pirate's chest. Instead of backpedaling and yanking them free, Lod shoved forward, using the heavy body to knock other pirates aside.

At that point, Lod freed the sword. He had to leave the spike-shield, but scooped up a fallen cutlass. With the two weapons, he began to cut a swath through the enemy.

The cutlass smashed an enemy spearman's face, sending him reeling back. The sword of Tubal-Cain sheared through a helmet and much of the skull beneath. The two weapons slashed a big spearman, cutting his neck and forehead.

Pirates and spearman shrank back from the wild man of Elohim. Lod's demeanor was awful to behold as he spoke in a low voice, quoting holy words, and his eyes shined with the madness of a desert prophet seeing rivers of enemy blood in his mind's eye.

Then, the enemy attack was over as the last pirates in this area broke and ran back for their side on the other side of the mammoths. Lod almost gave chase after them.

"Lod! Lod!" Joash called. "In the Name of the Most High, I order you to regain your senses."

A cold wave of something struck Lod. He staggered, and the fires of bloodlust in his heart slackened. He blinked, looked back at Joash, struck anew by the young man's holiness. In that moment, Lod feared Joash.

Strangely, Lod did not feel exhausted. He had gone into the berserkergang and out, without losing his reserves of strength needed for the rest of the day.

He nodded to Joash, and then Lod would not look back at him. Is this what Lord Uriah had always sensed in Joash? It was wondrous and fearsome all at once.

The greater battle progressed as the bulk of the Shurites flowed against the enemy's left flank. On the right flank, Huri archers stood at a short distance from the Pildash spearmen, drilling arrows into the milling formation.

Uriah in his chariot finally discovered where Gog's city guard and the Arkite mercenaries were—at the back of the Army of Gog, making sure the host of spearmen and pirates attacked. The city guard held whips and hot irons. The Arkites waited on the right of the guard formation, tall men with their ancestral weapons ready.

Uriah gawked at the whips and hot irons. Had the guard driven the main army onto the battlefield? Did the pirates and men of Pildash regard the mammoths with that much terror?

That must have been the case. For now, the great Army of Gog shuddered as it if were a single man. Fear was filling pirate and Pildash hearts to the breaking point. The mammoths had proven simply too much for the men. The bravest pirates and spearmen had already died, slain by tusk and mammoth foot or rider spear. Few of the mammoth riders still lived, but that wasn't changing the situation.

As the two chariot wings converged on the rear of the Army of Gog, the city guard dropped their whips and hot irons and drew their weapons. The Arkites readied themselves for a fight.

There were Nephilim and half-Nephilim among the city guard. These were Gog's elite, and they had trampled across many a battlefield, butchering hosts of normal men through countless years and decades. The Arkite mercenaries were mountain-men champions who had often fought under Gog's banner and shown their worth.

The commander of the Army of Gog shouted orders. The city guard faced left while the Arkite mercenaries faced right. Then, as a huge Nephilim shouted, the two formations charged the chariots.

Luckily for the charioteers, there was plenty of space for them to maneuver. That's exactly what happened as the chariots wheeled away from the racing enemy attack. The drivers attempted to remain near the enemy but just out of spear and sword range. The charioteers hurled iron darts and javelins, and if they raced near enough in passing the enemy, they leaned over to thrust with long lances.

Then, eight-foot Sakard Axe-Slayer and his brother Rekard the Bold raced like cheetahs at the swirling chariots of the left flank attack. The two Nephilim were incredibly fleet of foot despite their size. Sakard used his great axe and sheared a horse's head from its body. The chariot crashed and the charioteer and driver tumbled out. Sakard slew them with a single mighty sweep of his weapon.

Rekard scooped javelins from the ground, hurling them one after another at passing chariots. He slew someone at each cast because he was too near to miss.

Sakard and his brothers drove off the left flank chariots. The Arkites dealt boldly with the right flank chariot-attack. Those charioteers took note and likewise turned as a whole, the horses thundering away from the rear of the Army of Gog.

It didn't look as if the Nephilim-led army was going to be encircled and butchered to the last man after all.

Still, the chariots had won a different sort of victory. Uriah's assault had forced the city guard and mercenaries to face sideways and charge to the flanks. That had a horrible effect upon the greater army.

The rearmost pirates and Pildash spearmen kept looking back over their shoulders to see how their Nephilim masters were doing. In looking back, they started to drop back. The men in front of them noticed, and they began looking back too, wondering what was so terrible back there.

The clash of weapons, neighing of horses and shouts of champions and men that drifted to them preyed upon their minds. *The Elonites must have encircled the army.* If that was true, they were trapped here, and they were going to die to the mammoths.

The individual thought, multiplied a thousand times, began to flow throughout the army. As the Shurites and Huri continued to slaughter the flank-placed men, and the mammoths continued to apply pressure on the front...it finally proved too much. The Army of Gog lost its nerve as the rear-rank pirates and spearmen began walking away from the fight.

"Stop!" shouted Sakard Axe-Slayer. "Face the enemy, you fools."

One pirate lost his head, charging the city guard in his desire to get away. A Nephilim cut him down, and another spat on the pirate's corpse.

At that point, the pressure burst as floodwaters through a dam, and more pirates and spearmen fled from the fighting on the right, left and front. Some threw away their weapons as terror took hold.

131

They wanted to get away as fast as possible and didn't want anything to encumber them.

The Army of Gog was beginning to melt away because their cohesion was gone. Perhaps as important, the Shurites, Huri, spearmen of Bomlicar and Carthalo and the Elonites saw the enemy losing heart and felt that victory was within their grasp.

Fighting knife to knife, sword to sword or spear to spear and all the possible combinations was a terrifying process. Being cut and maimed for life, and maybe even killed, put horrible mental pressure on a man. That terror and fear he had to master or he would unman himself in front of his friends. That terror never really left as long as enemy warriors thrust at him. So, once his enemy turned away and fled, a surge of elation filled the man. He thought like an animal at that point, one that saw a fleeing foe. The released fear and terror now bubbled up. To kill his foe in retribution, without having to worry about being maimed or dying in turn—as the terror left, great elation flowed in its place. That caused the electrified warriors in the Host of Elon to chase the enemy. The warriors yearned to kill those who had caused such awful fear to build in their hearts.

Nephilim and their offspring were wonderful warriors. They understood battle and its effects better than anyone alive. Those in the city guard of Shamgar weren't going to check the Elonite impulse at this point, and maybe Sakard Axe-Slayer and his Gog-spawned brothers realized it.

The Nephilim also realized that Gog hated failure. Thus, Sakard and Rekard put into effect a last-ditch plan that might yet win them a reprieve from their First Born father.

-6-

Earlier, the chariots raced away from the city guard and mercenaries, moving along the great flanks of the two warring congregations where Shurites slew and demoralized the pirates and Huri archers used their last arrows to pincushion spearmen of Pildash.

The city guard of Shamgar together with the Arkite mercenaries marched away from the pirates, Pildash spearmen and remaining Nebo tribesmen. More than a few Nebo had already managed to slip away from the fight and raced for their swamps, there to spread the terrible news of defeat.

The Shamgar city guard and Arkites moved up the gentle slope to the trees back there. Hidden in the shadow of the trees were huge covered wagons. During the week before the battle and the morning of, the beastmasters of the last set of creatures had bitterly argued with the commander, creating division and hostility between them. The commander had believed he could win the battle without the last set of beasts. Now, the commander swallowed his pride, realizing he needed the beasts if he hoped to save the army and later his life when he gave his report to Gog.

A few beastmasters waited in front of the covered wagons, including Sagoth of Great Apes. A half-Nephilim messenger raced to Sagoth and informed him of the commander's wishes.

The apish Nephilim scowled. Now was a fine time for the commander to realize his errors—Sagoth hooted softly. He could see what was happening in broad outline, and he would have to give a report to Gog as well.

133

"Yes," Sagoth grunted. "I hear and obey."

The messenger sprinted back to the city guard marching toward the trees. He sprinted in order to speak with the commander.

As the messenger departed, Sagoth shook his apelike head. This was a black disaster, and it was the arrogant commander's stupid fault. The Army of Gog could well perish in its entirety. The commander was now trying to place the burden of that on him. How would his father Gog view all this?

Fear welled anew in Sagoth's heart. Gog abhorred failure. His father would hate it even more if mere men managed to besiege Shamgar. It was time to act, doing his best to placate his often-angry father.

Sagoth shuffled to three other beastmasters, giving orders. They nodded with understanding, hurrying to obey.

As they left, the chief necromancer rushed up, a lean individual of the fourth generation with a black cowl hiding his sinister features.

"What should I do?" the necromancer whispered.

"We are releasing the bears."

"Surely it is too late for that."

"Wrong," Sagoth said. "You will use sorcery to goad the bears into even greater fury. They must fall upon the charging horde, giving our shattered army time to slip away."

"Slip where?"

"To Shamgar, you fool," Sagoth said. "All is lost here. Now, you and I are going to ensure that we get as much of the army back to Shamgar as possible. There, Gog will rebuild for the next campaigning season."

"Then, you and I should flee now," the necromancer said.

Sagoth showed his apish teeth. "Run away before I give you leave and my great apes will catch you and tear your limbs from your torso. You and your devotees will goad the bears to fury. Do you understand?"

"I will obey, Lord," the necromancer whispered, bowing his head.

"Then, get to your equipment and begin your spells."

The necromancer hiked up his long black robe and ran back to his wagon, to his fellow sorcerers and their necromantic pile of skulls.

With his red cape flowing behind him, Sagoth hurried to the beastmasters, shouting orders.

The others began releasing huge altered cave bears. The shaggy monsters weren't as big as one particular beast that had traveled several years ago to the Isle of the Behemoth. But these cave bears might yet help the commander save more of the army than otherwise.

**

The Army of Gog fled, but it did not happen in an instant, and some men were braver than others and managed to form a fighting retreat.

A curious thing also happened among the mammoths. They did not give chase as a predator would in such a situation. The mammoths had proven their courage. They had protected Joash. They now trumpeted at the fleeing warriors, taunting them.

The mammoths, in other words, just stood there, proud of their achievement but not understanding the importance of destroying a beaten army so it couldn't gather itself later and do everything all over again.

The great beasts from the plains of Elon acted as a bulwark and became an obstacle to the rest of the Host of Elon. The spearmen of Bomlicar and Carthalo not only lost cohesion as they chased the fleeing Army of Gog, but the individual soldiers had to thread between the great beasts.

Perhaps it didn't matter anymore. The entire enemy army was on the move as they streamed away for the trees in the near distance. The Shurites and Huri Men had an easier time chasing the enemy. They were already past the mammoths. The charioteers had it the easiest of all, as this was the moment for one of their greatest powers—that of running down and spearing fleeing enemies in the back.

However, the forest would naturally stop the chariots from racing much farther. Thus, the charioteers had to do their work now, before the army disappeared into the woods.

Uriah and his captains blew their rams' horns. The chariots wheeled and raced along the flanks of the streaming fleeing army. Some charioteers hurled javelins. Most leaned over the side and stabbed with their long lances. They had a field day, and their butchery thinned enemy numbers considerably.

The city guard of Shamgar and the Arkite mercenaries had already marched off the battlefield and moved into the forest. The first pirates and spearmen were now following suit.

As the Shurites, Huri Men and city spearmen sprinted to catch their enemies, a new development occurred.

Necromancer-ordered sliths wheeled overhead and released packets from their tiny talons. The packets plummeted to the ground, bursting so clouds of yellow powder spread. Men ran through the drifting clouds and some clouds burst upon racing warriors. One thing was the same. Every warrior that inhaled particles of yellow lotus soon found himself thrashing on the ground, convulsing to death or screaming horribly from yellow-lotus nightmares.

That, however, was merely the prelude to something much worse.

Sagoth's beastmaster wagons had rolled away into the forest. But now, huge cave bears rose up and charged out of the tree line. The shaggy monsters thundered bruin challenges as spit flew from their gaping maws. The bears had tiny red eyes enflamed with something more than rage, radiating a primeval hatred for everything that walked on two legs. They bawled savagely, fifteen monsters altered into vile creatures of destruction.

These were greater than cave wolves or sabertooths. These were engines of death unleashed here at the end. If not for the bitter arguments between the beastmasters and the commander, the battle might have gone quite differently—if the cave bears had led the attack.

Sorcerous spells goaded the monsters, and men looked upon them in horror.

The fifteen beasts changed the complexion of the chase. They charged into the rushing masses, bowling over scores of men and buffeting with their huge claws to the right and left. Each blow shattered bones and often brought instant death.

The carnage was drastic and happened with amazing speed. Two thousand men perished fantastically fast, and more would have surely died if champions had not taken up the challenge.

Lod recognized the danger, and with heavy hurled spears, he slew two altered cave bears even as the beasts murdered another hundred warriors.

Thoar riding the lone mammoth to give chase slew another altered cave bear, the tusks goring the bruin as the Mammoth Man sat above and hurled one dart after another into the roaring and maimed beast.

Joash's faced shined with holy radiance as he boldly approached three such cave bears one after another. With calm words, he stilled the animals and bid them leave. Those three cave bears did so, running away into the woods to live out their lives as best they could.

Groups of charioteers, Shurites and Huri warriors slew the rest. By that time, however, many of the fleeing warriors of Gog had gained a greater separation from Uriah's forces than they could have otherwise achieved.

The cave-bear attack had also acted like a bucket of cold water on an excited man. Lord Uriah and Lod now worked hard to reignite the fire in many of their men, and the Host of Elon gave chase for another hour. Without the altered cave bears, though, the chase might have lasted the rest of the day. The bear attack had drawn the wild elation from the victors much as one might suck out viper poison from a wound.

It was possible the victors could have ended the war right there by slaughtering eighty to ninety percent of the enemy soldiers. The cave bears stopped that from taking place.

In the end, the Host of Elon lost almost four thousand warriors, with half those casualties coming from the yellow-lotus packets and cave bears. Others bore ugly wounds. Perhaps another four hundred would die from wounds or infection in the next few days.

By counting corpses later, it was evident that the Army of Gog had lost 11,000 battlefield-slain. Most of those deaths occurred during the final rout and chase. It was likely another two or three thousand wounded would die later. Some of those who escaped would surely head to Pildash. Others would race to Shamgar, and many might flee to parts unknown or to the Nebo swamps.

The cave bears had saved thousands of the enemy, and that might prove a bitter blow in the end, if the Elon-led warriors hoped to trek to Pildash and later Shamgar, capturing both cities during a torrential rainy season.

PART THREE
SWAMP SIEGE

Few of the surviving Pildash spearmen returned to the coastal city in time. Combined with Nar Naccara's fleet rushing the port, the Host of Elon stormed the walls and captured Pildash in a day of riotous victory.

It rained for weeks after, and hot debates raged among the warriors living off the plunder. Most suggested it was time to go home as victors. They had shattered Gog's throttlehold on the southern coast and could live like princes on their accumulated loot. What need was there to risk all that by attempting to enter the swamp around Shamgar?

A few still wished to follow Lod to the pirate city and finish it, ridding their part of the world of the terrible First Born, who had plagued the region for centuries. That would also rid the Suttung Sea of the pirate base that launched too many robbing galleys every spring.

In the end, Lod, Lord Uriah and Joash convinced the bulk of the victorious warriors and the sailors in Nar Naccara's fleet to head for the Hanun Delta, there to work through the floodwaters with the mammoths so they could besiege the swamp city. No one expected it to be easy. Gog and his sons would likely rage like wounded beasts in their lairs, but there would probably never be a better opportunity to slay Gog and his sons than now.

What none knew yet was that this was a golden opportunity. Gog's known rages frightened his sons, the commander of the army and Sakard Axe-Slayer chief among them. The repercussions of their fear meant...well... that little was well in the retreating Army of Gog and in Shamgar this winter.

-1-

The defeated Army of Gog tramped through marshy terrain, men and oxen drawing the supply wagons. It rained all the time and soldiers were dying from pneumonia, exhaustion and festering battle wounds.

The smattering of Nebo primitives were the first to slip away. They were the best swamp trekkers, and they knew the region better than anyone else did. On no account did they want to live the winter in Shamgar, the butt of Nephilim frustration. They were already tired of upset and moody Nephilim and half-Nephilim striking them at the slightest provocation. Each time a Nebo and his friends successfully slipped away, they congratulated each other on their daring.

The Arkite mountain men took note of the primitives slipping away and the inability or indifference of the Nephilim to stop them. The Arkites began to speak to each other during the march and at night. They'd retained the majority of their warriors and were thus still a cohesive force. There were eighteen hundred of them, more or less. How should they handle the army's grim defeat?

The argument went something like this: Perhaps two thousand spearmen of Pildash yet remained with the army. The rest had died or slipped off in order to race home and defend their city. None knew yet that Pildash had already fallen. The Nebo had all departed, and thus there were no trackers to follow anyone else who fled. Sagoth's great apes could give chase through the trees, but the Arkites knew how to deal with a few of those. Three thousand or so pirates complained bitterly about all this marching. The pirates

141

wanted to build rafts and float to Shamgar. None of them would ever track Arkites overland if they left for their mountains.

Would a band of Nephilim and half-Nephilim chase them? Eighteen hundred Arkites were probably too many for a small band to attack. The city guard as a whole desired to return to their barracks in Shamgar. If the entire guard gave chase, it was possible the enemy would reach Shamgar before they did.

The question then was: would Gog send his champions and guardsmen later to harry Arkite Land for what the First Born might perceive as desertion today? The chiefs doubted it. They had often fought in Shamgar's army for pay, and Gog would need mercenaries more than ever if he could survive the winter.

The final question then was this: would it be better to slink off at night or demand their pay and march with their heads high, saying they would return for the spring campaign?

The chiefs held a night council, and the oldest mercenary suggested a quiet leaving would be wisest. During the marching and fighting, most of the mountain men had pitched aside their stone weapons and now carried iron swords, or hatchets or iron-tipped spears in their place. Such weapons were worth more than soft silver or gold. Nephilim like Sakard Axe-Slayer and his brother Rekard the Bold might hope to soften Gog's anger against them by bloody actions against those they would call traitors and cowards.

"We are not cowards," a young chief declared hotly.

"I know," the oldest mountain man said. "But defeated battle-chiefs often lie to their master in order to put themselves in a better light."

The young chief nodded. He could understand that.

The mercenary chiefs voted afterward, and the Arkites slipped away on the rainiest night, marching for several days without slowing. Finally, the mercenaries reached an Arkite hill fort and there slept long and ate ravenously upon waking. No warrior of Gog appeared, and thus the mercenary host split up, each warrior going his separate way into the mountains.

Their part in the fight was over.

That left the city guard, sorcerers, pirates and a few Nebo, spearmen of Pildash, and those Arkites who had remained for whatever reasons. In all, that was a little more than five thousand individuals. In other words, instead of boasting 22,000 effectives, the Army of Gog was a pittance of its former self.

Gog would be highly upset.

Still, five thousand men able to wield sword, spear or bow—combined with those yet in Shamgar—would prove a formidable force.

Hot words between Sakard Axe-Slayer and the army commander, Kregen Iron Arm, led to ill feelings and finally an eruption after the desertion of the mountain men became known. More spearmen began to depart after that, claiming their city needed them.

In any case, Sakard and Kregen were on a bar of land between marshy mires and towering cypress trees. Kregen bore a gnarly staff of command given him by their father. A ruby glittered at its end, said to possess magical powers. Sakard was empty-handed, although his famed battle-axe was slung across his back.

Rekard was with Sakard, while several human attendants awaited Kregen's bidding.

"Do you understand that failing to halt the Arkites is yet another error?" Sakard accused the commander.

Kregen wasn't as tall or as massive as Sakard. He wore a belted tunic and glittering rings on his big fingers. The commander was seven and a half feet tall and known for his brilliance in many matters. After Gog, he was likely the smartest person in Shamgar.

"Brother," Kregen said. "When addressing me, you will watch your tongue or I'll have it torn from your mouth."

Sakard sneered. "No one would dare."

Kregen pointed the ruby-topped staff at him. "One word from me, brother, and you will never speak again. That will be a blessed relief for all of us. You spout just to hear yourself speak, and you're as dull-witted as an auroch bull in heat."

Sakard blushed angrily. "You're a prancing fool who lost the army our father put in your soft hands. I'll let him know you overruled me at every turn. How do you think that will sit with Gog?"

Kregen knew how it would sit, and he feared returning home and facing Gog under the Temple. It was why the march had taken as long as it had. His temper had also become worse as the small army neared Shamgar. How had everything turned in his hands? It had

143

been those mammoths. It would have been wiser to first slay Joash and Lord Uriah. They had been the brains and the soul behind the enemy's resistance.

"You failed me, Axe-Slayer," Kregen said in a stern voice. "You disobeyed a direct order. I told you to scatter the chariots and fall upon the Shurites from behind. Instead, once the chariots turned, you marched back behind the army instead of facing danger and winning glory like a true son of Gog should."

"Bah!" Sakard said. "You only gave the order so the enemy would slay me. It would have been the height of folly for the guard to expose itself as you'd suggested."

"Firstly, I did not 'suggest,' I ordered you to lead the guard. Secondly, I'm astounded to hear you admit that you feared the cattle and turned and ran away."

"Watch your mouth," Sakard snarled.

That was too much. Kregen's temper flared. He'd had enough of this over-muscled and self-important boor. Sakard had failed him at the most critical moment. If the guard had driven off the Shurites and Huri Forest Archers as he'd decreed, they would have won the battle. Now, the oaf dared to tell the commander to watch his mouth. That was a slur on his Gog-given authority.

Kregen stepped close and with the staff of command, he struck Sakard across the face.

The Axe-Slayer's black eyes shined with murder-lust. He knew Gog would make all of them pay for Kregen's mistakes, and that knowledge had turned him anxious and therefore easily triggered— and maybe he should have attacked the Shurites. Would Gog view his retreat as cowardice or prudence?

Without thinking it through, Sakard reached back and freed his axe.

"Sakard," Rekard said. "Stop. This is madness."

Sakard did not stop, but stared at an open-mouthed Kregen and saw the fear there. Before he could halt himself, Sakard swung, chopping off the commander's head so it toppled onto the ground, bounced and plopped into the miry water. The corpse jetted blood and toppled with a thud.

At that point, Sakard stared in horror at the axe in his hands. He noticed the ruby glint from the staff of command lying on the wet grass. Gog would never forgive him this outrage. His father would see it as an attack against his own authority.

"You're doomed," Rekard said, confirming the worst.

Sakard turned to his brother with the cunning of fear. "You were here. You didn't stop me."

"I just tried, remember?"

With an oath, Sakard jumped over the corpse and slew the shocked human attendants with three well-placed blows. They would never bear witness against him.

"Have you lost your mind?" Rekard shouted.

"No," Sakard said as he trembled at his daring. "We must flee the swamp and flee Shamgar as long as our father...rules." He had almost said *lives*. Gog would learn about his inner thoughts in time and send assassins to slay him.

"What are you saying?" Rekard demanded.

"Gog's rule is over in Shamgar. We must take others with us to begin elsewhere."

"Where else?"

"Far from here. We will raise our own city and rule there as gods."

Rekard blinked several times and finally nodded. "We must move with haste, brother."

"Yes. But first we must use cunning to gain a fighting force to help us."

The Axe-Slayer washed the blood from his weapon and tied stones to Kregen's and the human corpses, pitching them in the mire so they sank out of sight. Then, he went to his closest friends and talked them into slipping away with him. Rekard spoke to others.

In all, Sakard and Rekard took twenty-four half-Nephilim and Nephilim heroes, five hundred pirates and two hundred city guardsmen. They fled and built rafts later, poling deeper into the swamp and out of the saga of Gog of Shamgar.

Confusion reigned in camp afterward, until Sagoth picked up the staff of command and gave orders. He did not do this fast enough to prevent other defections. But he did do it quickly enough to save some of the army.

Five days later, Sagoth reached Shamgar with fifteen hundred pirates, one thousand guardsmen and half the champions who had left on the campaign. Bearing the staff of command, Sagoth headed for the Temple of the Oracle, there to give Gog an account of what had happened.

-2-

Cain knew things had changed for the better when a human jailor opened his cell door and guided him to a luxurious pool in a building aboveground. There, beautiful slave girls bathed him, kneading his muscles with oil afterward. He took one into an alcove and used her well, her moans of pleasure a welcome relief after endless weeks of listening to rats squeal as they fought over garbage scraps, or cave hyenas whine as they cracked the bones of the dead and consumed them.

A servant—a man in a short brown tunic—took him to a hall with foods piled on a long table. Cain ate until he was bursting. It felt good to be full again.

He slept on a soft bed, a slave girl slipping in to keep him company for the night. In the morning, an Enforcer's attendant took him to an armory. There, Cain selected armor and weapons, outfitting himself until he bristled with expensive weaponry, including a Bolverk-forged sword.

Finally, the attendant took Cain into a room where he selected a dark cloak, boots and other gear.

Cain looked every inch the warrior again, a massive man with thick yellow hair and beard, like a lion in its prime, and the cold black eyes of a killer.

Minos met him in the hall, the half-Nephilim Enforcer raising his eyebrows. "You almost look dangerous, Cain. I hardly recognize you."

It was true that Minos was taller, broader and likely stronger than Cain. He had the blood of the high in his veins after all. He was a

147

grandson of Gog, which made him the great-grandson of Magog the Accursed, a *bene elohim*, a fallen angel of Heaven that presently lay deep in an off-world prison in Tartarus.

Cain held his tongue. He had been in the dungeons under the Temple of the Oracle for too long. He rued coming to Shamgar, realizing now he should have slain Sagoth of Great Apes when he had the opportunity in the forest. Lod…Lod had escaped him—

"Are you brooding?" asked Minos.

The Enforcer had been his jailor, coming to mock him at times. Now, Cain debated whether he could draw his sword fast enough to gut this arrogant son of Sakard Axe-Slayer.

"I see your hate," the half-Nephilim said. "At least you have the balls to act like a warrior in my presence. I'll give you that."

Cain waited, wondering why Gog had given orders to release him. He knew the First Born did not have a conscience, not as humans conceived of such things. No. Gog wanted to use him. That would be the only reason to let him go instead of ordering his head cut off for failing to bring Lod to Shamgar.

"I ought to beat you for your insolent stare," Minos said. "When one of us asks you a question, you must immediately answer."

Cain allowed himself a mocking smile.

"Why you…" Minos said with heat, drawing his sword, possibly intending to put the tip against Cain's throat. Instead, Cain drew and parried, sparks flying as their blades came together.

Minos scowled, which crinkled the black tattoos on his broad face. He launched an attack, maybe thinking to beat down Cain's defense. Instead, Cain held his ground, using his Bolverk-forged blade to meet the half-Nephilim's attack and stop it with parry after parry.

Finally, Minos stepped back and lowered his sword.

Cain did not step back as the custom demanded. He allowed another mocking smile to dominate his face. He noted the beads of perspiration on Minos' face and knew the half-Nephilim was winded by the exchange.

"I could kill you," Minos said in a low voice.

"Yes," Cain said. "If I sheathed my sword and took off my armor, you could do it after an hour of tough battle."

Minos looked as if he might choke on his ire, and it seemed he would renew the assault. At the final moment, he sheathed his sword with a snap and threw back his head, barking three short snorts of laughter.

"You have balls, Cain, big old pig balls. Are you sure you're still human after all these centuries?"

Cain sheathed his sword but kept a hand on a dagger hilt hidden up a sleeve. He didn't trust the half-Nephilim. He also didn't like the question because he had begun to wonder the same thing after all this time. Time weighed on his soul. Time weighed on his existence.

"Are you pissed off?" Minos asked. "Did your stint in the dungeon sour you on Shamgar?"

"Did Gog's Army lose the battle?"

The humor drained from Minos as he stared at Cain. "Think you're smart, do you? Well, you're going back into the dungeon, although you're not going back to your cell. Gog wants a word with you. Seems he's not going to kill you after all."

"Ah," Cain said. "I see the army did lose. Is Gog going to ask if I'll fight for him?"

"Watch your mouth."

Cain shrugged. "I can win this war for Gog, if he wants."

"I doubt it. Now get going. You had a good night's sleep and your fill of tail. And you almost look dangerous, like I said. Maybe it will impress Gog, but I doubt it."

Cain turned for the exit, seeing rain pouring outside. Could Lod and his confederates really be trying to lay siege to Shamgar in this weather? If so, did he owe Lod a good turn because Gog had let him out of the dungeon cell?

Maybe it was time to find out…

-3-

As on his last visit, three drugged priests bore torches as they led Cain deep under the Temple of the Oracle on Shamgar's central acropolis. Darkness pressed in against the torchlights, and a depressing weight sought to smother Cain's soul, growing heavier the deeper the four of them traveled.

The outer sounds of life diminished, as did the screams of the damned, the tortured, and the prisoners. Soon, only their footsteps sounded in the Stygian gloom that circled the puny flickers of torchlight.

The drugged trio groaned in dread, each of them in turn dropping his torch and bowing his head, covering it with his arms. One after another, the priests dropped to their knees, moaning and lying flat on their faces before the awful presence that dominated the darkness.

"KNEEL, CAIN," Gog boomed.

The oldest human in existence felt the elephantine presence towering just inside the darkness. The three fallen torches still fought to provide light. He had given up his weapons earlier—except for one hidden dagger—but he still wore his mail. If Gog was going to kill him, at the very least, he would injure Gog.

Where weapons are forbidden, there one should carry weapons. Cain had long-ago adopted the ancient adage.

"ARE YOU DEFYING ME, WORM?"

"I am not, O Gog," Cain said. "I just wonder why you need me to kneel to you. I don't worship you like your sons and subjects do. I worship nothing save for my own will."

"DEFIANCE," Gog thundered.

"I came to Shamgar because you requested it," Cain said, feeling Gog's anger and knowing he jeopardized his life doing this. But why should he kneel to Gog when he had defied Elohim at the East Gate of Eden? He would die as he'd lived, and if that meant death by tentacle, well, he would cut the First Born if he had the chance.

"PREPARE TO DIE, CAIN."

The sense of doom grew, and Cain had to lock his knees lest his legs buckle and he shame himself.

A tentacle slithered from higher up, snaking for Cain.

Even though he quailed within, Cain crossed his arms, watching the python-sized tentacle come closer and closer. At the last second, he would whip out his dagger and slash, charging into the darkness to fight to the death. Gog might be bigger, perhaps even greater, but did that mean Cain would bow to him?

"AH," Gog said, withdrawing the black tentacle before it reached the man. "YOU ARE BRAVE. I FIND THAT IMPORTANT, AS IT IS SAID ONE CAN TRUST THE WORD OF A BRAVE MAN."

Cain nodded, impressed with himself for guessing right.

"CAN I TRUST YOUR WORD?"

"If I give it."

"ARE YOU HOLDING A GRUDGE AGAINST ME FOR YOUR TIME IN THE DUNGEON?"

"Yes."

"WORM, I AM GOG. I AM THE GOD OF THIS PLACE. NONE DEFIES ME HERE AND LIVES TO TELL OF IT."

The words vibrated through Cain's flesh and made his bones shake. The pressure against his soul increased, and suddenly, Cain cried out. His knees unlocked and he crumpled to the floor. He did not mewl for mercy, but he found it hard to breathe and hard not to beg for life. He'd never felt anything like this. The pressure—

It abruptly relented.

"IMPRESSIVE," Gog intoned. "NONE OF MY SONS HAVE RESISTED THAT STRONGLY. YOU ARE UNIQUE, CAIN. YOU ARE NOT QUITE HUMAN ANYMORE."

As he lay on the floor, Cain closed his eyes with relief. The awful pressure lessened even more.

"Is that better," Gog whispered.

"Yes," Cain said, as he pushed up to a sitting position.

Silence filled the chamber. Slowly, the three priests began to revive. Each sat up, regarded Cain and the others and then quietly picked up a torch.

"Follow them," Gog said softly.

Cain climbed to his feet, following the priests. The three priests reached a wall, stretched as one, each fitting his torch in a wall-holder. After that, as if receiving silent commands, the priests entered the darkness.

Cain heard their footfalls as they walked away, the sounds diminishing. In their place, he heard Gog breathing slowly, like a hippo or some other large animal might do.

A black tentacle pushed a chair into the tiny radius of torchlight. Cain sank onto the chair. A moment later, a black tentacle pushed a table with a map of the city of Shamgar tacked in place.

"Study the map," Gog intoned softly.

Cain did so. The city was circular after a fashion with canals crisscrossing everywhere. The outer compounds had high walls. Cain noted that each compound was a fortress in itself. Given the swamp and rivers outside the city, Shamgar would be difficult to besiege. The attacker would need galleys and barges, at the very least.

Cain sat back finally.

"Listen, Cain, as you open your mind."

Cain blinked and a force, a power of will, struck his mind. He resisted, but this time that proved impossible. A panorama of sights, sounds and smells invaded his consciousness. He did not know it, but he saw from a variety of angles, including sliths and Nephilim. He witnessed the Battle of Mammoth Field, noting the enemy victory. It was impressive. He saw some of what had occurred afterward.

Then, as abruptly as the images had impinged upon his mind, they ceased, and he found himself deep in the dungeons of the acropolis.

"Your army lost," Cain said simply.

Gog did not reply.

"It would appear that only a fraction returned to Shamgar."

"It is a small thing," Gog intoned softly.

152

Cain did not believe that. He had been among the Elonites and had been with Lod for a time. He wondered at the wisdom of pointing that out. Finally, the man shrugged.

"O Gog, Lod is coming with the victorious Host of Elon."

"Of course," Gog intoned.

"Without your army, who will defend the walls?"

"I have an army."

"Is it numerous enough to defeat the coming besiegers?"

Gog snorted softly, a thing of derision. "I am going to be candid with you, Cain. I am doing so for a simple reason. None has lived as long as you and I have. Between us, you have lived longer, although I am many times greater than you are."

Cain waited, knowing there was more to this.

"The Arkites are gone. The Nebo are cowering. The pirates fear what is going to happen. My sons, grandsons and great-grandsons wonder if my time has finally come. They do not realize the truth yet. I'm sure you have no inkling of what is really going to happen."

Cain continued waiting, sitting in an attitude of respect.

"The trouble with my sons is arrogance. They are bigger, stronger, smarter and quicker than humans. They hold the humans in contempt, which is justified most of the time. Yes, a host of my foes is coming. Lod leads them, or Lod is among them, in any case. I long to hold him, cradling him to my bosom and telling him the agonies of his death that will soon be coming. I will still sacrifice Lod on the altar and tell you your future, Cain. First, though, you must capture the seraph for me."

Cain nodded slowly.

"I am thinking about giving you the command of the humans in my service. My sons will continue to command the city guard. But the rest of the humans will obey you, Cain. Legends say that you are a great war-leader."

Cain dipped his head. It was not only a legend; it had proven true many times in the past.

"Can you defeat my enemy?"

"I don't know their numbers."

"Does that matter?"

"It certainly does."

"Do you know what is really going to happen?"

"I'm not an oracle."

"Then learn, Cain. I have tricked my greatest enemies into converging upon Shamgar. I have lured them here. Do you think I did not know my army would taste defeat?"

Cain didn't know the answer to that, and it bothered him. Gog could see the future, men said. But how did the procedure work in reality? Were all of Gog's visions accurate? Cain suspected that was not the case.

"You are silent, and your manner implies you don't fully believe me."

"I'm withholding judgment," Cain said.

Gog breathed heavier in the hidden darkness, until he said, "Are you trying to anger me?"

"No. I'm being as honest as I think you can bear to hear."

"I should slay you for that. A First Born can bear to hear *any* truth. I am not afraid of what is."

Cain did not respond, as he didn't believe that. Gog had ruled in Shamgar too long to listen to unpleasant truths from others.

"Yes, you are attempting to goad me. I do not understand why…unless you are angry for staying in a cell for so long."

Cain waited quietly, as he saw no reward for saying more.

"I will refrain from punishing you," Gog intoned. "Instead, I will show you my generosity because despite your low birth, we are alike in a critical way. You have defied him whose name we will not speak. You are, perhaps, a precursor to us. Is that not strange?"

Cain nodded. It *was* strange.

"I am going to give you command of the human soldiers in Shamgar. With them, you will hold off Lod, Uriah and that dreadful boy Joash and their warriors from profaning the streets and canals of Shamgar. You will do so long enough for the great trap to snap shut."

"What trap?"

"Oh, ho, the ancient one stirs with curiosity. Cain, do you not realize my greatness? Do you not realize that I know all?"

"You're omniscient?"

"No one knows everything, even though our great celestial foe tells the fools who listen to him that he is all-knowing and all-powerful. Clearly, that is false. If he above had such power, he would have already conquered us. If he knew all, he would never have allowed our fathers to revolt against his rule."

154

Cain grew uneasy with such talk.

"Why do these words trouble you?" Gog asked.

"I'm not sure."

"Do you not understand that one greater than I stands behind me? I refer to the Morning Star, of course."

"Lucifer," Cain said softly.

"There are plots within plots, Cain. You yet have an opportunity to rule a kingdom like a god. Does that interest you?"

Cain nodded, for how else could he answer such a question?

"Good," Gog said. "Know, O man, that the giants of Jotnar are even now on the march. The Gibborim of Yorgash have reached the shores of the Suttung Sea with the galleys of Poseidonis."

"There is no sea lane from Poseidonis to the Suttung Sea."

"The Gibborim carried lumber and parts overland. The galleys have been rebuilt and sail to gather the giants of Jotnar. More are coming, Cain. This is a trap to smash the host of Elon and others, and to capture the seraphs and learn secrets that will give us all the means of turning the Great War back in our favor."

Cain frowned. Was this true? Did giants and Gibborim march to save Gog? Or was the First Born raving because he could not stand the thought of losing and possibly dying in the days to come? Yet, the more Cain thought about it...the more likely it seemed. If there had been a miscalculation on Gog's part, it was on the need for the lure to be as good as it was. Uriah was a cagey seraph. He would need to see the evidence of Gog's weakness. Maybe the First Born had over-calculated, losing too much of his army, and that's why he needed Cain's help, at least for a time...

Cain began to nod.

"You accept commission in my service?"

"I will lead your army—"

"Only the humans," Gog said, interrupting.

"Fine, just the humans, the bulk of your army."

"The humans have the numbers. My sons are the greatest strength of Shamgar."

Cain said nothing.

"I will pay for your service with visions," Gog said.

"I also demand payment in coin."

"Oh?"

"That has ever been my custom."

Gog breathed heavily in the darkness. "I will pay you coin and allow you to make what changes you think are necessary in the human force. But one thing remains constant. You must capture Lod for me."

"I will."

"Then, let us toast as you swear allegiance to me."

Cain almost snorted. He would say the words, but they would not mean anything. Cain's allegiance was to himself and none other. He would take command of the human element in Shamgar and see what would develop. If in swearing he was forsworn because he did not swear in good faith, what did he care?

Soon, Cain raised a goblet of wine. He swore a pretty oath and drained the cup, and he listened as Gog swore in turn, promising vile punishments if Cain failed or disobeyed, and then Gog slurped heavily in the darkness, sealing the bargain between them.

-4-

It rained endlessly, pelting everyone with heavy drops of cold winter showers. That raised the delta waters and would have made it impossible for a host slogging through the swamp on foot. But that wasn't the case with the warriors moving by land and sea and with the help of big bull mammoths.

Joash had persuaded the bulls with less-serious injuries from the battle against Gog's Army to help one more time.

Nar Naccara led the galleys from the League of Peace. He only had half the numbers that had fought their way into the harbor of Pildash. But he and other sea captains had listened to knowledgeable seamen of Pildash. They had suggested barges to ferry the host up the delta to Shamgar.

Lord Uriah had collected all the barges in Pildash harbor, and those barges had sailed, rowed or been towed by league biremes along the coast to the delta. Now, the barges floated against the current of the fast-flowing winter streams. At other times of the year, these were slow and often sluggish channels, but not with these rains.

It might have proven too much for human muscles. But once again, the Mammoth Man Thoar came up with the solution. The great bulls allowed men under Joash's guidance to hook them into special harnesses. The shaggy beasts from the plains of Elon waded through the cold rushing streams, their gargantuan strength towing the barges.

That left the regular rowers to propel the galleys upstream. The galleys carried specially constructed catapults they would use against

157

Shamgar, and they held the majority of the food stores that would feed the warriors as they brought down the worst First Born left on Earth.

Lod and Uriah stood on such a galley as the rowers strained to move the bireme past dripping swamp trees towering around them. The white-haired seraphs each wore an oiled campaign cloak with the hood thrown over his head. Water dripped before the cowls and water pooled around their soggy boots.

"Foul weather," Uriah complained.

Lod did not respond. He had been soaking in the sensations ever since they entered the Hanun Delta. Long, long ago, he had escaped from the canals. As a lad, he had received visions from Elohim that he would return a victorious warrior. Not so long ago—just before Mimir the Wise and Tarag of Sabertooths had struck out for Eden— Lod had snuck into Shamgar. He had roused many of the pirate captains to revolt, and there had been a bitter fight in the swamp. Lod had believed that was to be his moment of victory. Instead, it had led to bitter defeat and his captors dragging him like a slave through the streets of Shamgar. There, on the flowered streets and before mocking throngs, he'd healed crippled Keros in Elohim's name, and there Gog had entombed him deep in the Catacombs. He'd known terror, shoved and plugged into a tiny shelf of stone. It had almost unmanned him, but Keros had slipped into the Catacombs and freed him and many rebellious pirate captains. That had been a glorious day as he'd driven a spear into Gog's sole eye. Lod had fled from the city, though, and he'd wondered if Elohim would ever allow him to really come back and defeat the First Born for good.

Now, though…now must surely be the time. Lod realized he'd acted prematurely back then. He had tried to force Elohim's hand. But that was not the right way to do it. He had to wait for Elohim's timing. He was the blade of the Most High. He was the sword of vengeance bringing fire and woe to the foes of the Creator.

Lod wanted to laugh in glee. In truth, he hardly noticed the endless rain. A fire had built in his heart, and it roared hotter every mile closer to Shamgar they came. Would Elohim allow him to slay Gog? More than anything in life, Lod wanted to kill the First Born and watch him bleed out his life!

Lod laughed.

158

"What is it?" Uriah asked.

Lod blinked, realizing he stood on a bireme working upstream, that Lord Uriah stood beside him.

"You must concentrate, Lod," the older man said. "I know you've had visions, but men must work hard to gain their dreams."

"Yes," Lod said, his blue eyes shining. He'd worked hard as rat bait, a galley slave, a charioteer, a scout in the forests—all his life had been endless toil and strain. As he stood on the galley deck, he cracked his knuckles, and he forced himself to live again in the here and now. It wasn't always easy doing that.

Lod turned to Uriah. "I'm surprised there haven't been any raiding parties hitting us. Is Gog going to keep his men behind Shamgar's walls?"

"We have warriors combing ahead. They've seen a few great apes watching us from high in the trees, but no Nebo, Arkite or pirate has set an ambush against us."

Lod inhaled as his waking dreams began to take hold again. "I smell victory," he intoned. "It is the stink of burning flesh and spilled blood. It sounds like breaking bones and tearing flesh. I hear the cries, the pleas for mercy." Lod shook his head. "For the evil ones, there will be no quarter. For the slaves and indentured servants of Shamgar, it will be a time of great rejoicing." Lod's blue eyes burned brighter. "I see darkness ahead."

"Disaster for us?" asked Uriah.

"No. It is the darkness of the tunnels under the Temple of the Oracle. There in the cold darkness, I march, hunting for the First Born. Our torches refuse to flicker brightly, but I am using my ears, listening for the soft tread of him who fears his coming doom. He fears what awaits him after centuries of evil and defiance against Elohim. He will meet his Creator. He fears that day. Does he realize that I will help him take the first step into a new plane of existence?"

Lod laughed again, and it was a mirthless sound.

"Men and Nephilim live as they please in this life. But there is a day coming when they will answer for each word and deed. Some will soar like eagles on that day. Some will wriggle like gigged worms. The day, Lord Uriah..."

Lod could no longer speak, caught up in his waking visions, the prophet of fire and sword, master of refusing to quit even as the lash opened his back or a giant canal rat tore out bites from his flesh.

Endure as you press on for the great goal. Fight on your knees, if you must, but fight with all your heart, get off the floor when knocked down even if every bone aches and all your muscles throb. Perhaps you will die that day, but you will have lived as a man of valor. And perhaps luck or God Above will see and allow you another chance.

"Gog," Lod whispered on the slick deck. "Gog, I am coming for you."

Uriah shuddered at the quietly growled words, and he knew that Lod was not like other men. What man set such a goal as to slay a giant First Born who made others cringe in terror? What drove Lod to such madness?

Uriah did not know, but he was glad that Lod fought on their side.

-5-

Cain did not have long to train his men or assert his authority over them. The Host of Elon and its galleys, barges and mammoths had just reached the delta when Gog gave him command.

Minos commanded half the city guard, while a Nephilim Defender of Gog named Dark Nath commanded the other half. Each of the guard commanders had a different part of Shamgar under his control. Cain was the third commander, but neither Minos nor Dark Nath paid him any heed. The necromancers went under the Temple of the Oracle. No one had any idea what spells Gog was ordering the sorcerers to cast.

The enemy hadn't reached the walls yet...

Cain went on a tour of the outer defenses and then inspected the galleys laid up in their wooden-roofed slips. Finally, he gathered the pirate captains in a long hall. He spoke to them and asked their opinions. None of them dared speak up.

Cain inspected the pirates, along with the handful of Arkites that had finished the journey and the few Nebo heroes who had refused to slink away. The firstborn of Adam had become a good judge of character. He chose several fellows and dueled with them, each in his favored manner.

He fought the Nebo hero Brunt knife to knife, stopping only after he tripped the squat champion, put him on his back and held the knife against Brunt's throat.

"You are better than me," Brunt said.

Cain gave him a hand up and slapped him on the shoulder. "I like you, Brunt. Stand with me."

161

Brunt nodded his shaggy-haired head.

Next, Cain wrestled a wide-shouldered Arkite known as Dan Back-Breaker. Dan was the taller of the two, with impressive shoulders. Cain was thicker in the chest and had heavier arms. They strained on the mats, and Dan knew clever moves. In the end, Cain lifted Dan high and crashed onto the floor on top of him, twisting an arm behind Dan's back until the other grunted, "Uncle."

"Do you hold grudges?" Cain breathed in the Arkite's ear.

"For besting me in an honest wrestling match?" asked Dan, surprised.

Cain nodded.

"You are like iron," Dan said. "No man I've ever met could best you. There is no grudge from me. I respect you, Cain."

Cain got up and let Dan rise. "Stand with me as you guard my back."

"I'll do so with pleasure," Dan said.

Finally, Cain dueled with three pirate champions. That was the most spectacular of the events, for he fought them as a trio. He did not use steel, though. Instead, he handed each pirate a wooden sword tipped with hot tar. Cain took up a similar sword so stained.

"Each time you touch me," Cain told the three, standing with them before a packed throng in a large area covered by a snapping awning, "I'll give you a gold coin. If you don't want the coin, I'll give you the prettiest slave girl of your choice."

"We must tar you?" the largest pirate asked.

"If you can," Cain said.

"What if we knock you unconscious?" asked a pirate known as Dog.

"You'll get a sack of coins."

The three pirates grinned, nodded or glared with gleaming eyes, each as his character dictated.

Cain picked up his wooden sword, saying, "Start."

Dog and the biggest pirate charged. Cain tripped the largest pirate, sending him sprawling, and he parried Dog's blows and painted both the man's cheeks with tar.

The watching pirates roared with laughter at that.

The last pirate judged the situation and circled Cain until the big pirate scrambled back onto his feet and Dog finished trying to wipe the tar from his face.

The three pirates moved together this time.

Cain moved to the left, attacking and likely surprising them. He clouted the smart pirate a hard blow on the head, knocking him down. He struck Dog's sword so hard it went flying onto the floor. And he dueled the biggest pirate for five clacking passages. Then, he tarred both cheeks and struck such a stunning blow on the man's hip that the pirate went down in a heap.

"Again?" asked Cain.

Someone dashed water on the smart pirate. From on the floor, he rubbed his head and blinked, and he said he couldn't see straight anymore.

"My hip," the big pirate said, not meeting Cain's eyes.

Dog had reclaimed his sword and charged wordlessly.

Cain parried and tripped him.

No one laughed this time.

Dog climbed back to his feet. He eyed Cain purposefully, and he flinched when the killer-fire lit in Cain's eyes. Without a word, Dog backed up until he picked up the big pirate's wooden, tarred sword.

"It's just me, then," Dog said. "But I got two swords. That acceptable to you?"

Cain said nothing.

"Fine," Dog said, charging. No doubt, he expected Cain to try to trip him again.

Instead, Cain fought against the two-sword attack, parrying and countering every move Dog made. The pirate tried everything until he panted, exhausted from his many efforts.

With two stunning blows, Cain knocked the wooden swords from Dog's hands. Then, he touched his own tarred tip against Dog's chest.

"I am dead," Dog said between pants.

"You are," Cain said. "But I can teach you to fight better. Are you interested?"

"I am."

"Will you be my man and obey my commands?"

"I will," Dog said.

Cain pointed at Dog with the wooden sword. "This is the best pirate in Shamgar. Does anyone disagree?"

No one had the balls to challenge Cain's word.

Cain started the training that day. Mainly, he wanted the best pirates under his command. But he wanted them working with those they had worked with for many years. He chose teams, had the teams fight and made his decisions.

Two days later, he decided he might as well make his first reconnaissance against the invaders and test the mettle of his chosen ones.

He went to Gog first and asked for information. Gog sent him to Sagoth, the chief of the beastmasters and necromancers.

Cain wasn't sure, but Sagoth looked thinner than he remembered, the apish face more gaunt than before and the eyes red-rimmed and haunted. What had this Nephilim in such straits? Cain decided not to ask, concentrating on the great-ape scouting missions instead. Sagoth started a detailed explanation of their findings.

"Can you show me on a map?" asked Cain, unrolling one in the elegant chamber.

Sagoth pointed out what he knew, making estimates regarding the number of enemy galleys, barges and warriors.

"Fifteen to sixteen thousand warriors," Cain said. "And half again as many rowers, you say?"

Sagoth nodded.

"We could be in trouble," Cain said, watching the Nephilim as he did.

Did fear well in the beastman's red-rimmed eyes? The Nephilim might even have trembled the slightest bit, but Cain couldn't be sure.

Then, Sagoth straightened, bringing the edge of his rich red cape around. He sat on a glittering chair in a chamber rich with expensive tapestries and paintings. His cloak and furnishings were quite at odds with his beastly bearing.

"There will be no trouble," Sagoth said. "We have Cain. We have the city guard and sorcerers with an unlimited number of death-skulls. Besides," he added hurriedly, "we only have to hold for three weeks. By then, the galleys of Poseidonis and Jotnar's giants will arrive. We'll butcher the attackers and rid ourselves of Uriah, Lod and Joash for good."

"Have the sliths seen these galleys?"

"You doubt Gog's word?" Sagoth asked haughtily.

"Who said anything about that? I asked if you've seen the galleys."

164

"I'm not one of your pirates, Cain. Don't question me as if I have to answer you. You'll die fast doubting Gog's word."

Did Sagoth speak for an unseen audience? Was he playing a part? And if so, why bother? What undercurrent troubled the Nephilim?

Cain couldn't decide, so he dropped the question. "I'll take that as a no," he said. "No slith has spotted a Poseidonis galley. What about the giants? Has a slith spotted one of them?"

"I'll tell Gog of your doubts."

Cain refrained from saying more on the subject, and he began to wonder more deeply about Gog's boast concerning other First Born coming to aid Shamgar in its hour of need.

Afterward, he hurried from Sagoth's chambers, deciding he would use three galleys instead of the two he'd planned.

-6-

Cain had lived longer and fought in more wars than any Nephilim or man alive. He knew that simply sitting behind tough defenses, fighting when the enemy chose the time and place, was a good recipe for defeat. A good defense meant sallies against the enemy, swift attacks to upset their timing and mental balance. That meant allowing the enemy an unhindered march up to Shamgar qualified as poor generalship.

Gog said they needed time for the galleys of Poseidonis and the giants of Jotnar to arrive, springing a deadly trap on the three seraphs leading the Host of Elon.

After talking with Sagoth, listening intently to what the great apes had witnessed, Cain concluded that the enemy set great store by the mammoths. Human muscles could only do so much. Mammoth brawn allowed the enemy greater than ordinary maneuverability, dragging barges and galleys through raging streams and muddy morasses alike. If he destroyed the damn mammoths, the enemy would slow their advance considerably.

There were two ways to achieve the objective: kill Joash, who controlled the mammoths in some unnatural manner, or kill the individual animals one by one. Slaying Joash should be theoretically easier than butchering huge mammoths one by one. But the wily Uriah likely had many layers of protection encircling the unique young man, which meant theory was wrong this time. Thus, Cain decided to kill enough mammoths to slow the advance and change the way the enemy used the great beasts. Butchering thirty of them should do the trick. If the enemy were truly stubborn, maybe he

166

would have to kill forty. The thing he had to figure out was *how* to kill thirty to forty mammoths fast enough to slow the invasion.

Cain debated the issue with himself. The enemy wasn't going to allow his pirates to walk up close and hurl endless volleys of heavy spears. How else could he kill mammoths?

The answer came as he watched wheeling gulls and a Nebo with a sling bring one down with a perfectly cast shot.

The primitive couldn't have thrown a stone that hit with enough killing force to bring down the gull. Instead, he had used a device that had multiplied his strength and increased his stone-hurling range.

Long ago, Tubal-Cain had invented the first javelin thrower. It had proven instrumental in many of Cain's victories against the hated Sethites of that era. Could he remember how to build one, and were there the right resources here to do it?

Cain went to work, finding pirates with mechanical understanding. Under his guidance, they constructed three great javelin hurlers. Each was the same. A massive bar of iron was set crossways upon a great wooden trough. A steel cable was strung onto the curved ends of the iron bar as if it was a giant bow. A windlass with ratchets clacked back and back, pulling the steel cable until it locked into place. The pirates had constructed a swivel bolt underneath the trough and mounted that on a heavy wooden tripod on the prow of each of three chosen galleys.

Cain tested the javelin throwers. Each could fire a heavy iron javelin over five hundred paces. The javelin hit with sickening force. A javelin fired through the forehead should kill a mammoth. Several through an animal's side would likely do the trick as well.

Soon, three pirate galleys exited the city canals and maneuvered through the delta, hunting through the rain for the enemy vanguard. Several of Sagoth's great apes swung ahead in the trees, acting as scouts. A beastmaster stood near Cain on the rear deck. The beastmaster would interpret ape chatter when the time came.

The pirates rowed their own galleys. These were smaller and lighter than the League of Peace biremes. Each of those vessels had a fully covered deck, and they were much heavier and therefore not as maneuverable in the swampy delta.

Time passed as the galleys and great apes hunted. Shamgar's walls were long gone behind them, and—

A great ape dropped from an overhanging tree, landing on the catwalk in the middle of the galley. Pirates at the oars shouted, shrinking back from the monstrously hairy beast. It moved on all fours to the lean beastmaster standing on the rear deck beside Cain. The ape chattered at the beastmaster, and the creature used its manlike hands to gesture as it talked.

The beastmaster nodded, understanding the animal noise.

Cain found that unsettling. He could tell the watching pirates found it even more so.

Finally, the beastmaster turned to Cain. "Several mammoths are nearby pulling barges. There is an open channel of water we can use that will put our galleys behind the enemy in relation to Shamgar."

"The ape told you all that, did it?"

The beastmaster was of the fourth generation, and he was almost skeletal beneath his cowl. "They are intelligent creatures," he replied.

"Can it lead us to the channel?"

"Indeed. That is what it proposed."

Cain didn't like the idea of placing the galleys behind the enemy. He wanted a clear line of retreat in case things went badly. But by coming up from behind, he should gain total surprise. That could count for a lot.

"Let's do it," he said.

The great ape shambled to the prow, which indicated it had understood Cain. The beastmaster followed the creature. Cain did likewise.

As the galley passed swamp trees, the ape turned at times and chattered with the beastmaster. The beastmaster relayed the messages to Cain. Soon, the ape led the galleys through a narrow, sluggish stream where the ships had to go one at a time. Twice, wooden sides scraped against bark as a galley brushed against an intruding tree. Three times, a hull scraped the muddy bottom, slowing them until the ship had passed over the area. Perhaps three-quarters of an hour later, the lead galley burst through a curtain of foliage and came upon a larger scene than Cain had anticipated.

Ahead of them to the left, six mammoths strained in harness. The great beasts pulled three barges full of warriors. It had stopped raining, which might hamper the ambush. The mammoths waded through muddy water, their shaggy coats dripping with brown mud.

The rope lines hummed as the great beasts dragged the flat-bottomed barges across the muddy realm.

Cain looked back. There were no enemy biremes visible behind them.

The ape turned to the beastmaster, hooting urgently. The beastmaster told Cain, "This is the moment to strike."

Cain eyed the ape, not sure that he wanted to accept advice from an animal, no matter how intelligent. Despite that, the ape spoke sense, matching how Cain felt himself.

Cain gave quiet orders that passed from ship to ship.

The three pirate galleys maneuvered until they were abreast of each other and closing upon the barges. Cain nodded. Daring brought great reward. Hesitation was an enemy at a time like this.

He raised his right hand and made a circle in the air.

The trained pirate teams were watching him. On each galley, they whipped back oiled tarpaulins, revealing the heavy javelin thrower at the prow of each ship.

Cain's heart began to thud. Many pirates hunched forward with worry etched on their faces.

At any moment, enemy warriors might look back and recognize the different type of galley. Cain spied Lod. The oaf shouted encouragement to the mammoths. With keen eyes, Cain searched for Joash. An iron javelin through the young man could solve a host of problems, but no, he didn't spy the young seraph.

The pirate galleys slid from behind toward the barges and mammoths. They were lighter than the barges. The heavier craft scraped against the muddy bottoms, needing the mammoths to pull them across.

A pirate from another galley hissed and dared to call out. Cain turned, looking at the pirate. It was Dog. He pointed behind. Cain craned his neck, looking back. *Damnit,* four biremes turned a distant bend, coming into view. The biremes were headed this way. The channel must be deeper over there. Likely, the mammoths would have to pull the biremes through this section too. If the biremes reached the exit to the side channel the pirate galleys had used to get here...

Cain estimated they had time for one volley, at best two. Then, they would have to maneuver back to the side channel and race back to Shamgar.

"Fire at my command," Cain told the pirate teams, his words drifting to all three vessels.

At each heavy weapon, two pirates turned a big windlass as a ratchet clacked, pulling the steel cable as it bent the giant iron bow. The shooter adjusted the entire weapon on the swivel bolt, aiming, picking his mammoth and the target on the big beast.

Cain visibly checked each team, waited and finally saw that the other two javelin teams were ready, as were the men on his galley. He raised his hand and chopped down hard.

The shooter on his galley pulled a lever. That released the ratchet. The toothed wheeled spun fast as the bent iron bar straightened, yanking the steel cable that shot the heavy iron javelin. It slid along the wooden groove and left the device, sailing in an arc through the air. The heavy javelin hissed past a mammoth as the beast dropped its head at the wrong moment. The javelin sailed into foliage, disappearing.

The other two javelins hit, but the shooters had each targeted the same mammoth. The javelins sank into the beast's shaggy side, staggering the animal as it trumpeted in pain.

"Back oars," Cain shouted. This had been a botch. "Let's get the hell out of here."

The shot mammoth keeled over onto its side, splashing and sinking out of sight.

At that point, Cain lost interest in the mammoths. He was worried about getting his three galleys back to Shamgar.

-7-

Lod jerked upright as a mammoth screamed with agony. He'd seen something blur past his head but hadn't thought much about it. Then, the great beast trumpeted and fell sideways into the miry swamp.

Lod whirled around as warriors shouted all around him. He peered past the dripping foliage and saw three galleys. At first, he didn't realize what he saw. Then it hit him. Those were Shamgar pirate galleys. They were open craft, unlike the decked biremes of the League of Peace.

Then, Lod saw Cain's yellow hair. He saw pirates throw canvas over—javelin throwers. Those were javelin-throwing machines.

With an expert gaze, Lod understood that the lighter galleys would have greater maneuverability here. Did the pirates know the waterways better? He was sure that was so.

"Thoar," Lod shouted, cupping his hands.

The Mammoth Man turned back to him from a different barge.

"Free those mammoths," Lod shouted. "I have an idea."

Thoar looked at him blankly.

Lod motioned the Mammoth Man to get over here. After a moment, Thoar started.

Lod looked back at the three Shamgar galleys. Yes! He saw them maneuver for a hidden channel. Just as important, he saw four biremes giving chase. This might actually work.

It took time for Thoar to jump his way from barge to barge. Once the black-haired Mammoth Man reached him, Lod outlined his plan.

171

"That's madness," Thoar said. "The pirates slew one of our beasts. What's to stop them from killing the others if we do as you suggest?"

"Nothing," Lod said. "The key is to slow them down enough for our biremes to catch them."

"And if those biremes don't give chase?"

"They are," Lod growled. "Now, do as I tell you. This is our chance to capture Cain and grab three enemy galleys. We'll also learn what transpires in Shamgar by questioning them closely."

Thoar searched Lod's eyes, and whatever the Mammoth Man found, he nodded seconds later. "You're in charge here. I will obey you."

"Then skip to it," Lod said. "Time is critical."

***

It took too long, but the rest of the mammoths dragged a single barge full of Shurite warriors. Keros was among them, and he cheered them on.

Lod rode one of the pulling mammoths. Thoar was on another, and different mammoth riders were on the rest. The great beasts strained as they dragged the single barge faster than the animals had pulled the greater number of vessels earlier.

The mammoths dragged the barge through streaming raging water and muddy fields alike. Lod was searching for the waterway Cain and his three galleys had used to get behind the barges.

Drizzle began to fall. That didn't change a thing. War was a matter of nerve and daring and hoping that risks paid off. Uriah had known of Cain's legendary generalship. Leave it to Uriah to have pierced Gog's thinking. The First Born must have given generalship of the defense to Cain. In that way, Gog hoped to cheat his destiny. Lod would do just about anything to make sure that Gog died this time.

"There!" Thoar shouted, pointing with a javelin. "I see galleys."

Lod laughed maniacally, and he slapped the great beast carrying him. He wore mail under his oiled campaign cloak, and he had the sword of Tubal-Cain belted at his side.

"How many galleys are there?" shouted Lod.

"Three," Thoar said. "It's them all right."

"Praise be to Elohim," Lod said. "Now, let's set the barge in their path. Maybe the biremes are following. Maybe it's all up to us now. Are you ready to fight?"

Thoar nodded.

Lod laughed with glee. "Come on. Let's get a move on. This is the break we've been waiting for."

***

The barge made it as the mammoths struggled in the current. Shurites readied themselves on the flat-bottomed barge, waiting for the galleys to reach them.

The three pirate galleys fought their way upstream, but they came on strongly, their oars slashing the water as drums beat the time.

"I see biremes farther behind the pirates," Thoar said. "We have them trapped like you planned."

Lod had a shield on one arm as he continued to sit on his mammoth. This was a risk—

A heavy iron javelin sailed from the prow of a pirate galley, and hissed past Lod, striking barge wood behind him.

Shurites shouted, many of them shaking their weapons at the approaching galleys.

"That's a far shot," Thoar said in wonder. "They can hurl a javelin three times the distance a man can throw one."

"Don't worry," Lod said. "Their advantage isn't going to last long. They're in a tight spot—duck!" Lod roared.

The seraph had kept an eye on the pirate galleys and seen two javelins hissing toward his mammoth. Lod dove from his beast, pitching into the water. He had barely done it in time, as two javelins pierced his beast's forehead.

With an animal groan, the mammoth crumpled into the water.

Lod jerked his arm free of the shield and despite his chainmail, he swam strongly for the barge. His years as rat bait had made him one of the strongest swimmers alive. On the way to the barge, he grabbed the back of the jerkin of a floundering Thoar. A javelin had killed the mammoth he'd been riding, too.

Keros must have given orders. Shurites cut the lines anchoring them to the dying or dead mammoths. Some Shurites pulled at long sweeps, trying to maneuver the ungainly barge.

The barge held approximately half the number of warriors that was bristling on the approaching Shamgar galleys. Behind the light galleys came three biremes, their oars moving smartly, propelling the heavy ships after the fleeter pirates. The fourth bireme must have mired somewhere.

Shurites reached down, giving Lod and Thoar a hand up onto the barge. The soaked seraph spun around. Heavy iron javelins slew the last mammoths.

"Watch it, boys," Lod said. "The pirates will turn the javelin throwers on us next. Dodge if you can. Get fighting mad because when those galleys try to pass us, we're jumping aboard and swarming them."

Lod accepted a new shield and drew his sword. Then, he waited in the front rank, and his prediction came all too true.

As the pirate galleys neared, a trio of heavy javelins hissed at the barge. One sailed overhead, plopping into the water behind them. One thudded with murderous force against the wooden hulk, and one plowed through the crowded deck, slaying five Shurites as men shouted in fear and consternation.

Now, however, the pirate galleys were going to have to make a choice. The barge was in the middle of the fast-flowing stream. There was little room on either side of the barge. Behind the galleys charged the three biremes. Maybe the rowers over there knew this was their best chance of catching the pirates.

Lod saw Cain, and he aimed his sword at the son of Adam. The distance was near, and Cain stared at Lod. It was hard to know what the other—

With a nearly physical shock, Lod felt the murder-lust in Cain's stare. The mark of Cain—Lod knew a moment of awe as the realization struck him. Then, he grinned crazily as his grip tightened on the sword of Tubal-Cain.

Once more, at almost point-blank range, the javelin throwers hurled their heavy darts. Lod leaned left as one grazed his side. Shurites behind him screamed as the javelin killed four of them. The barge deck was awash with blood, gore and the moans of the dying and injured.

"Here they come," Lod said. "Pay them back for what they did to your friends and brothers. Don't let the murderous scum get away."

Now, the enemy's hope became obvious as the first galley aimed directly at the barge. Pirates were jumping out of the first galley and into the other two.

A crash and splintering of wood told of the head-on collision between the first galley and barge. Lod stumbled as the deck heaved beneath him. Some Shurites pitched overboard into the raging water. Many warriors fell down on the barge.

As the Shurites scrambled back onto their feet, the next galley slid past on the right. Then, the other began sliding past on the left. Pirates heaved javelins, boat hooks and darts into the confused mass of Shurites.

"Kill them," Lod thundered. He picked the nearest galley, hoping Cain was in it. Lod gathered his legs under him, ran and sailed over the gunwale into the enemy galley. He crashed against a pirate, using his shield to bash the other. The pirate fell back, and Lod was among them. Without conscious thought, bellowing at the top of his lungs, Lod hewed right and left. His sword bit flesh, and a pirate howled in agony. The sword hacked out wood from a shield barely thrown up in time.

Then, Keros and other mountain warriors of Shur landed over the gunwale among the pirates of Shamgar. A bloodbath began as warriors and pirates chopped and thrust at each other. This was close-quarters fighting without room to maneuver. Men raved, shouted, bellowed, screamed, killed and died.

Lod's near-berserk attack created a zone around him, and it gave the Shurites time to gather their wits as more mountain warriors surged onto the galley.

Then, a fierce warrior with two swords charged Lod. The man snarled, leading other pirates behind him.

"Kill him, Dog!" a pirate shouted.

Lod met the two-sword attack with his shield, shoving the other back, back—Lod dashed the sword of Tubal-Cain against a flashing cutlass. The cutlass shivered into pieces. Before Dog could recover, Lod thrust into the pirate's face.

At that point, the Shurites howled, enough of them on the galley to start using their superior numbers. Darts hurled at short range did murderous work. Tomahawks thudded against pirate skulls and chests.

175

But not all the mayhem went the Shurite way. Mountain warriors died, torn apart with boat hooks or their brains dashed out by a cutlass stroke.

Even so, Lod and the Shurites cleared the galley of pirates. A few dove overboard, there to die by cast javelin volleys. A few at the end attempted to surrender. The Shurites were having none of that, although Lod managed to save two cowering pirates.

He wanted them for questioning.

At that point, Keros shouldered his way to Lod. "What now?" the mountain warrior shouted.

Keros was dark-haired and well-muscled, a rangy warrior with rugged features.

Lod looked where Keros pointed. A lone pirate galley had made it past the barge. That craft literally bustled with pirates so that the normally light craft presently moved sluggishly. The keel likely scraped the bottom of the passage.

Then, the galley floated free as the oars shoved against water.

Lod spied Cain. The bastard had gotten away, maybe with half or three-quarters of the pirates who had started the mission. In the other direction, the biremes were slowing, as the channel was shallower there.

"It's time to take stock," Lod said.

"We lost six mammoths altogether," Keros said.

That was bad, but they had hurt the first pirate raiding party. That had to count for something.

"What about those javelin throwers?" Keros said. "That was clever on their part."

Lod glowered, and he saw the lone pirate galley take a bend in the channel and disappear from view. Six mammoths lost—that was going to hurt.

-8-

Two and a half days later, Cain found himself marching deep under the Temple of the Oracle. No priests guided him this time. As he marched through the darkness, Cain had time to think and ponder.

A definitely leaner and haggard Sagoth had led Cain into the temple and handed him a torch. "Go," said the bleary-eyed Nephilim, indicating a spiraling set of stone stairs that led down into darkness.

Cain had regarded Sagoth with his scarlet cape.

"What are you staring at?" Sagoth had demanded.

Cain had shaken his head a moment later, taken the torch and begun the descent on the spiral staircase.

Surrounded by darkness, as his torch flickered and hissed, Cain brooded yet again about the raid. He'd lost Dog and Dan Back-Breaker, leaving him with Brunt. Cain had decided earlier that those three had been the best human fighters left in Shamgar. One foray had cost him two out of the three. Maybe as bad, there was something evil going on in Shamgar. Since the foray, Nephilim teams had roped off avenues and canals, saying no one was to go in those areas of the city. Every night, there were high-pitched screams coming up from the earth, the sound of lost or tormented souls.

The sounds unnerved his men. They had begun unnerving Cain, too. The Nephilim continued to block off more parts of the city, and a sense of doom, of death, had grown exponentially.

Cain had already concluded that he wasn't going to be able to forge the pirates and other men into a formidable fighting force. He simply wasn't going to have the time to do it or the right atmosphere.

The evil in Shamgar, a spreading thing like a tumor, was making brave men start at shadows and turning already-uneasy men into terrified cowards.

The javelin throwers had been a good idea. With them, his men had slain six mammoths, if the great apes could count correctly.

Six dead mammoths could have been a good start. But upon reentering the canals with the lone galley, Gog had sent word to him through Sagoth. There would be no more pirate forays against the enemy.

In the darkness, Cain reached a landing. He raised the torch. There was only one way to go. He took it, striding along a musty corridor deep under the earth. He was a man, a strong and cunning man, but he did not have the so-called blood of the high in his veins. He was beginning to think that difference was the key to understanding Shamgar.

At that point, the presence of Gog overpowered his thoughts. Cain halted, barely managing to lock his knees in time and barely able to hold the torch aloft.

"I HAVE BEEN THINKING," Gog boomed.

The harsh words made Cain's bones shake and breathing difficult. Was it worth trying to remain standing? Fierce pride welled up. Cain did not buckle, but forced himself to stare toward the source of the awful drumming words.

"THE GNAT STILL HAS WILLPOWER, I SEE."

Cain did not speak, could not speak, as he struggled to inhale the putrid air. Yes! The realization slammed home. The very air stank of *death*. A feeling rolled over him then, an awful sense of futility—

"I will relent," Gog whispered.

Some of the pressure departed, and Cain breathed easier. He no longer smelled putridness in the air, but there was a sense of...of...*wrongness* down here.

Cain tried to decipher why he felt this, and he realized something pressured his thinking. With the awareness came a shift in his thoughts. He wanted to ask what he'd done wrong to have angered Gog so, but such words did not pass his lips. His pride was too strong for that. He was the army commander, and Gog had given him freedom of action. If Gog wanted a military miracle, the First Born was going to have trust his general.

As if reading his thoughts, or maybe even guiding them, Gog intoned, "You lost too many soldiers with your costly stunt in the delta."

Here, alone in the dark before Gog, Cain steeled himself to act the part of a man. He refused to cower, and he used centuries of pride and the tricks he'd learned to stiffen his resolve.

"Are you revoking my authority?"

"I am demanding an accounting of your actions."

Cain bristled inwardly, although his features remained placid. "That's not how it works, O Gog. You gave me authority. You have to trust my ability or find yourself a different general."

"There is no more room for error, Cain. That is why I entrusted the humans to you. My sons err when given charge of men. You are supposed to be a great warlord, and yet you cost me soldiers I cannot afford to lose."

Cain inhaled deeply. Gog wasn't human, but a hybrid monster of demon and woman, an elephantine creature imbued with supernatural power. He'd ruled a shadow empire for centuries, using his prophetic sight to bind tens of thousands of desperate souls to him. Gog had delusions of godhood… And yet, even given all this, Cain decided to say the words that needed speaking.

"O Gog, you say that you need men to man Shamgar's walls against your enemies. Yet…you or your sons are practicing necromancy to an inordinate degree, and through the practice you are weakening your army's resolve to stand and fight."

"Are you a sorcerer that you can know such things?"

"I've heard the tormented screams at night, rising as if from the very earth. I have felt the misery in the air, the stink of death that drifts through the city like a fog. Yes. I think I finally understand. Your sons have cordoned off areas of Shamgar. Your Enforcers have surely driven many people underground. There, the necromancers are killing the people to power some great spell."

"You are shrewd, Cain, perhaps too shrewd."

"You have soldiers to man the walls and galleys, and giants to trap the enemy. Why, then, do you butcher your own people to power a spell?"

"No one questions me. You would do well to remember that if you desire to keep living."

"I'm your general, O Gog. The unleashed necromancy is leaching the men's courage. If you desire the men to fight when Uriah's warriors boil against them—"

"The men will fight, or I will pulp their bones into powder."

"You rule in Shamgar, O Gog. I'm simply a hired sword. But I'm the deadliest sword and the hardiest champion among men. I'm telling you that you must make a choice between your spell and the men's courage—"

"GOG ALLOWS NO MAN TO DICTATE TO HIM. I AM GOG. I AM SUPREME IN SHAMGAR."

During the tirade, Cain bowed his head as if he faced a hurricane, and he went to one knee because the force was too much to resist while standing.

In the darkness, Gog breathed like a bull ready to charge, but slowly, over the seconds, he breathed easier and finally grew quieter.

"I am Gog," the First Born whispered. "I have ruled for an age in Shamgar. I await the Poseidonis galleys and giants, and I grow weary having enemy warriors camp around my city. My spell will weaken those gnats, and afterward the pirates will regain their courage. None of those things troubles me, Cain. What does trouble me is that by the reports, you almost slew Lod."

"Who told you this?"

"Do not question me, O man. Tell me. Is the report true?"

Cain thought quickly, saying, "During a fight on the battlefield, a tough man like Lod throws himself into the thick of it and—"

"No," Gog said, interrupting. "That is not the report I heard. Your javelin teams deliberately aimed at Lod. The seraph barely pitched himself aside in time, or a javelin might have pierced his heart, killing him."

Cain debated his next words. Lod was dangerous, he had seen, clearly too dangerous to handle with kid gloves. Cain had realized then he would not jeopardize his life in order to save Lod, so Gog could sacrifice Lod on an altar later and tell Cain his future.

"I must cradle Lod," Gog intoned. "I yearn to whisper to him before I begin his long years of torment. He will pay the most ghastly penalties imaginable for what he did to me years ago."

In that second, Cain realized that Gog would never sacrifice Lod on an altar for him. In that moment, Cain realized that Gog's promises were as good as Cain's own oaths. What surprised Cain was the anger that surged through him. He almost rose up to glare at Gog, but his cunning came to his rescue. He bowed his head, as if in fear of Gog.

"You will continue to lead the humans in Shamgar," Gog said. "Tell them to endure the sensations and sounds coming from below. Those will not last, but the coming spell will aid them against the enemy. You must instruct every human holding a sword, spear or bow that no one must harm Lod. I bid you to tell the humans bearing arms that each must let himself die rather than hurt Lod, or that one will wish he had died a million times over rather than to face my wrath."

"I will do that," Cain said, his head yet bowed and his voice pitched to please the First Born.

"I am laying a great charge upon you, General Cain: capture Lod for me."

"And if that means letting the Host of Elon break into the city?"

Gog began to breathe more heavily, and an aura of something mad vibrated in the air. It grew, a numbing sensation, and then boiled over as Gog intoned:

"Have I not told you, Cain? You must only delay the enemy. My brothers are sending their best to aid us. I will crush the humans and make them rue the day they believed they could beard Gog in his den. I have seen visions of fire and blood as my armies trample the Suttung coasts and destroy Elon, Shur and everyone in the forests of Huri Land. I will hang Uriah and Joash by their thumbs over a slow fire. O, Cain, how I long for the days of retribution to begin. The seraphs of him whose name I refuse to utter think they are coming to a great victory. Instead, they march to their eternal doom. I, Gog, will bring them down and stamp on their putrid carcasses. My armies, Cain—the victories I have witnessed in my visions—they are endless. After I have shattered the Host of Elon, I will unleash my sons as they seek the entrance to Eden. I will yet eat from the Tree of Life. I will live forever as Earth's greatest god. I am Gog, and I have spoken."

With his head bowed, Cain trembled. He did not tremble in fear, but in awe. Gog had gone mad with thoughts of death and defeat. The First Born must have retreated into his visions because he could not cope with reality. Would Yorgash of Poseidonis send his precious galleys overland to the Suttung Sea? It struck Cain as

181

preposterous. And what love did Jotnar of Giants hold for Gog the Oracle? From what he knew, the giants loathed the hidden Gog. Of all the Nephilim, giants most loved courage and high deeds of daring. That meant everything rested on Gog's great necromantic spell, and that was why his sons whipped the people under the Temple, leading them there to die horribly as they powered the coming sorcery.

"Go, Cain," Gog hissed. "Fulfil our bargain and bring me Lod. Then, I shall load you down with riches, and in the reaches of time, I will sacrifice Lod and tell you the moment of your doom. Is that not our bargain?"

"It is," Cain said roughly.

"Then arise and complete your appointed task as I decree. By this, men shall know that Cain serves Gog the Oracle."

"Let it be so," Cain said, already beginning to scheme for his survival in the coming slaughter.

9

"I know that sensation," Lod said in a hushed and anguished voice.

Several days had passed since the encounter with the pirate galleys and the battle on the barge. Lod, Uriah and Joash stood at the prow of one of the captured galleys.

It was nearing dusk, and past the cypress trees where the galley had anchored, they viewed Shamgar. The squat pirate city was like a boulder thrown into the middle of a mud puddle. The walls weren't high, but they looked thick and daunting. From the center of the city rose the great acropolis, with the mighty Temple of the Oracle dominating everything else. Great iron gates barred the canal entrances into Shamgar. On the thick walls, torches moved and spears were evident though their bearers were not.

To the galley's left at a distance of several hundred paces sat two great apes in a towering tree, watching them.

Behind the stolen galley by a mile was the main Elon encampment. The great sprawling site was part isle and part linked barge and bireme in a semi-floating city.

As Lod, Uriah and Joash looked in the deepening gloom upon dread Shamgar, the over-muscled lead seraph recalled that an epiphany had come after Cain's attack. He and Uriah had toured the dead mammoths and battle site. During the latter part, Joash had joined them.

"How awful," Joash had said, with tears in his eyes for the dead beasts.

Uriah had pointed at a javelin sticking up from a carcass. "That's the answer to the puzzle that's been troubling me for weeks. I should have seen it long ago. Isn't it ironic that Cain should provide us the means to finish our great task?"

"How so?" Joash had asked.

Lod had been too surprised to comment.

"Cain must have reasoned out how important the mammoths are to us," Uriah had said, "allowing thousands of warriors to advance through raging streams and muddy lakes. Cain must have decided he had to kill the mammoths quickly, and thus he had javelin throwers built."

"That was evil," Lod had said.

Uriah had regarded Lod closely. "Our great problem in the coming days is how can men defeat Nephilim champions? On the walls and in the city, such champions will reign supreme. Here, we see the answer to our dilemma."

"Ah…" Joash had said.

Lod had stared at Uriah.

"We will construct more javelin throwers," Uriah had said. "And we will fight the Nephilim as if they are beasts of the field. They are bigger and stronger than men. They would slaughter hundreds and maybe thousands of us on the walls and in the city, but with heavy javelins piercing them—we will slaughter them instead, wheeling the javelin throwers through Shamgar, hunting Nephilim like vermin."

Ever since the epiphany, metalsmiths and woodworkers had labored to construct javelin throwers, using Cain's throwers as the model. Since the epiphany, a foul stink had drifted from Shamgar. An unseen cloud of hate had risen from Gog's abode. That cloud had begun wilting the courage of the avenging Host of Elon.

Now, Lod, Uriah and Joash viewed Shamgar as the sun sank into the horizon.

"Listen," Joash said breathlessly, as he cocked his head. "I hear…screaming."

Uriah shook his head. "I hear nothing."

"You must listen closely," Joash said.

"I'm not sure I want to," Uriah replied.

"The sound is pitched just above human hearing," Joash said.

"Then, how can you possibly hear it?" Uriah asked.

Joash turned to Uriah in wonder. "I hear it just as I hear animals speak."

"I don't hear the screams," Lod said slowly, "but I know the sensation. I have felt it before."

Uriah's nostrils flared. It was possible, nay, certain. He did not want to know what they sensed.

"What's happening over there to cause the screaming?" Joash asked.

"Necromancy," Lod spat. His eyes glowed indignantly. "This is not normal necromancy either, but a great spell cast by a First Born. Many over there are dying in hideous ways. The First Born and his necromancers are slaughtering thousands to grease an evil spell of power. Gog must sense his doom, and he is resisting in the only way he knows how."

"We need time," Uriah said thickly, "time to construct more javelin throwers."

"Time has become our enemy," Lod replied. "We must attack Shamgar and sweep the evil ones from existence before Gog completes his great spell."

"Necromancy," Uriah said. "They use foulness to prolong their unnatural existence. Gog devours his own to—"

"No," Lod said, interrupting. "Gog is using people, not his own. Gog has never looked upon any man or woman as his own. He is demon-spawn, and we must storm Shamgar come tomorrow. I will go down into the crypt under the temple and slay the monster there."

"We will both go," Uriah said.

Lod glanced at Uriah before nodding. "So be it. We attack tomorrow?"

Uriah cocked his head and closed his eyes. "I can't hear any screaming."

"It's there," Joash said. "In fact, it's gotten worse as night deepens."

Uriah shuddered, opening his eyes. "Let us go and prepare the men, for tomorrow we attack."

"Tomorrow..." Lod muttered. "Tomorrow, the end begins..."

-10-

A fierce red glow pulsated from the Temple of the Oracle on the great acropolis of Shamgar. The foul stink continued to drift through the city, gagging many, making it impossible to sleep.

Cain paced in his room. He'd heard reports from his men. They had seen Nephilim and others of the blood whipping and herding weeping women and children up the stairs of the acropolis. No doubt, those poor souls had tramped underground, there to the waiting necromancers and their skinning knives.

The pirates and the few Nebo and Arkites that made up Cain's army muttered angrily and fearfully. None of them had dared to interfere with the city guard herding the populace of Shamgar into the dungeons beneath the Temple.

As Cain paced, he debated endlessly with himself. Gog was mad, but Gog was a vengeful creature. The First Born yet commanded his sons, and through them the city guard, and he commanded high-blooded necromancers and the art of supernatural magic that only a being of his powers could cast.

Dare he defy one like Gog? Dare he stay in the doomed city to face beings that regarded him as little more than a dog?

"I am Cain," he whispered many times that night.

Finally, it dawned on him that maybe the necromancy drifting through the city had unmanned *him*. The idea was as enraging as it was unbelievable.

Cain's head snapped up as he stopped pacing. In the oil-lamp light of his chamber, his eyes burned with murderous hate. Gog's great building spell, the horrible killing under the Temple, had caused a fog of terror to shrink everyone's courage.

"Not mine," Cain said through gritted teeth. Yet, he did not move. "Act," Cain hissed to himself. "Do something, man, before the monster devours everyone in its path, including you."

The Host of Elon, with Lod and the other seraphs, were all going to die in Shamgar. According to the latest report from the scouting great apes, the camp of Uriah stirred as if the warriors prepared to attack tomorrow.

A harsh laugh escaped Cain. He was the great killer, but he was also the great survivor. He would not be in the slaughterhouse come tomorrow. Oh, no, he would collect his chosen and get the hell out of Shamgar while there was still time.

187

-11-

The Host of Elon had practiced sudden marches many times, including night marches. Every warrior of the host knew what to do. So, even though the orders were still fresh, Lod led a third of the avenging host.

Torches flickered through the jungle morass of the delta swamp as mammoths and lightened biremes used pre-scouted channels to drag barges full of warriors. None of his crafts carried catapults. Instead, several of the barges had the newly-constructed javelin throwers.

Uriah and Joash's hosts had the catapults. Come morning light, Uriah and Joash's two-thirds would batter at the walls to create an opening for the warriors.

Lod's third was circling Shamgar in the dark. They were going around the city so they could hit from the direction opposite where Uriah and Joash would strike. Rowers, warriors and mammoths alike cast fearful glances at the hulk of the city. Shamgar was foul. On its walls, torches flickered with hellish light. No one here heard audible screams, but men and beasts shivered as an aura of doom rolled out through the pile of stones and the metal bars guarding the canal entrances.

Lod sensed the fear among his men, and Thoar had told him the mammoths were positively petrified of Shamgar. Removing his helmet, Lod looked up at the stars. He inhaled and spoke loudly so many could hear him pray.

"O Elohim, great Creator of the Earth, Moon, Sun and Stars, hear our cry. We seek to destroy Your enemies. We seek to destroy those who pervert the Earth with their evil. Give us courage, we ask. Give us a sign that You are with us. We are but men, created in Your image, O Elohim. Guard my warriors, I pray, that we may destroy those who have defied You, the Most High. In Your name, I ask You this, O Elohim. Amen."

"Amen," several men around him said.

"Listen to me," Lod shouted so even more could hear him. "We will prevail. This is our time of vengeance against the evil ones. Our enemies are frightened of us. It is the reason they devour their own. They know that our strong right arms are powered by our love of Elohim. We seek what is good, and that means destroying what perverts. The thing in Shamgar has hounded men far too long. When the sun rises, we will gain admission into the pirate city. When the sun sets later, Gog will lie dead in his dungeon, a thing of the past that will bother humanity no more."

The men didn't cheer as Lod fell silent, but the division continued on its way, using the delta maze to work around the dread city. Come morning, doom awaited many, and—possibly—doom awaited Gog of Shamgar as well.

***

"Lod," Keros said leagues later. "Lod, you won't believe this."

The biremes, mammoths and barges of Lod's force had circled the pirate city during the night and now headed inward toward Shamgar. The force moved through foliage and watery channels, and Keros raced from barge to bireme to barge until he panted before Lod.

"What's wrong?" Lod asked.

In the torchlight, dark-haired Keros grinned like a madman. "You won't believe it, but two pirate galleys are heading straight for us."

"A counterattack?" asked Lod.

Keros laughed. "I don't think so. Rather, these are deserters fleeing Shamgar before the bloodbath. But here's the best part. Cain leads them."

Lod's blue eyes gleamed. "You're sure."

"Come and see for yourself."

Lod made a fist. "This will be a wonderful start to the assault. First, we kill Cain and then—"

"What?" Keros asked, interrupting Lod.

"We'll kill Cain first—isn't that what you're thinking?" Lod said, surprised the mountain warrior didn't understand.

"No, no," said well-muscled Keros, a practiced raid chieftain. "Elohim has not only given you a sign, but a gift. A way into the city without fighting."

"What do you mean?"

"Isn't it obvious?"

Lod blinked several times, and he scowled. "I want to kill the bastard. He held me captive on the Suttung Sea. I have to pay Cain back for that."

"Don't you want to kill Gog more?"

It only took Lod a second. "Yes!" he said, clapping Keros on the shoulder. "You always were a cunning lad. I see what you mean. First, though, we have to convince the schemer to see things our way."

"Don't worry about that. In their fear, the pirates are moving fast. You'd better hurry, though, or our men will butcher Elohim's sign before the pirates can aid us."

-12-

Cain groaned inwardly as he spied barges, biremes and mammoths. That could only mean one thing.

It was almost dawn, and he had slipped out of Shamgar through a canal, leading two galleys full of pirates, including Brunt and several Nebo trackers. He'd headed in the opposite way from the camp of Elon. Who would have thought anyone could lead men around Shamgar at a time like this?

A bireme eased forward from the foliage where the rest of the enemy craft waited. There were thousands of warriors ready to attack, probably five thousand or more. He had several hundred pirates with him. This was a disaster.

"They want to parley," Brunt said beside him on the prow deck.

"Eh?" asked Cain.

"Lod waves a white flag," Brunt said.

Cain pulled his thoughts together, peering through the darkness. He could see in darkness better than any normal man could, and better than Brunt. It was Lod all right. The armored seraph waved a white flag from the prow of the approaching bireme. The vessel had several javelin throwers, primed and aimed at them. There were also many warriors with notched bows, Huri archers, by their headdress feathers.

"They must want us to perjure ourselves," Brunt complained.

Understanding lit Cain's brain, and it surprised him Lod had been cunning enough to see it.

"Get set, lads," Cain called. "If it looks like we're..." He let the words trail away. One wrong move could cause this to end in a bloodbath. He was going to tell them to kill Lod if anything bad happened. Lod had surely told his men the same thing about him.

Cain cupped his hands around his mouth and lowered them. He waited, even though waiting was tough.

Soon, the bireme's oars dug into water, slowing and then stopping the bigger ship. Lod put away the white flag while a warrior raised a torch above Lod's head.

Cain had a man do likewise to him on the pirate galley prow. Twenty feet separated them. The men on the galleys and bireme would easily be able to hear what passed between them.

"Had enough of Gog and his Nephilim?" Lod asked harshly. "Are you sick of the way they treat men?"

"Yes," Cain said in a rough voice.

"I understand. I grew up in Shamgar. I know the ways of Gog, the sneers, the beatings, the haughty bearing and the sheer contempt Gog and his ilk have for men and women. I know Gog is killing the people of Shamgar so he can weave a sorcerous spell. It stinks of doom, and you lead those who have the balls to slip away before Gog devours them. Do you not realize this is a sign from Elohim? You did not come here by chance, but to pay back Gog and his sons for all the years of vicious abuse they have heaped upon men. You are here to show us the way into Shamgar, to lead us through the city defenses so I and my comrades can slay the evil ones."

"You'll have to go down into the Temple dungeons to slay Gog," Cain said.

Lod laughed harshly, maybe even madly. "Do you think I fear that? No. I've waited a lifetime to lead an army under the earth and face the evil one with a band of hardy warriors. We will kill Gog. We will kill any of the Nephilim champions who dares to show his face. We will hunt them like vermin, using the javelin throwers you taught us how to construct."

"What are you saying?"

"That you have a choice, Cain. Lead us to an open canal. Show us the path through the city defenses. Take us to the acropolis, and you are free to leave as you wish."

"You'd have me believe that you'd let me go afterward?" asked Cain.

"If you live, you and your men may leave. And unless you raise a hand against one of us or betray us to the enemy, none of us will raise a hand against you or your men. I, Lod, have spoken."

"You swear this?"

"I have spoken, Cain. My yes is yes, and my no is no."

"You're mad to want to attack Gog."

"Don't try any of your defeatist talk on us, Cain. We've come to rid the Earth of Gog. Today..." And Lod fell silent, perhaps overcome with harsh emotions.

Cain turned to Brunt. "What do you say?" he asked quietly.

"They'll kill us if we say no."

Cain twisted back, looking at the fearful pirates staring at him. "It's a bum deal," he told them loudly. "But I'll take it. Gog is butchering the people of Shamgar. That means he's butchering some of your women and children. That dissolves our oaths to him."

Cain turned back to Lod. "How will you be able to tell us from the others of Shamgar?"

"I'll give you a red scarf to tie on your left arm. We have plenty of these. Each of your men will tie one around his arm."

"You've thought this through," Cain said grudgingly.

"Your coming here is a sign," Lod said. "The sign is the surety that we will win, come sunlight."

"It's good to be sure," Cain muttered. Lod was a madman, but he was a strong and cunning warrior just the same. If anyone had a hope of slaying Gog...it would be the warrior that had already blinded the First Born.

"Who says nay to this?" Cain asked his men.

None of the pirates said a word. They all must have realized that to say no meant to die here in the swamp. Who knew what would happen to save their lives once they reached the city?

"Fine," Cain said. "It's a deal."

"You'll join me on the bireme," Lod said.

"Who of yours will join my men?"

"No one," Lod said flatly. "We have the advantage here, and I plan to keep it that way."

Cain nodded after a second. Lod might be a zealot, but he wasn't stupid. "All right. I agree. Now, let's get started before the sun rises and spoils everything."

-13-

In the Temple of the Oracle, Sagoth of Great Apes listened to the hooting and chattering of three of his creatures. They had been lurking in the jungle during the night and had seen a strange sight. They had hurried back to the city, but ships and mammoths had passed through the night, reaching the canals, blocking several of their normal passages. Now, there was fighting in the streets—

Sagoth hissed angrily.

The three great apes cringed, afraid of their master's wrath.

Sagoth chattered at the apes, trying to come to an understanding of what they meant. The apes were big, each much stronger than a man. The apes were stronger than most half-Nephilim, but none was stronger than a full-blooded Nephilim.

The blood of the *bene elohim* granted more than mere strength, however. That was why Sagoth had been turning thinner and more haggard by the day. Although he was not a trained necromancer, he had great supernatural ability. Gog had put Sagoth and other Nephilim to work crafting the spells that would gird Gog with fell abilities once completed.

In answer to his questions, the apes hooted, chattered and screamed, making wild gestures. Finally, Sagoth understood. The enemy was in the city.

The apes hooted louder, one jumping up and down. The creature was clearly agitated.

"There's more?" Sagoth asked in the ape tongue.

The agitated ape spoke fast and gestured faster.

194

Sagoth kept blinking, yearning to understand— "Cain," he said. "Cain has become a traitor?"

The huge ape jumped up and down more excitedly than before. The ape nodded and flung his long arms wide.

"What?" Sagoth said somewhat threateningly. "Make sense!"

The ape jumped higher and higher—

"Lod is in the city?" Sagoth asked.

The ape hooted crazily, screaming in the affirmative as he nodded.

Sagoth sagged back, thumping into an ornate chair. This was blackest treachery. Gog must learn of this… Sagoth swallowed uneasily. Who should go tell Gog the bad news? *Not I,* he thought. The full spell was not yet completed. Gog would want to face the enemy host…

With sick understanding, Sagoth stood. He had to go tell Gog about this. As he stood, he wavered. The three apes watched him. Then, Sagoth of Great Apes came to a decision. It was a similar decision to the one Sakard Axe-Slayer and Ceto master of the Nidhogg spawn had made earlier.

Instead of heading into the dungeons, Sagoth called his great apes and headed for the Temple exit. It was time to flee Shamgar and live among his creatures for good. This spell-casting was not for him. In truth, practicing necromancy was killing him. Before he ended his single life, Sagoth wanted to live many more years.

Let someone else warn Gog. He knew the First Born's rages, and Sagoth did not want them directed at him.

***

Deep underground near the infamous Catacombs, Gog seethed with impatience. He was blind because of hateful Lod, but he had many powers and agencies that he could call upon. Lately, though, his visions had failed him, and he knew the reason. He had lost confidence, and that had caused his power to dwindle.

That was the reason he had driven his sons and grandsons and their children to practice necromancy to an inordinate degree. He had refrained from this art most of his life. It had bitter costs. Now, though, he did not mind the costs because he'd rather pay them than die!

The spells had been cast down here in the dark of the Earth—spells that had devoured the great supply of necromantic skulls with the seething magical fury stored in them. The need for more, more, more necromancy meant death, hard dying in blasphemous ways, to provide yet more skulls.

Gog had kept everyone hard at work killing and casting, torturing and spell weaving. Now, at last, the great Skull Crown was finished. His minions slaved to conjure so powerful a weapon. O ho, he would range the battlefield like a Titan, personally slaughtering the Host of Elon and their puny seraphs.

With massive tentacles that could crush a person as others crushed bugs, Gog lifted a mighty crown made of blackly pulsating skulls. The silken threads of necromancy and his own willpower held the skulls together. The First Born of Magog the Accursed raised the Skull Crown and placed it on his gargantuan head.

Gog moaned as sorcerous power swirled around him. That power invaded his mind and surged outward to his ruined orb, the single eye that had once seen as others see. It was mangled—Gog moaned as the necromantic power changed and shifted torn flesh and optic nerves. The pain seared like fire as the crown wove an ancient spell upon Gog.

By degrees, the mighty First Born blinked his single eye, and through it—

"I CAN SEE!" Gog shouted.

He raised his huge tentacles and shook them. He could see. He could see again. And now, the Skull Crown conferred other sorcerous abilities upon him.

Thousands, tens of thousands of people had recently died hideous deaths to give him these powers, but what did Gog care about them? At least the scum of Shamgar had died doing something useful.

Gog wanted to sing a ditty and dance a jig. He did not. He was too profound to indulge in such—

Gog's head jerked upward in the darkness. Not only could he magically see with his ruined eye, but he sensed in new ways. The Skull Crown was a hastily fashioned magic item, but the mass deaths had given it great powers indeed. Once Gog had his weapon—

"No," he whispered. In that instant, in a waking vision, Gog saw Lod and Cain marching through Shamgar together. They led a band of warriors, a mass of victorious fighters sweeping everything before them.

"No, no," Gog moaned bitterly.

The Lod-led force had swept aside the main defenses, allowing the rest of Uriah's host to gain admittance into the city. Why hadn't any of his people told him about this?

Gog gnashed his teeth in fury, using his newfound senses to range farther. Some of his sons and grandsons had fled, but there was still a hard knot of Nephilim fighters and city guard left.

In that moment, Gog knew what he had to do. The idea enraged him. Risking his sacred person in battle at this point…if he wanted to turn the tide and teach his enemies—the world—a lesson it would never forget, then it was time to take the fight to the vermin and stamp them so hard that no human would ever raise his head in a Nephilim's presence again.

Yes, he would create the needed weapon, using the power of the Skull Crown, and he would summon the last of the city guard, granting them berserk rage so they could tear into the unsuspecting host.

-14-

"Hold your fire," Lod shouted. "Hold it... Hold it..."

A band of seven and eight-foot half-Nephilim and full blood-Nephilim charged the vanguard of the Host of the Elon. These were the heroes of Shamgar, Gog's last hope to stem the tide of human victory.

Lod stood behind seven javelin throwers, big machines patterned off Cain's original. These throwers had a new addition, sleds—two big greased wooden skis—on the bottom of each. Men had hauled the throwers through the streets of Shamgar, others aiming and firing so withering bolts slammed against heroes of old who had dared to stand in their way.

Huri archers stood to the left of the javelin throwers. Mountain warriors of Shur were to the right. And armored charioteers of Elon stood on foot with their swords drawn and bloodied behind the seven engines. Cain and his pirates were behind the Elonites, while more of Lod's force guarded the pirates with lowered spears.

Lod and his vanguard had reached the great plaza of the Temple of the Oracle. Gog's heroes had just boiled out of the Temple and charged down the great stairs. The Nephilim and half-Nephilim bellowed as ones crazed, their eyes glazed with berserker zeal. The evil ones leaped and ran to close in a rush, eager to maim and kill.

The champions of Gog neared...neared...

"Now!" shouted Lod, as he air-chopped with the gleaming sword of Tubal-Cain.

Men jerked the latches on the javelin throwers. Ratchets whirled as the great iron bows drove the steel cables that flung the iron darts.

In a withering blast, well-aimed javelins struck the charging champions of Gog. At the same time, Huri archers let fly their steel-tipped arrows that hummed through the air.

A few Nephilim and half-Nephilim pitched backward to the ground, driven by the force of the javelins. Huri arrows peppered others, but none of Gog's heroes went down because of them.

At this point, city guardsmen raced from around the corner of the Temple. Hundreds of soldiers dressed in black mail and carrying shields raced at Lod's force.

More Huri arrows hissed at point-blank range, and Shurite javelins powered by human muscles added to the mayhem. Each side drilled the charging heroes, but few of the berserk warriors went down.

Minos the half-Nephilim reached the line of javelin throwers. He smashed one with a heavy hammer in one hand and cut down a charioteer of Elon with a sword in the other.

The city guard, the pitiful remnant yet remaining, was a mere fifth the number of Lod's force in the great plaza. Yet with the handful of raging Nephilim heroes, the guard might yet prove enough once they reached the fighting.

Lod hewed at a Nephilim as he stood with the charioteers rushing up to defend the javelin throwers. He faced a great bear of a warrior of Gog, one with a blood-dripping trident tattoo on his forehead. The towering Nephilim parried the sword blow with a blade, and he swung a mace in his other hand that would have dashed out Lod's brains if it had hit his helmet, but the seraph intercepted the blow on his shield. The crashing mace driven by berserk Nephilim muscles shocked Lod, numbing his shield arm and driving him down onto one knee.

The bear of a warrior laughed insanely, raising his two weapons to finish off the stunned Lod.

Huri archers fired, drilling arrows into the roaring face. Arrows pin-cushioned the face, with an arrow sticking out from each ruined eye. The bear-like Nephilim screamed, swinging wildly. The mace pulped a charioteer, killing the man, while the sword chopped clear down through a skull, the curved blade embedding in the man's neck.

Lod witnessed the gruesome scene, and he roared, enraged. From on one knee, he sprang forward at the monster, driving the sword of

Tubal-Cain through the Nephilim's armor and into his gut. That still wasn't enough to kill the berserk champion, though. The bearish Nephilim swung the mace, but Lod was in too close. Instead of the mace striking him, the Nephilim's fist buffeted Lod mightily on the right shoulder. The blow numbed his arm and drove Lod down onto the plaza bricks.

From farther back, Cain witnessed the duel, entranced by the madman taking on Nephilim champions. Not sure why he bothered, Cain used his considerable strength and hurled a spear. As the blind, bearish Nephilim bellowed his fury and continued to strike, his weapons getting closer and closer to the dazed Lod, Cain's spear crashed into the Nephilim's face. The force was enough to cause the bearish warrior to stagger backward, finally collapse, and die on the plaza.

The racing city guard reached the battle line, and Minos son of Sakard Axe-Slayer took charge, leading them. The half-Nephilim proved that he was a fantastic swordsman, cutting down one Shurite after another as he and the guard pressed against their band.

Keros slid up and tried to kill Minos, and fell back with blood streaming from his chest, his mesh-mail parted by an unnaturally sharp sword. Keros might have died as Minos locked onto the Shurite raid chief, but others behind him dragged the wounded warrior out of the fight.

The half-Nephilim roared with berserk mirth, reveling in the battle, at the apex of the city guard, driving against the greater number of warriors and pushing them back, and back again.

Could Minos sweep the plaza of Gog's enemies? At that point, it seemed more than possible.

Luckily, Uriah arrived with more warriors and wheeled javelin throwers. Under the cunning old seraph's guidance, his thrower teams aimed and fired a deadly volley. Three heavy javelins pierced Minos's armor, killing him on the spot and taking out several city guardsmen beside him.

Cain roused his band of pirates, leading them into the fight. A revitalized Lod energized those around him, and together, the two swordsmen stabilized the line, halting the Nephilim and city guard advance and then beginning to drive them back.

All the while, Uriah's javelin-thrower teams picked off those Nephilim and half-Nephilim still fighting.

"Soon," Lod shouted. He meant that soon they would kill the last of the Temple defenders. Then, they would begin the great hunt *under* the Temple of the Oracle. Lod was sure that he would die today, embracing death to kill Gog as the First Born cowered deep in his hole.

But that was fine with Elohim's madman. Lod's visions were coming true today. He had indeed marched through Shamgar, torching buildings, shattering enemy teeth and breaking the bones of countless defenders. He'd almost died a few minutes ago, but now the lads were doing it.

"One more push will do it," Lod roared. "We'll rout these bastards and—"

HAHAHAHAHA! HAHAHA! One gargantuan peal of LAUGHTER after another shook the battlefield and cut off Lod's ranting. The laughter was terrible and terrifying, and it stilled the fighting with its volume and sense of purified evil.

The last of the city guard used the break, retreating in ragged order as they kept their shields and swords aimed toward the enemy.

Another gargantuan peal of mirth rang out. This time, Lod and others placed it. The vile laughter came from within the Temple of the Oracle.

A bloody, panting Cain stepped up beside Lod. Both men were hulking brutes compared to the others around them. Both of them clutched bloodied swords and both had burning eyes, one pair those of a killer beyond time and the other the blade of Elohim come to exact vengeance from those with the blood of the high on Earth.

"It's Gog," Cain said flatly.

"He's here?" asked Lod, amazed.

A tread that sounded like doom itself boomed through the ground. Then, a strange and terrible sight that made no sense to the viewers began to emerge from the vile Temple of the Oracle...

-15-

In mingled horror and awe, the remnant of the city guard of Shamgar and the human invaders led by Lod and Uriah watched a strange sight indeed. Smoke poured out of the great oaken doors that had flown open as if by an unseen power. The smoke held together, though, and it advanced down the stairs, each step a tread of heavy approaching doom.

"What sorcery is this?" Lod demanded indignantly.

"You're seeing Gog." Cain could see better than others and perhaps his gaze could pierce the roiling smoke.

Lod glanced at Cain. "Make sense, will you?"

Cain laughed bitterly. "Don't you understand yet? The smoke wraps around Gog like a cloak. He's inside the darkness so that he can dare to walk in the light. He has come out of the Earth to terrorize us."

The smoke swirled and shifted, and it seemed to hold something within. Lod judged its height, and it towered over them like a giant of Jotnar. Then, a black tentacle, the size of a giant python, snaked for a moment from within the smoke. The tip of the tentacle pointed at Lod and then retracted.

"I SEE YOU, WORM," Gog roared.

Most of the city guard and the Host of Elon fell down at those words. The words not only boomed loudly, but also had a fear-inducing power.

"He's using sorcery against us," Cain panted.

Lod felt the weight and the pressure of the death-magic. It was heavy indeed, and it stole the power of speech from him. Even so,

202

Lod struggled to form words, and at last, he bowed his head, silently beseeching Elohim to aid him.

"YOU SHOULD HAVE STAYED OUT OF MY CITY, DUNG OF THE MOST HIGH. NOW, YOUR DOOM IS AT HAND, LOD."

Lod did not look up as the sorcery-fueled words hammered at his soul, at his resolve. The force of it battered him again and again. He felt his determination shrinking, his anger wilting. With greater sorcery than he'd ever faced, Lod's inner seraph power simply could not compete.

Then, someone touched Lod's left shoulder. The touch was warm, and there was something more: hope flickered in Lod's heart.

"THAT ISN'T GOING TO SAVE YOU, WORM."

Then another hand gripped Lod's other shoulder, the one that pulsated with hurt, where the bear-like Nephilim had hammered. The words of Gog still pained him, and they sapped more doggedness from him. But... From the two hands flowed warmth and something more. Lod opened his eyes. Joash stood one side of him and Lord Uriah stood on the other.

"We are the seraphs," Uriah whispered.

Young Joash's face shone with a strange light. "Gog comes at us in his power. We are here under the guidance of Elohim."

Strength, resolve and the sense of a mighty and high purpose surged from their hands into Lod. The blade of Elohim laughed, a rich and manly sound. Hope sprang anew in his heart, and he stood straight. He looked around the plaza of the Temple and saw that all the men were on their bellies, facing the towering column of roiling smoke.

One other struggled to rise: Cain. He was on his knees, mumbling to himself.

"There is little power in yourself," Lod told Cain. "You must stand in the power of Elohim if you hope to face the demons."

"DO NOT SAY THAT NAME HERE."

Lod's head whipped about so he faced the roiling tower of smoke. "Elohim!" he shouted. "I say His name because I come against you in His name. You have the blood of the high in you, Gog. You have the power of many souls surging at your command. But it will not be enough to save you this day."

"I HAVE SEEN YOU LYING SENSELESS IN SHAMGAR. I HAVE SEEN—"

"I am the blade of Elohim. Prepare to meet your maker, Gog."

And with that, the puny man with the sword of Tubal-Cain in hand charged the towering column of smoke that stood on the stairs of the Temple of the Oracle.

Uriah and Joash sprang together to a javelin thrower. Uriah cranked it madly as Joash placed a heavy iron javelin in its groove.

At the same time, Gog hidden in smoke—in sorcerous darkness—descended the stairs to meet Lod in battle.

"I SEE YOU, WORM. I SEE YOU THROUGH THE POWER OF THE SKULL CROWN."

Lod was beyond speech as his blue eyes blazed with the murderous wrath of a prophet about to pronounce and bring death to a demon.

Then a long, flaming whip snaked from out of the smoke and struck at Lod. He ducked just in time, although he felt the blaze of heat across his back.

Gog roared with mirth, and the whip struck again and again. The last time, the fiery whip slashed Lod on the left arm, burning him. The burnt flesh sizzled and bubbled.

Lod howled in pain, and the fire burning along the whip seemed supernatural, draining him of strength and the desire to inflict death.

"OH, HOW I HAVE WAITED FOR THIS DAY, WORM. YOU HAVE NO IDEA."

Before Gog could say more, a heavy iron javelin lofted from the thrower Joash aimed. The javelin hissed through the smoke—and Gog grunted as the missile entered his flesh with a wet sounding thwack.

The grunt of pain ignited something in Lod. He ached all over, and he knew then that he could not defeat Gog in the manner he wished. He was just a man, and before him was a creature of fallen angelic cunning and power, strengthened further through necromantic sorcery.

"Please, Most High, grant me this boon. Give me the strength I need and deliver the enemy into my hands."

Lod inhaled, and although he did not feel any stronger, a sense of righteousness filled him with his old resolve. He began to run at Gog hidden in the smoke.

"Guide my aim, Lord." Then, as Lod ran, he drew back his sword arm and did a most foolish thing. He hurled the sword of Tubal-Cain with all his remaining strength. The sword forged long ago spun end over end. It flashed once as sunlight gleamed upon it. Then the spinning missile entered the smoke at giant height.

For a second, nothing happened. Then, a terrible and thin-pitched scream came from the roiling smoke. Heavy footsteps crashed upon the steps of the Temple. It seemed as if Gog, still hidden in the smoke, staggered backward.

A roaring screaming shriek of agony rent the air.

Lod clapped his hands over his ears. Uriah and Joash did likewise. Hundreds of soldiers from either side writhed in pain upon the plaza bricks. A few managed to cover their ears, Cain included.

Hidden yet, Gog staggered up the stairs, and perhaps he turned in the smoke. He went back into the Temple, and there, Gog collapsed upon the stone floor, with the sword of Tubal-Cain embedded in his single eye all the way to the hilt.

At that moment, a terrifying and awful thing happened. Gog's will no longer held the Skull Crown together. It was a unique crown of necromantic power that needed a supreme sorcerer to wield it. As Gog's will receded, the individual skulls with their black power broke the chain. In that breaking, the soul energy of tens of thousands of slain people erupted at once.

Gog screamed one last time. Then, the great First Born was consumed in a fiery holocaust that roared upward and downward at the same time. The column of dark fire destroyed and devoured more necromantic spells and skulls in the dungeons under the Temple of the Oracle. In that terrible moment, a great power was unleashed. It exploded with purifying cleansing. It destroyed the works Gog's hands had created over the many centuries in the dungeons. Old bones, still-working necromancers, prisoners, chained and altered animals, all died in the blast of sorcerous power.

That power also rose in a column of fury. It devoured the great Temple of the Oracle and Gog's flesh and bones with it. The unleashed holocaust boomed once, creating a hole where the Temple and dungeons had been. Like a magical volcano, it devoured all of Gog and his realm, and all without going beyond the circumference of the magical column.

Gog was dead, and he and his Temple and dungeon disappeared with the fantastic passing Lod had prophesied.

-EPILOGUE-

-1-

"It doesn't have to end like this," Lod said the next day.

Cain stood in a pirate galley packed with desperate pirates eager to get away from the victorious Host of Elon. The city of Shamgar was in ruins, the former acropolis now a hollow smoking pit filling with brackish swamp water. Lod, Uriah and Joash had ripped the heart out of the city by killing Gog, and his sorcery had backfired in a ghastly necromantic holocaust.

There were no more Nephilim or half-Nephilim left alive in the city. There were those of the fourth, fifth and sixth generation of the *bene elohim*, although they were hiding among the befuddled fugitives.

Lod wanted to scour the people for them and hang the lot of them. "Brand this evil with fire, burning out the root," he said.

Uriah had said it was a time for mercy. Joash had agreed. And so, that had settled the matter for now.

From the galley prow, Cain eyed the battered Lod. The man was a mass of bruises and swelling, and he moved in a pained way, but that wasn't stopping him.

"We have unfinished business," Lod said. "I gave you my word, and you fought with us at the end. That's what counts."

Cain waited.

"*They* fought with us," Lod said, pointing at the crew.

As Lod's gaze swept over the pirates, many of them stirred uneasily.

207

Lod pitched his voice louder as he spoke to the crew. "Here's some good advice. Once you leave, don't take up your old trade. The League of Peace is going to hunt down pirates and hang them all. Start over now that you have this chance. In fact, for your own good, I doubt it's wise for any of you to even leave in a pirate galley."

"You're going to break your word then and keep us here as prisoners?" asked Cain.

Lod shook his head. "Old habits die hard. You must know that. Now is the time for them to change their path. It's time for you to do the same."

"You can kill me," Cain said, scowling. "Just don't lecture me on something you know nothing about."

The two hulking brutes stared at each other.

Lod shifted painfully. His right arm was stiff and overly tender. Despite that, something welled up in him. The words seemed to pour out of their own accord.

"You were the first murderer, Cain, but being first is really all that makes you unique. You set your face against Elohim and His ways, and you've lived a bitter existence because of it."

"Oh?" Cain asked sardonically. "You do realize that I just happen to be the oldest person on Earth."

"I realize. But do you realize that maybe your great age just shows the mercy of Elohim waiting to extend even to you?"

A hot retort bubbled up, but Cain had enough presence of mind to hold the thought. Instead, he said, "You have your beliefs, seraph. I have mine. Let's see how long yours work for you."

"I agree that's a good measure," Lod said, "but don't just take this life as the measuring stick, but also the one to come."

"Like I said, Lod, you believe what you want. We'll see if there's anything after this. Maybe it's nothing at all."

"One way or another, you're right, we'll see. I don't want to argue with you about it. You saved my hide yesterday, Cain. That makes me glad I gave you the offer in the swamp. Even with my visions, you never know what tomorrow is going to bring."

"You're a tough man," Cain said. "I'll give you that. You actually slew Gog. I didn't think anyone could. So…what's next for you?"

"Joash says I should rejoice in the great victory." Lod grimaced as he shifted, glancing around before regarding Cain again. "I grew up in Shamgar as the most pitiful of slaves, destined for an early death, to be devoured by giant canal rats. Joash says it's time for me to put that demon to bed. Maybe I'll help the rat-bait people we set free, help them find trades so they can grow up to be regular people."

"I doubt that's what you're going to do."

"For a little while I will...maybe. But..." There arose a strange gleam in Lod's eyes. "I owe another First Born. I owe Yorgash of Poseidonis for the thousands of whip scars crisscrossing my back. I tried to storm his isle once, to set the captives free. It didn't work that time. Maybe it's time to reevaluate the possibilities and try again."

"Forget about that. Joash is right. Enjoy your win. It was a long time coming. You'll never taste something like this again."

Lod stirred uneasily.

"Does the idea bother you?"

"Good-bye, Cain. If you want my advice, you should turn to—"

"Lod," Cain said loudly, interrupting.

The over-muscled seraph nodded. "I know. You don't want to hear it. Well, it's your life, and it's been a long one. Go in peace, and for the sake of your crew, don't lead the poor souls back into piracy."

Cain said nothing.

Lod looked as if he wanted to say more. Instead, he turned abruptly and walked away.

That was Cain's cue. He gave the order, and the pirates in the galley shoved away from the dock. Soon, oars slid out and the drum beat sounded for the oarsmen. The galley headed for a canal that would take it out of ruined Shamgar.

"Which way are we headed?" asked Brunt.

"The way I first came to Shamgar," Cain said. "I want to get as far away from here as possible."

Brunt looked as if he wanted to ask why, but he didn't. Instead, he passed the order to the first mate, a former pirate lord. That man bellowed the orders that guided the galley in the direction of the Hanun Mountains.

-2-

That might have been the end of Cain in the story of Shamgar and its aftermath. But he had one other small part to play.

The galley left the shattered city, left the pall of smoke hanging over the ruins of Shamgar and the smell of death and decay that permeated everything for leagues on end. The pirates worked the oars, heading deeper into the swamp, and succeeded mainly because it was still the wet-season winter. Finally, several days later, the waterways became too shallow, and the galley mired in mud.

"This is no good," the lean first mate told Cain. "We have to go back."

"You want to head back to Shamgar?" asked Cain. It was the middle of the afternoon, and swamp trees towered around the mired galley.

The first mate shook his long head. "Back to the Suttung Sea," he said.

"You're going to become a salt trader, are you?"

The first mate became shifty-eyed, no longer meeting Cain's gaze.

Cain laughed darkly. He wore mesh-mail, had on a long, oiled cloak and a Bolverk-forged sword belted at this side. "You want your captaincy back, don't you?"

"I'm content being first mate," the former pirate chief muttered.

Cain noted several pirates had slowly moved to stand behind him. They seemed innocent enough, but he knew they were the former captain's loyal men. Should he kill the first mate, the former captain, for scheming? *And then what will I do?* Cain asked himself.

Lod had tried to give the pirates good advice, but the seraph had realized these scoundrels could never do honest work.

"The galley is yours," Cain said. "I'm leaving." He turned suddenly and shoved the pirates behind him. They fell over the gunwale into watery mud. Then, Cain vaulted over, also landing in the mud, but feet first.

"Hey!" the first mate shouted from the galley.

Cain waded through the mud as he headed for a shore, the sticky substance getting worse and trying to suck his boots from his feet. The mud failed in the end and Cain climbed onto a rocky shore, still sporting his boots.

"What about us?" the first mate shouted from the galley.

"Luck to you," Cain said. Then, he disappeared into the tree line, leaving the pirates and the galley to their fate.

A half mile later, Cain whirled around, drawing his sword, ready to kill the skulker behind him.

Brunt broke through the foliage. "Don't kill me, Cain." Several other primitive trackers stayed behind him in the shadows.

"What do you want?" asked Cain.

"To go with you," Brunt said. "There is nothing left for us at home."

Cain eyed the squat, hairy tribesman and felt an odd sense of camaraderie with him. "No, Brunt. There's no life for you with me. I'm a wanderer, passing through an endless existence, at times bored to tears. I played a game in Shamgar, and it helped pass the endless time that seldom varies. I enjoyed the thrust and parry of fighting, and maybe I'll find a different battle somewhere in several years. Until then...I live alone."

"You chose me."

"You chose yourself by being better than the others. Go back, Brunt."

"And be a pirate?"

"Knowing Lod, I doubt that would be a good trade at this time in the Suttung Sea. Why not take charge of a tribe and learn new ways?"

"Lod's ways?" asked Brunt.

"If they work for you, why not?"

Brunt scowled, but at last, he said, "Good luck to you, Cain. And goodbye."

"So long, Brunt." Without another word, Cain turned away and left Brunt and his fellow Nebo to their fate.

***

In time, Cain sat in a wet jungle at night. It rained hard. He was a under a jink tree with his oiled campaign cloak over his head. He chewed on hardtack, sitting cross-legged—

He stiffened, sensing a hostile gaze directed at him. In the dark jungle, Cain looked around. Even with his superior night sight, he could not pick out anything, anyone. Yet, the sense of being watched intensified.

Cain probed his instincts. The watcher was near, very near. Once more, Cain twisted around under his upheld cloak. He should be able to see someone—with a flash of understanding, Cain looked up just in time to see a soaked great ape drop from the jink tree above him. A second ape and a third dropped down as well.

Cain put his left hand around the hilt of the sheathed Bolverk-forged blade, and he let go of the cloak so it dropped to the ground. Cold drops struck his head and shoulders.

At that point, a thoroughly soaked Sagoth dropped from the tree. He landed among his three creatures, and he wore a soaked red cloak. There was a heavy short sword in Sagoth's right hand.

"Cain," the Nephilim said in an ugly voice. "This is an ill-met night."

Cain did not reply, although he shifted so his back was to the jink-tree's trunk. He sensed other great apes above him. They held something in their hands—he believed that was true because he sensed urgency from them.

"Where's your arrogance now, Cain?" Sagoth asked.

"You're ill," Cain said, hearing it in the beastmaster's voice.

"I'm wasting away," Sagoth said. "I hate it, but I can't seem to stop it."

Lightning cracked above, causing it to thunder an instant later. In the harsh light, Cain had seen Sagoth's thin cheeks and the emptiness in the Nephilim's eyes.

"Do you miss your father?" Cain asked.

"What do you mean?"

"Haven't you heard the news?"

"No. Tell me."

212

"Gog is dead."

"I don't believe it."

Cain shrugged.

"Why lie about something like that?" Sagoth demanded. "I know Gog is hunting for you. What's the reward for your capture?"

"A gut-full of steel for trying," Cain said.

Sagoth laughed, and it did not sound altogether sane.

"Gog is dead," Cain said. "I saw him die."

"Tell me more."

Under the jink-tree, under the threat of the Nephilim and his great apes, Cain did just that. He gauged his chances as he spoke, and he laid his plan.

"Shamgar is gone," Sagoth said hollowly. "How strange. What am I going to do now?"

"Keep on living."

Sagoth laughed bitterly. "No, Cain. I'm dying inside. It's the price of practicing necromancy. I never should have done it."

"You aren't doing it anymore."

"But I am," Sagoth said. "There's a new hunger in me. I hate it. I despise what it's doing to me." The Nephilim cocked his head. "Didn't you practice sorcery ages ago?"

"I did."

"And?"

"And I stopped doing it, maybe for the same reasons I suggested you stop. Magic warps the spell-caster. Necromancy does it worse than any other form."

"Why is that?"

"I don't know," Cain said. "It just is."

"I want to stop."

"So do it."

"But I cannot," Sagoth said. "I need people to kill slowly so I can siphon off the spiritual power. You must surely hold a great store of necromantic power in you."

In that second, Cain exploded into action, drawing his Bolverk-forged blade and thrusting into the nearest great ape's chest. He twisted the blade, killing the creature so it screamed.

Others above cried out in rage, dropping rocks.

213

Cain had already moved. The rocks thudded harmlessly on the ground where he had been. Cain was among those on foot, thrusting, slashing and killing another massive ape.

Then, the sharp steel sliced deeply into Sagoth's left arm. The Nephilim howled, trying to claw-attack with his other hand. Cain lopped off that hand and thrust again.

Great apes dropped and landed on Cain. In their rush to attack and save their master, the creatures tried to pummel the son of Adam, but ended up mostly hitting each other.

Sagoth was screaming in the dark, sickened about his lost right hand and badly maimed left arm. The screams were of such intensity that the apes left Cain lying on the wet soil, rushing to help their injured master.

Cain lay bruised and half-dead on the ground. The ape blows that had struck had hit with numbing force. Despite the pain and bruising, the throbbing of his aching head, he heaved up off the ground, staggering away, watching the enemy. The hairy beasts attempted to minister to their Nephilim beastmaster. Instead of running away as any sane person would, a terrible rage spurred Cain into action. That caused his head to throb even worse. He gripped the sword with two hands and charged silently, thrusting and slashing, killing two beasts in a rush and hacking Sagoth's skull almost in two.

Two great apes launched themselves at Cain. The rest bore Sagoth, shuffling him away from the maddened human.

There, under the wet jink tree, Cain fought one of his bitterest duels. Several ape buffets, nails breaking against his mesh-mail, came as near to slaying him as anything had. Despite the awful ape-strength, Cain slew those two.

The fight left him panting and reeling, grinning as blood poured from a head wound. He did not follow the band in the dark. Instead, he turned, picked up his fallen cloak and, using the Bolverk-forged sword as a cane, he limped into the night.

In doing so, Cain staggered out of the story of Shamgar and its fallen First Born. The first murderer on Earth continued life as a wanderer, seeking meaning for his long existence…

-3-

Eight and half months after the fall of Shamgar, Lod sat on a tree stump in a swamp-jungle camp. The seraph and several hardy Shurites—a healed Keros included—trained seven former rat baits in the warrior arts.

The rat baits were passing from boyhood, and they had radically changed in the time Lod and others had been training them. Even the rope scars around their necks had healed. Shamgar had fallen, and no one had attempted to rebuild it. No one lived there anymore.

Lod had searched through the ruins twice already to make sure.

Joash, Uriah and most of the host had long ago returned home. A band of warriors followed Lod in his latest quest. He had taken time out to help train these lads. The rest of the time, he hunted Nephilim, half-Nephilim and those of the blood of the high who lived in the local area and continued to make trouble for regular people.

One result of this had been a slow turning among a few of the Nebo tribesmen. Some of the stone-age primitives had stopped practicing their Nephilim-fostered shamanism in order to follow the ways of Elohim. The manner of the death of Gog had gone a long way to shattering their former confidence in the *bene elohim.*

In any case, as Lod sat on the stump, telling a tale that would end with a moral to the seven candidate-in-training warriors, commotion among the Shurites caused the seraph to cut his tale short. He stood, putting a hand on a sword hilt. The former rat baits scrambled to their feet, all picking up spears and lowering the points as they turned around.

Three squat Nebo tribesmen broke through the foliage around the camp. These three were heavyset primitives with broad shoulders and outthrust heads. Each had a beetling brow, wore a loincloth and sandals, and each had an iron sword belted at his waist.

"I know you," Lod told the leader.

The leader was a mite taller than the other two, thicker muscled and tougher looking.

"My name is Brunt."

"That's it," Lod said. "You were one of Cain's champions."

"That is true. I followed Cain from Shamgar, and I spoke to him just before he left us."

"Cain is gone?" asked Lod.

"I would not be here to speak to you if that were not so."

Keros broke through the foliage, having gone to investigate in the nearby jungle. "It's just these three, Lod," the raid chieftain said.

"We are here seeking your aid," Brunt said.

"You're starving because you don't have any honest work?" asked Lod.

"No. I am a chieftain of a Nebo tribe. I took our people far from our former lands. I wanted a new start. So did the tribe."

"Where did you go?"

"Where Cain trekked," Brunt said. "We no longer live in swamp land, but in jungle land. Unfortunately, a Nephilim is killing my people, picking them off one by one."

Lod perked up. "Do you know the Nephilim's name?"

"Sagoth of Great Apes."

"Ah... Go on."

"Sagoth murders my people, eating their flesh and using their bones for sorcery."

"Come here," Lod said. "Put your hand on mine. Then tell me the truth."

Brunt stared at Lod. "My yes is yes, and my no is no."

"Well spoken, Brunt. Yes. I'll help you. Do you wish to kill Sagoth?"

"And his man-eating apes," Brunt said.

Lod pursed his lips, thinking. "This is what we shall do..."

-4-

The first attempt to kill Sagoth and his man-eating great apes proved a dismal failure. Although Brunt and his warriors were keen trackers, they were inept compared to the jungle apes in their home environment. Lod attempted several ruses, but they proved as fruitless as those of the Nebo primitives.

Finally, Lod admitted temporary defeat. He left Brunt's tribal area, traveled through the Shamgar swamp and sailed along the Suttung coast until he reached Elon.

There, Lod enlisted Joash's aid.

Adah pleaded with her husband to stay home this time. Joash asked for her patience just a little longer. Then, the seraph who could talk with animals left with Lod on a long journey.

A year and three months after the destruction of Gog and Shamgar, Lod, Joash and Brunt trekked through dense jungle foliage. Several big hunting dogs trailed the humans, but the hounds weren't tracking great apes. Instead, Joash had befriended two leopards of the jungle. The great cats roamed ahead through the trees, hunting for the great ape colony.

"I remember a female beastmaster called Nyla the Knife who had a leopard," Lod said later in the day. They sat in a small clearing, eating supper. "She's still in the Sea of Nur as far as I recall, living as a pirate."

"What happened to her leopard?" Brunt asked.

Before Lod could answer, a beautifully spotted great cat landed on the sward before them, having leapt from a nearby tree. Lod jumped to his feet and drew his sword, all in one motion. The big shaggy hounds also jumped up, growling low in their throats.

The leopard ignored both Lod and the dogs, going directly to Joash, sitting on its haunches and leaning its head forward. Joash put his head forward until they touched. Abruptly, Joash jerked back.

"Sagoth is coming," the young seraph said. "In fact—"

Great apes screamed from the trees circling the clearing. Branches shook and leaves rustled. Then a heavy thing catapulted from the trees and landed with a thump on the ground before Lod.

It was the carcass of a slain leopard, the brains eaten from it.

The living leopard snarled up at the apes. Coconuts launched down, striking the leopard.

"Go," Joash told it.

The leopard spun around and leapt into the foliage, disappearing from sight.

"Sagoth," Lod shouted, cupping his hands to do so. "Sagoth, do you hear me?"

The great apes hidden in the trees grew silent.

The hounds looked to Joash. He motioned them to silence. The big hunting dogs hung their heads.

Brunt had strung a bow and had selected three arrows. He stood behind Lod, waiting.

"Sagoth," Lod shouted.

"I hear you," the Nephilim said from high in the trees. "What do you want?"

"I slew Gog. I killed your father."

"What is that to me?" Sagoth shouted.

"You belonged to Shamgar. Now, you lack a home and have become a wanderer."

"Wrong," Sagoth said from his hidden location in the trees. "This is my home and you are in it uninvited."

"What kind of home is it if you devour men like a cannibal?" shouted Lod.

"Men are flesh and bone. I devour those so I can grow strong."

"You have become a cannibal."

"I gain strength like a cannibal and as a necromancer. I am Sagoth of Great Apes. I rule in the jungle. Did that little Nebo Brunt curry your favor? I will devour all of his tribe and then I will eat him, too, using his skull to hold stored magic."

218

"I defy you, Sagoth," Lod shouted.

"You are a dim-witted fool, Lod. I know your game. You seek to get me to come down to you. I am here, untouchable. I respect your battle prowess enough to leave you alone. You did slay Gog, after all. But once you are gone, Lod…"

Lod laughed loudly, pointing at a great ape descending from a tree.

The huge hairy ape stared intently at Joash. The young seraph's face shined strangely. The ape looked at the hounds eagerly watching it.

"They won't hurt you," Joash promised.

The ape hesitated only a moment. Then, it dropped the rest of the way, shambling to Joash until the seraph touched the ape on the shoulder.

The ape sighed as if with relief.

"What is he doing to my ape?" Sagoth shouted.

"Releasing your ape from its chains," Lod said. "Letting it go from your perverted bondage. It is no longer yours."

Another ape slunk down from the trees.

"Stop," Sagoth told it.

The ape slowed its descent.

"You're safe down here," Joash called to the ape. "Look. Your friend is free."

The ape eyed Joash and the contented ape. Then, it continued to descend.

"Stop," Sagoth ordered. "I command you to stop."

Joash cupped his hands. "Your practice of casting spells has weakened your beastmastering skills, Sagoth. I can feel that from here."

"No," Sagoth shouted. "That's a lie, a lie. I am Sagoth of Great Apes."

"You're a doomed creature that devours men," Lod said. "Your time is over, Sagoth. Gog is dead. He was your shield. Now, your shield is gone."

"Attack!" roared Sagoth. "Attack, my lovelies. Kill them. Then, we can feast upon their flesh and gain their strength."

At that point, a band of screaming, man-eating great apes descended in a swinging rush from the trees. Brunt acted fast, notching and firing an arrow, the first missile hissing into an ape's throat.

That creature let go of the tree and plummeted down to flop against the ground.

Lod had several javelins at his feet. He picked one up and hurled it, skewering a great ape.

"Kill him!" Sagoth roared.

The Nephilim plummeted from a tree, landing hard on the ground. He was missing a hand, and he looked awful, sickly. His other arm and hand worked fine, though, and he held a sword.

The huge hunting dogs rose up, attacking the apes as they landed on the ground. The leopard reappeared, jumping on an ape's back and ripping it with his claws.

Joash bore a sword and shield, but he stared at various apes, stilling some so they slunk near under his protection.

"I am Sagoth," the Nephilim monstrosity shouted, charging Lod.

The blade of Elohim rose up to engage the Nephilim, and it turned into a horribly uneven contest. Cain had lopped off Sagoth's dominant hand, leaving the Nephilim as an indifferent left-handed swordsman. Thus, after several passages, Lod stepped in close and thrust his sword deep into the Nephilim's gut. He shoved the blade up higher into the body cavity, and Sagoth's foul breath exploded in Lod's face.

With a roar, Lod shoved Sagoth from him, and so died the last Nephilim to perish in this region, falling down dead at Lod's feet.

Soon, the surviving great apes surrendered after a fashion, going to Joash. The hunting dogs and leopard had killed the rest. These apes…these Joash washed with his strange power, expunging their desire for human flesh. Afterward, the young seraph sent them back into the forest, there to begin anew.

-5-

Lod, Uriah and Joash had slain Gog the Oracle. Shamgar became a ghost town, a ruin, and over time, the swamp reclaimed it.

Cain had shown up for its death, and that sustained and continued the wanderer's awful legacy of destruction rather than growing or building things.

Many pirates released at Shamgar's end returned after a year or two to piracy, finding themselves unsuited to a civilized lifestyle. The vast majority of them died, hunted down and slain by galley crews outfitted by the League of Peace. However, other pirates returned to a normal life and became productive citizens of various cities and towns. The Nebo tribes as a whole became more civilized. Taken altogether, the general Suttung Sea region knew several decades of peace and real prosperity.

As for the fate of Yorgash of Poseidonis and Jotnar of Giants, those stories lay in the future as the war between Nephilim and men continued in the Pre-Cataclysmic Age before the oceans rose to destroy the world that was…

THE END

Fantasy Books by Vaughn Heppner:

LOST CIVILIZATION SERIES
Giants
Leviathan
Eden
Gog
Behemoth
Lod the Warrior
Lod the Galley Slave
Cain

THE ARK CHRONICLES
People of the Ark
People of the Flood
People of Babel
People of the Tower

OTHER FANTASY BOOKS
Warrior of the Blood
Rhune Shadow
Dark Crusade
The Dragon Horn

Visit www.Vaughnheppner.com for more information.

Made in the USA
Las Vegas, NV
06 January 2023

65140814R00135